Esme Dooley
&
The Kirkkomaki Circus

D1550605

Also by the Authors

Esme Dooley

ESME DOOLEY

&

The Kirkkomaki Circus

WITHDRAWN

Jane Donovan and Holly Trechter

with illustrations by Jane Donovan

Sky Candle Press

ESME DOOLEY AND THE KIRKKOMAKI CIRCUS

ISBN 978-1-939360-05-2

ESME DOOLEY

&

The Kirkkomaki Circus

To Leah and Joe and Bannen, with love.

And to Dave, who has a shining heart.

JUNE 1904

And so it was that a plump moon wandered through the purple dusk until it reached the Zumbro River. There it illuminated the iron bridge and touched the ripples, making them glitter. Softly, the moon sailed over pastures, where drowsy cows knelt to sleep. It swept along new telegraph lines that were already starting to sag, and after a time, it visited the village. As it hovered over a shimmering peony, the last petals of spring fluttered to the ground.

Close enough to touch, the moon floated by windows, where farmers slept, while their wives dreamed of blue ribbons at the Minnesota State Fair. Outside their doors,

I

fireflies sparked in groves of apples and fields of corn. Summer was definitely here.

Only one soul was awake in the valley, and that was Hatch Dooley. Newly sprung from jail, she was stirring something disgusting on her brother's stove. She grouched and growled and grumbled and griped, brewing for Esme a brutal revenge.

Not far away, Tommy Dooley and his twelve brothers and pa were sleeping in their new home at the inn. It had taken a good while to settle the paperwork for the title to the inn. As one week after another had passed, Tommy had fretted and worried. However, the law had been on their side, and in the end, they had won their battle against their murderous Aunt Hatch.

Tommy's cousin Esme was also at the inn, sharing a room with her grandmother. They too were asleep, so they did not hear the moon knocking on their window. Its silvery light streamed into their room, almost missing Esme, for even though she was eleven, she was very, very tiny.

Esme turned over in her sleep, jostling the sparkling locket around her neck. Her grandma had given it to her, saying it had belonged to Esme's mother. From the moment Esme had first seen the locket, she had imagined it was brimming with love and power. She had clasped it on, and instantly, she had felt safe.

Now the moonlight shifted, catching the gleams in Esme's chestnut braid, which curved across her pillow. She smiled in her sleep, for her heart was full of thankfulness. She no longer had to live with Hatch, she had a loving home with Tommy's family, and best of all, she had the grandmother she had always wanted. After years of enduring the greatest pain and misery, she was finally happy.

Later, when everyone looked back, they all agreed that this was the calm before the brink of calamity. But for now, Esme was sleeping innocently, oblivious of the new season and unaware that this would be her only peaceful night of the summer.

ESME

"Faster, Tommy," Esme yelled to her cousin. She was dying to see how quickly she could go in her new roller skates. If she could only get moving, she was sure it would feel like flying — at least, a close-to-the-ground sort of flying. That was why she had dug out her wings.

She held onto the end of a long rope. The other end of the rope was tied to the collar of Tommy's pony, Bess. Tommy was riding on the back of Bess, trying to coax her to go faster. *But at this rate,* thought Esme, *we couldn't outrun a glacier.*

To encourage Bess to giddy up, Tommy extended a long stick with a carrot hanging from it, and the vegetable dangled right in front of Bess' nose. So far, this contraption wasn't working. Bess trotted along at her usual leisurely pace, ignoring everything around her — even the carrot.

They were on a back road that led to Zumbro Falls. Due to the recent lack of rain, the dry dirt was packed down, creating the perfect surface for trying out Esme's new skates. She shouted, "Can't you hurry her up, Tommy?"

He yelled back, "I reckon Bess only has one speed today." As he rode, he patted the bib of his overalls, where their pet raccoon was dozing.

Esme raised her green eyes to the clouds and sighed. Not only did she long to learn how fast she could go, but she was also in a hurry for quite another reason. She wanted to find Grandma, who had galloped off to the village for the third time that afternoon.

Esme suspected the reason for these frequent trips was that Grandma was expecting a telegram. But the topic of that telegram was a dark mystery, so Esme's curiosity burned!

It had been like this since yesterday afternoon, when Esme had accidentally interrupted Grandma and Tommy's pa. They had been on the porch, whispering something about the telegraph office, and they'd hushed up completely when they saw Esme. Grandma's green eyes had twinkled mysteriously, and Esme knew right away that something was brewing. *Grown-ups,* she thought, *aren't very good at keeping secrets.*

Now, as she rolled along — unbearably slowly — she reminded herself that things could be worse. Tommy could still be mad at her. A couple of weeks ago, she had given him a terrible haircut. It had all been going perfectly until their raccoon had jumped at Esme, and suddenly Tommy had a big bald spot where his bangs used to be. Oh, he was so mad! He slapped a hat on his head and didn't speak to Esme for eight days, or in other words, 192 hours. It had practically killed her.

Grandma finally sat down with them and talked about forgiveness. She said it heals the forgiver as well as the person who needs to be forgiven. Her wise words must have affected Tommy because the next morning, he broke his silence and joked with Esme about needing to find a decent barber. Before long, their friendship fell back into place, just the way it was supposed to be.

Now, as Esme was (still) rolling slowly along the back road to Zumbro Falls, she admired the wild lilies in the grassy ditches. She remembered how she'd helped gather flowers for Lavinia Hobbs' wedding last month. Suddenly, she was reliving the excitement of the wedding day, which was a dazzling event with more than a few surprises.

Despite the wedding's unexpected moments — like when Mr. Hobbs accidentally crashed into the outdoor altar with his horseless carriage, or when a storytelling cowboy shot and popped all the balloons — Esme thought the day had been just heavenly. Not even their raccoon, the wily Mr. Wright, who had gobbled the top tier of the wedding cake, could take anything away from the joyous occasion.

After the wedding, Esme stumbled upon the book *Pride and Prejudice*. She adored it! She read it twice, and now she considered herself to be somewhat of an expert on matters of matchmaking and love in general. She had grand designs of matching all of Tommy's twelve brothers, so she'd have twelve weddings to attend. *And best of all,* she thought, *I'll have twelve new sisters!*

Shifting on Bess, Tommy turned around and smiled down at her. His blue eyes crinkled into half-moons, and his unruly, orange hair stood on end. Even though they were both eleven, he was a lot taller than she was. Now that his tooth had been fixed, and his glasses had been replaced, and his hair had finally grown back, it wouldn't be long before she could look for a match for him too. *Make that thirteen weddings to plan!* She covered her mouth to stifle a giggle.

Tommy's eyes narrowed with suspicion. "What are you up to now, Esme?"

She simply smiled.

As they passed a meadow of nodding daisies, she pondered what kind of girl he would someday marry. *She will have to be pretty special,* thought Esme. *To be good enough for Tommy.*

Peals of laughter reached them. They were nearing the first building in Zumbro Falls — or the last, depending on which direction you were heading. As Bess pulled Esme past

Mackey's General Store, the laughter grew louder. People milled about outside, guffawing about Farmer Wiebusch's entanglement with his wayward bull. He held up a pair of pants with a ripped-out seat — much to the merriment of the gathering. Esme waved to the farmers, and they all waved back.

"Is that a new mode of transportation?" someone hollered, teasing her from the boardwalk.

Esme was just about to answer when a shrill whistle pierced the village, coming from an approaching train. Shocked by the blast, Bess took off like she was in the Kentucky Derby! Esme lurched forward but somehow managed to hold tight to the rope.

They were off!

They sped down Main Street, causing a rumpus that would be talked about for days. Up ahead, Esme spotted Mrs. Adams, who kindly delivered meals to invalids in Zumbro Falls. She was carrying a tray, and Esme caught the tantalizing aroma of her award-winning fried chicken. "Mrs. Adams!" she cried, hoping to warn her of the coming catastrophe.

Mrs. Adams turned, and Esme would never forget the look of shock on her face. The saintly woman veered sideways, but Esme still smashed into her tray. It flipped into the air, raining chicken legs. "I'm sorry!" Esme called back, as she and Tommy and Bess raced onwards.

And then, oh, mercy! Esme had to duck to avoid a flying stick with a carrot. *What in the world?* Was Tommy throwing things at her? "Tommy!" she wailed. She turned to watch the fate of the vegetable missile. To her horror, it struck

Pastor Eriksson square in the head! The blow knocked him backwards, and his armful of red hymnals soared and plopped one-by-one in the horse trough.

Oh, jiminy! Before Esme could pull her eyes away from that waterlogged scene, the toe of her roller skate struck the base of the boardwalk by the train station. Instantly and unexpectedly, she was thrown in the air, flying over the platform to the railroad tracks.

Terrified, she landed smack dab on the tracks, in front of a whistle-shrilling, steam-blowing, not-stopping-soon-enough locomotive!

TOMMY

Holey buckets! By the time Tommy finally slowed Bess down, turned her around in the right direction, and made it back to the depot, Mr. Mackey was carrying a very limp Esme off the tracks.

Even though there was no splattered blood, nor arms nor legs scattered about, Tommy felt just sick because he'd never seen anything that looked deader than Esme. A ten-day-old fish would look more lively than she did. Even the dead and not-so-merry Widow Winkler showed considerably more life at her funeral than Esme was displaying at that very moment.

Tommy peered at Mr. Mackey's face, but the man's expression wasn't giving anything away. So Tommy gulped and asked, "I-I-Is she dead?"

"No, no," muttered Mr. Mackey, "but by all accounts, she should be." *Oh, thank goodness,* thought Tommy, *she's still alive!* Mr. Mackey continued, "When the locomotive finally stopped, it was touching the very tip of her roller skates. She couldn't have been any closer to that train!" He laid Esme on the bench.

With a low moan, she opened her eyes. As she rubbed her new locket, Tommy thought, *Maybe she's right. Maybe that locket does protect her. Maybe it kept her from the undertaker today.*

Gently, Mr. Mackey scolded Esme. "You need to watch where you're flying, young lady. Your landings are downright disastrous." The whole village was still gossiping about Esme's escapade last month, when she smashed through a window at the church and terrified the tuneless Ladies' Choir.

Draped on the bench, Esme managed to say, "Sorry . . ."

Mr. Mackey patted her head. "I'm glad you're all right, child. Yes, siree, it could have been much worse."

Suddenly, they heard Mrs. Mackey calling to her husband from the General Store. "Thaddeus!" she hollered, in her booming voice. "Thaddeus Mackey, where are you?"

Mr. Mackey glanced back and forth between Esme and his store. It didn't take him long to decide that his work here was done. He departed.

Tommy knelt at Esme's side. "Are you okay?"

Nodding, she gasped, "Wind knocked out . . ." Still struggling to breathe, she sat halfway up and started to unbuckle the skate strap around her ankle.

Quickly, Tommy fished the skate key out of his pocket and loosened the metal sides that gripped her toes. "I thought you were a goner. Are you sure you're alive?"

Hesitantly, she gave him a smile. "Need my breath back," she wheezed. "Then find Grandma." Esme patted Mr. Wright, who was peeking out of the bib pocket of Tommy's overalls.

As they removed her skates, Tommy heard mumbling from the crowd that was gathering on the platform. Whispers of "orphans" reached his ears. Esme must have been starting to recover because she hopped up, more like her normal self. Standing on the bench, she tried to peek into the train, but she was too short. "Tommy, I can't see. What's going on?"

So he climbed on the bench. From there, he could peer inside the train windows. "Kids are leaving their seats and forming a long line in the aisle." He glanced at Esme, who was hanging onto his every word. He went on, "A woman is walking along the line, combing each kid's hair." Unconsciously, he smoothed down his own orange hair. "And now she's brushing off a collar. And straightening a boy's suspenders. And tying a girl's braid."

After a pause, he blurted out, "I reckon it's the Orphan Train!"

PAPUZA

Sunlight streamed through the windows of the telegraph office, where Esme's grandma, Papuza, sat in an unsteady chair, too stunned to speak. Her black braids were quivering, and her hands held the telegram she'd awaited so anxiously. *How can this possibly be? Can I even dare to hope?* Her heart beat wildly.

Facts she had been led to believe for more than sixty years were false. Or were they? She had to gain control over her heartbeat, or surely she would perish in this very office.

Suddenly, she began to chuckle. And then she chuckled some more. The children would love another journey! Papuza knew that Tommy's pa would approve, for she had spoken with him yesterday about travel possibilities.

My stars! The last time she had felt this wonderful was when she'd held Esme in her arms for the very first time. She rose from her chair and strolled to the desk, where a dapper clerk leafed through a newspaper.

"Please, my dear sir," said Papuza, "I need to send a telegram."

ESME

The Orphan Train! Esme had read about it in the newspaper last week, and it had completely captured her curiosity. But so much had happened since then. She whispered to Tommy, "I've been so busy thinking about Grandma's mystery that I forgot all about this!"

Standing on the bench, she watched intently as children shuffled down from the train and lined up on the platform. Esme counted. There were twenty in all, half boys and half girls. All of them seemed a little embarrassed, and many cast their eyes down at their bare feet. Esme's heart went out to them.

That could be me, she thought. *Both my parents are gone, and I'm an orphan.* Granted, she was an orphan with a very large family. But still, she felt a strong connection with the poor children who stood before her. "Oh, Tommy," she whispered. "I don't know if I can watch this." These children's lives were about to be decided.

And what will happen to the ones who won't get picked? The newspaper said these orphans were passed from one town to another in hopes of finding homes. "Free Children" was the title of the newspaper article. Yet Esme couldn't help but think, *They are the very furthest thing from free.*

Even though her conscience told her it wasn't her place to watch, she simply couldn't help it. She was spellbound. Would all the orphans find loving homes in Zumbro Falls? Anxiety rushed through her, as her fellow townsfolk looked over the line of children.

The gentle hat shop owner, Miss Bass, paused in front of a little boy and asked him his name. A moment later, Esme felt crushed, as Miss Bass turned away from him and stepped to the next child, a thin girl with pale braids.

Oh, how that poor boy must feel right now! He was looked at, judged, and passed over. It must have been a terrible experience. Esme didn't think she would be able to bear the expression on the girl's face if she were turned down too.

Esme closed her eyes and crossed her fingers to send secret good luck wishes to the girl. When Esme couldn't stand the suspense any longer, she opened one eye and peeked. How wonderful! The girl was strolling away, hand in hand with Miss Bass!

And then the kind woman took the hand of the boy she had previously passed, and the three of them

headed towards the agent in charge. Thank goodness! A sunny feeling washed over Esme, and she clasped her hands to her heart.

Then she got a brilliant idea! "Oh, Tommy, we need to talk to Grandma and your pa about adopting an orphan. In fact, we could adopt a few! Why, when I get all your brothers married off . . ."

"What?" Tommy's jaw dropped in surprise. Esme knew he'd be utterly shocked if he had any inkling of her many elaborate matchmaking schemes.

"We've been fortunate, and we have so much." Her eyes began to fill with grateful tears. "So much — "

A sinister voice interrupted her. "So much, so much." It imitated Esme in a scathing falsetto.

Jumping Jupiter! Esme spun around to look for the speaker. She already knew it was her wicked Aunt Hatch.

HATCH

"So much, so much," Hatch spat out in a venomous whisper. "Well, of course you have a lot. You stole it all from me!" Itching to throttle Esme, Hatch reached out to grab her, but the girl was too quick. Esme jumped off the bench and raced away.

So Hatch turned her hawkish gaze to her nephew Tommy, who stood frozen with his jaw hanging open. *He looks about as bright as my nitwit of a brother,* thought Hatch. As Tommy managed to flee, Hatch hissed after him, "Just because that sniveling cousin of yours didn't appreciate my generosity doesn't mean *these* children wouldn't love to work for me." She stomped over to the row of orphans and opened the mouth of one of the girls, to inspect her teeth.

Yes, thought Hatch, *the indignity is just too much.* She had returned from her jail sentence, only to find she'd been

thrown off her property. *So what if I never actually owned it?* Until last month, her relatives hadn't known that measly detail, so they hadn't been missing anything. And now that little toadstool had the gall to whine about having "so much"? A blood vessel throbbed in Hatch's forehead.

Glaring, Hatch spun around to check on her brother, the moonshiner Billy Groggs. He was leaning against the depot. Or was he sleeping? That stinky scarecrow was nothing but a bag of bones, covered in filthy, ragged clothes. *It's a disgrace to be seen with him.*

Hatch swooped over and gave him a shove. Apparently, he must have been sleeping because he crumpled, falling facedown on the platform. Hatch took this chance to give him a swift kick in the side. "Get up, you slug."

He rolled out of range of her boot. As he rose to his feet, he muttered, "Ornery cow."

How dare he! Hatch whipped out her pearl-handled pistol. She longed to shoot at his feet to make him dance, but she was low on bullets, so she settled for snarling, "Come on, you hellish hat rack."

It was time to get started on her revenge.

TOMMY

Mighty eager to put a lot of distance between himself and Hatch, Tommy hightailed it after Esme. Gosh-almighty! Hatch had looked even madder than the last time Tommy had seen her, back in Wisconsin, when she'd tried to kill Esme. Or to be more exacting, when she'd tried to kill all of them, but she'd *especially* tried to kill Esme. As Tommy ran towards his pony Bess, carrying the wings and roller skates and Mr. Wright, he was ecstatic to note that Hatch and Groggs were heading away from him, in the opposite direction.

"Wait, Esme!" he hollered ahead.

But his cousin kept right on running, with her brown braid swinging behind her. She was tiny yet fast, and she didn't stop until she reached the telegraph office, where her grandmother's horse was tethered. Then, and only then, did Esme finally glance back to check if she was safe. She leaned over and rested her hands on her knees, panting to catch her breath.

"I tried to get you to stop," wheezed Tommy. He could barely talk because he was panting too. He thought, *Running **and** pulling Bess **and** toting roller skates **and** carrying crumpled wings **and** bearing Mr. Wright ain't exactly easy.* "Hatch went the other way, Esme, after you lit out of there."

"Oh, Tommy, wasn't that terrible? Where did she come from? What if she picks one of those poor kids?" Esme's green eyes flashed with outrage. "There ought to be a law against someone like her getting a child. An orphan would be better off without any home at all."

Tommy nodded in complete agreement.

Papuza stepped out of the telegraph office, looking radiant! She seemed happier than Tommy had ever seen her, and he'd seen her mighty happy. But he and Esme must have

looked fretful, or tuckered out, or something worrisome because right away, Papuza asked, "What's wrong?"

She knelt down by Esme while she took Tommy's hand to pull him closer to her. "What's wrong?" she asked again, searching their faces.

"We're fine, Grandma," said Esme. "We ran into Hatch at the depot. She tried to grab me, but I got away. It's fine, Grandma."

Tommy said, "But tell her what happened when you roller skated . . ." He stopped mid-sentence when he saw the pleading look that Esme was sending his way. He realized she didn't want Papuza to worry about them horsing around.

"It's fine, Grandma!" Esme hurried to say again.

"No, my dear, I think not." Papuza's lilting voice was quiet yet determined. "We're heading straight to the sheriff to let him know that Hatch is threatening you."

Esme gave her grandma a grateful hug. Then she pulled back and asked, "But first, can you tell us if you got your mysterious telegram?"

Tommy chimed in, "Yep, what happened?"

"Hmm," said Papuza, glancing back and forth between the two of them. "I can't imagine how you found out. But yes, I did indeed receive a telegram. I'll tell you all about it when we get home. I think I'll call a family meeting, for Tommy's father and brothers might want to hear this also. It's an unusual turn of events. And more importantly, you two should start packing."

"For what?" they asked at the same time.

Papuza chuckled. "I do believe you'll be traveling."

Esme and Tommy let out happy whoops and cheers. "Where? And when?" they pleaded.

Mysteriously, Papuza said, "We're going on a journey in search of a dead person."

ESME

"A dead person?" Esme was definitely puzzled. This was the last thing she'd ever expected to hear. *Are we going to a cemetery? Or maybe to a funeral? Where will we go to find a dead person?*

Grandma laughed. "Well, dead to me, at least. Or so I've thought for more than sixty years."

"But who is it?" asked Tommy.

"I think the story should wait until we get home, where I'd like to show you some letters that I've been storing in my dresser drawer.

But first, we're paying a visit to the sheriff."

With her skirts swirling, Grandma mounted her horse, Zinjiber. Her black braids swayed as she trotted along. Esme and Tommy followed on Bess.

On their way to the sheriff's, Esme and Tommy tried to coax Grandma to tell them her secret, but she was so firm that they knew it was a lost cause. Even so, they were blissfully delighted about the prospect of another journey. Esme wondered, *Where will we go this time?*

After Grandma talked with the sheriff, they stopped by the blacksmith's to buy some nails, and then they headed home. They pestered Grandma again with questions, but she refused to budge. Instead she wanted to hear about their run-in with Hatch and Groggs.

As he recalled those two scoundrels, Tommy glanced uneasily over his shoulder. "I swear, Hatch looked even meaner than the last time I saw her."

Esme nodded. "Grandma, ever since you had that talk with us about forgiveness, I've been trying to forgive Hatch. But honestly, when she tried to grab me today, all I could think about was how she'd wanted to cut me up in little pieces and stuff me in a pickle jar! I don't know if I'll ever be able to forget that."

Grandma murmured, "Forgiving and forgetting are two different things, my dear."

Esme pondered this for a while. Finally, she said, "Hatch was inspecting the orphans at the depot, Grandma. She should never, ever be allowed to keep another child. Those children should go to happy homes, like we have!" And that's when Esme told Tommy and Grandma her idea about adopting an orphan. Or maybe two. Or even three.

Grandma listened carefully, beaming with pleasure. "Without a doubt, it's a wonderful idea! Of course, we'll have to talk it over with Tommy's father, but I would be in favor of helping those poor children."

"Yep, I reckon it sounds okay," said Tommy. After a moment, he added, "As long as I wouldn't have to share my room with anybody." Grandma regarded him with amusement.

Well, of course he won't need to share, Esme thought. They had space to spare. And anyway, she thought they should adopt a girl. There were already enough boys in the Dooley household.

When they arrived home, Grandma told them to gather Tommy's pa and brothers and meet her in the kitchen in ten minutes.

It didn't take them long to round up the entire Dooley clan, even though it meant interrupting a wrestling match or two. Tommy's brothers came eagerly when Esme told them, "Emergency Family Meeting! Grandma has big news to share!"

They gathered in the kitchen around their new harvest table. With her ten-minute head start, Grandma had made two plentiful platters of strawberry jam sandwiches. She knew all too well that they couldn't pay attention if their stomachs were grumbling.

Esme gobbled down her sandwich in record time and fed one to Mr. Wright as well. Now she was ready to get down to business. "Who is this dead person, Grandma? And where will we find him or her?"

The Dooley clan stopped munching. They were all ears.

Grandma said, "I fear it may get confusing if I don't start at the beginning. Would that be acceptable, my dears?"

"Oh, it *must* be from the beginning," said Esme. "There's no better place to start than at the start!" Having read oodles and oodles and oodles of books in her short lifetime, she had very certain ideas about the makings of a good story.

Everyone around the table agreed with her, so Grandma cleared her throat and began. "Do you remember how I received a package two weeks ago from my attorney in Cornwall?"

"Yep!" Tommy said enthusiastically. "I saved all the colored stamps!"

"Well, as I told you then, the package was filled with some rather boring legal documents. However, as I sorted through them, I found these letters." She pulled out some old-looking papers from one of her many, many pockets. "I wrote these letters to my dear cousin Arthur during my winter at the logging camp."

"You lived in a logging camp?" asked George Washington Dooley. He was one of Tommy's older brothers.

"Don't be so surprised," teased Grandma. "Don't I look like your average, run-of-the-mill lumberjack?"

Everyone around the table cried, "No!"

"Well, contrary to how I may appear, I did indeed live and work at a logging camp. It was soon after we left Fort Crawford, and I wrote to Cousin Arthur to tell him all about my experiences. He must have shared them with my dear Gran, for somehow they got jumbled up with my legal papers." She pushed the bundle of letters over to Esme.

"Do you want me to read them out loud?" Esme asked, eager to finally uncover the mystery.

"If you'd be so kind, my dear." Grandma gave her an affectionate smile. So carefully, Esme opened the top letter and began to read:

October 14th, 1837

Dear Arthur,

I am sorry it has taken me so long to write. I truly hope that you and everyone else at home are the very picture of health.

Much has befallen since I last wrote to you from Fort Crawford. I remember telling you how Father and I galloped away from the mining camp on the horse of that murderer, Blackdeath Jackson. I shall take up the tale from there.

Right after I posted you my letter, I saw Father's face on a Wanted poster. To my horrible dismay, he was charged with horse-nabbing, which carries the punishment of hanging. Thus we needed to make ourselves scarce again immediately!

Hence Father struck a bargain with three voyageurs, who agreed to take us north in their flatboat. But heaven help us, we had barely left the fort when masked bandits attacked us! The voyageurs put up a fierce fight, yet I am certain they would have lost their vessel if it had not been for Father. Oh, Arthur, you should have seen him! He leapt into action, knocking away the bandits' weapons and punching those rascals so hard they fell backwards into the river with a mighty splash. So thankful were the voyageurs for Father's help that we all became steadfast friends.

27

We continued paddling up the Mississippi River, past many and many a beautiful sight. There are bold bluffs and countless springs that gush from rocky cliffs. 'Tis mighty pretty country here, Arthur. Oh, how I wish you could see it!

At night, we camped along the riverbanks. The three voyageurs were named Louis, Jacques, and Jasper. Louis was my favourite, for he played the concertina by the evening fire, and he told the BEST stories!

One night, Louis kept us spellbound as he told stories of this region just a few years past. At that time, the commander of Fort Crawford was Captain Zachary Taylor . . .

Tommy interrupted, "Hey, he became President!" He nudged Zachary Taylor Dooley with his elbow.

"I know," said Esme. "Your ma named all of you after presidents . . ."

All thirteen of the Dooley boys chimed together, ". . . so we will amount to something in life!"

Breaking into a grin, their pa said, "Well, I'm still waiting to see about that."

With a smile, Esme continued reading aloud where she'd left off:

Well, Louis fell in love with Captain Taylor's daughter, but she eloped with a soldier named Jefferson Davis. So Louis is now pining over a Sauk Indian maiden. He has been trying to learn her language, and in the process, he taught me a few words. I can say "bird" and "sky" and "water" in Sauk. He even taught me how to say "nincompoop," which I practice every day, so I shall be ready the next time you try to play a prank on me, Arthur.

We traveled north with the voyageurs until we reached Fort Snelling. Father and I shall rest here, but our voyageur friends have already taken their leave to go further on to the Elk River. I was sad to say farewell because I shall miss all of them, especially Louis.

Fort Snelling reminds me of Fort Crawford, for it has voyageurs, Indians, and fur traders mixed amongst the soldiers. However there is a most striking difference: I see no Wanted posters for Father here, and for that I am very relieved. He holds fast to his dream of somehow making his fortune in this new world. He is very determined, so I do not know when I shall see you again, Arthur — unless of course, you come and join us!

At supper last night, Father and I made the acquaintance of a man who may change our fate. His name is Oskar Olsson, and he hails originally from Sweden. He has red-gold hair and a bushy beard. He is a large man like Blackdeath Jackson, yet happy am I to say, he does not possess Blackdeath's meanness. Father and I warmed to him right away. Oskar came to Fort Snelling with a group of men who will be heading north to try their hand at logging. Settlers are venturing into that area, and Oskar believes they shall stand in need of lumber. "Houses and stores," said he. "Cradles and coffins."

By the time we finished our meal, we had reached a decision about our future. We shall venture north with Oskar's logging crew to work in the forests of the great white pines. My life as a miner is over, Arthur, and I will become a lumberjack! We are heading out tomorrow.

If my hand were not so tired tonight, I would tell you about the trapper we met who was trampled by a herd of buffalo.

Until my next letter . . .

Love,
Adara

TOMMY

"Who's Adara?" asked Abraham Lincoln.

"That was Papuza's original name," Tommy declared, proud to know these facts about her. "Then when she was twelve, she became Ade and disguised herself as a boy, so she could work as a miner." Out of the corner of his eye, he noticed that Mr. Wright had helped himself to another sandwich.

"Is that so? Well, when did you become Papuza?" asked James Monroe.

"Oh, dear me," she answered, "I have many names. Someday I can tell you all about them. But for now, shall we read another letter?"

Eagerly, they all cried, "Yes!"

So Esme began to read the next letter aloud:

Dear Arthur,

I hope this letter finds its way to you. I am sending it with a fur trader who promised to post it for me at Fort Snelling.

We have finished our journey, and at present we are living in a lumber camp by the St. Croix River. Our trip here was slow, for we traveled in a wagon that was pulled by a team of oxen. It was a mighty beautiful journey, Arthur, with leaves of red and gold falling around us. The forests were awash with colour, and I thought of you often, for I know how much you love autumn.

Once we arrived in this forest of white pines, the men built a slapdash bunkhouse, which serves as both a cookhouse and our place of lodging. The plan is that the men will cut wood all winter, storing up logs on the riverbank. When springtime comes, and the ice on the river melts, we shall float the logs downstream to sawmills in the South.

On our way here, we stopped at a trading post near Taylor's Falls to stock up on provisions. Oskar said that during the winter, it will be hard to make frequent trips to town, so he bought supplies that will keep, such as salt pork, beans, molasses, flour, dried apples, tea, and coffee.

I like all the loggers. In number, they are ten, including Father, and they are a much cheerier bunch than miners, perhaps because they get to work outside in lofty forests instead of toiling underground in the dark. Three of the men are Swedes, two are Irishmen who came here from Canada, one is German, one is Finnish, one is Polish, one is French, and of course, Father is Cornish.

Since Father is brand-new to logging, he does not receive the best tasks in camp. Although he works hard at his job of hacking branches off of fallen trees, the best pay goes to the loggers who actually chop down the trees. Swinging their axes, they hew the tall pines, and the trees fall with such terrible crashes that the ground beneath my feet rumbles. The best loggers can usually make a pine fall exactly where they wish. Yet not always! Hence I worry that Father could get crushed beneath a falling tree. He tells me I must not fret.

However, I am really writing to share a most wonderful thing that has befallen. I have a friend! And she is a girl!! And she is the same age as I am — twelve!!! You probably fail to realize how very rare it is to see another child in this remote wilderness. I am not exaggerating when I say it is quite unusual. I count myself lucky to have met Katrina.

I like her very much, Arthur. And that is a good thing because we work all day together, and we also share a straw mattress at night by the cookstove. Her father is the camp's cook, and Katrina and I help him prepare and serve meals. His name is Pekka Kirkkomaki, yet everyone just calls him "Cookie." His wife came from Norway, but she passed away last year. Both Katrina and I know how it feels to lose a mother.

Katrina is a pretty, blonde girl, and — give me leave to say — I know you would be fond of her, if you have learned to like girls now. She is much taller than I am, even though we are the same age, and she is very good-humoured. We have shared many laughs in the short time I have known her. She feels like the sister I never had. The only way I could be happier would be to have you here with us!

Katrina and I carry hearty lunches out to the loggers in knapsacks that we strap upon our backs. Each day we set out for a different spot of ground, wherever the crew happens to be working, and we build a fire to heat up the coffee. Then we try to warm the tin plates, but they cool quickly, for the weather is turning cold. Katrina and I feel that we have truly accomplished something if we manage to serve the men a hot meal.

At nightfall the men come back to the bunkhouse, and after a long day of working in the woods, they are cold and wet and weary. Clotheslines stretch by the cookstove, so the men can hang up their shirts and socks, which must be dry by morning. I have to say, the steaming clothes do not smell like a bed of roses.

When we are not helping Cookie, or mending the loggers' clothes, Katrina and I dream up our own games to keep us occupied. I am proud to say we fashioned scraps of wood into a checkerboard, and we organized a checkers tournament for everyone in the bunkhouse. The Frenchman, Remy, won. He was so pleased that he proposed a chess tournament next. He has been carving chess pieces for us, and we are only four pawns short of a complete set.

Sometimes the men play cards, and even though they do not realize that Katrina and I are listening and learning, we certainly are. I will teach you how to play poker when I see you again!

Now I must tell you what passed today, Arthur. Cookie fears that a sharp frost is not far off, so he sent Katrina and me into the woods to forage for any plants that could serve as greens, before winter claims them. Hither and thither we wandered, away from the bunkhouse, and as night began to fall, we realized we were lost.

Thank goodness we had a moon to plainly see by, yet little did it help as we cast about for our way back. I greatly feared we would need to spend the night in the ghostly woods. Katrina was brave and cheered my spirits as we kept searching and crying for help.

Finally we heard voices calling, and we yelled back and tried to set out in the direction of their shouts. We were merry and laughing at my fears, when alas! We came face-to-face with a wolf!

There he stood, a mangy-looking animal with frightful eyes that glowed in the dark. I froze, holding my breath. It is my firm belief that if it were not for Katrina, I would not be here to write to you now. Bravely she picked up a stick and waved it at the creature to scare him away. Then she took a step towards him and shook the stick some more.

The wolf did not move. It was as if he were trying to decide whether we would be worth eating. He must have made up his mind, for suddenly he made a lunging leap at us! We jumped as far away as we could, but Katrina had been closer to him, and he landed on her and knocked her over!

Then gunshots filled the night as Father and some of the other loggers rushed up and saved us! They killed the wolf.

I was quite shaken, and it was a goodly relief to see that Katrina was fine. She had only suffered a nasty scratch on her arm. But then, as we looked down upon the dead wolf, the strangest thing befell. Katrina threw herself upon his carcass and wept as if her heart would break. She felt terrible that the wolf had died. She had never wanted that to happen because she loves animals. She had only wanted to scare away the wolf, yet things had turned out ill.

Wilmer, the German logger, gathered Katrina in his arms and carried her all the way back to camp. Her father was overjoyed to see her, although he grew as pale as ashes when he saw her injury. Here I could help, so I washed her wound and bandaged her arm.

I must leave off for the present, Arthur. Give my best to your parents and Gran.

Love,
Adara

ESME

As Esme folded up the letter, Millard Fillmore asked in awe, "A real, honest-to-goodness wolf?"

Grandma beamed at him fondly. "Yes, indeed. A real, honest-to-goodness wolf."

Esme asked, "Did Katrina's arm heal, Grandma?"

"Well, my dear, you shall need to read on and see."

Tommy prodded, "Come on, Esme!" From the murmurs of agreement around the table, his brothers wanted to hear more too. So Esme picked up the final letter and began:

February 15th, 1838

Dear Arthur,

What a glorious day! Oskar and Cookie made a trip to the trading post and purchased the same provisions as before, plus hominy, eggs, and potatoes. Yet more importantly, they came back with letters for us. I was so happy when Oskar handed me a letter from Gran, and even happier when I read the news about you and your father. You two are coming to join us! What joyful tidings! Katrina and I cannot wait. She feels she knows you almost as well as I do, for I talk about you all the time. Maybe someday you will marry Katrina Kirkkomaki, and then she will truly be part of my family.

However I should warn you that if you do end up together, you must be prepared for a life in the circus, since that is what Katrina is determined to do when she grows up. She wants to make a home for abandoned animals, and the name of her show will be "The Kirkkomaki Circus." She has it all planned out. Her father will be the cook, and she will be the animal trainer. She said I could be the doctor of sick people and animals because she was so impressed with how well I bandaged her arm.

Katrina has been taking care of a motherless baby squirrel she found in the woods. The poor thing was half-dead, and she dotes upon it, constantly asking me for medical advice. I have to say, Gran's medicinal lessons never covered animals, so I hope the squirrel will not be the worse for my care. Father says it will be a miracle if the tiny thing survives. I hope for Katrina's sake that I can save it.

I know you will like all the loggers, Arthur. We spend enjoyable evenings around the stove, telling stories and reciting poetry. Last night, while Father was mending his boots, Clancy, the Irishman, sat near the kerosene lamp and read us passages from Tennyson. He read with such emotion that we were all crying. It was a sight to see these large men reduced to tears by the lovely words of that great poet.

Some nights we play charades. The best player is a big Swede named Gustav. His mimicking and gestures are so funny that we end up roaring with laughter.

I think we shall have music in our spare hours tonight. Father will play his fiddle, Clancy will play his harmonica, and Cookie has been trying to learn how to play the banjo (although I think he makes better flapjacks than music). The men are holding another contest to see who can sing the best song. Katrina will be the judge tonight. I was the judge last time, and it was hard to pick a winner. Most of the songs were not in English, and I had no idea what the men were singing about. I picked a song that I thought sounded very pretty, but later I learned it was all about pigs. Not that I have anything against pigs, but I did not expect them to inspire such beautiful melodies.

After the singing contest tonight, I think we may have some dancing. The Swedes and Germans like to clog, and I have even seen Father venturing a step or two. Jakob has taught Katrina and me how to waltz, but we do not have enough room in here to really fly, so we are heartily looking forward to dancing outdoors when winter ends.

The men talk of springtime, when the river will melt, and they can float their logs downstream to sawmills. They make it sound very exciting. Yet scary! Clancy told us he came close to dying in a logjam in Canada, for he slipped between two logs and almost drowned before he found a space where he could reach the surface again.

Spring will also be syrup time. Cookie has found some sugar maples in the woods, and he's promised to teach Katrina and me how to catch the sap and boil it to make sweet syrup. I was quite excited to taste syrup at Christmas. Cookie traded flour and salt pork to some passing Chippewas in exchange for cranberries and maple syrup. The next day, he surprised us by setting a little pitcher of the precious syrup upon the table to pour over our flapjacks. You will adore maple syrup, Arthur. I have not forgotten how much you like sweets.

It is such a wonder to wake and see snow resting upon the boughs of the tall white pines. It has been so very cold of late. Last night, the temperature dropped to thirty degrees below zero, so Oskar took down the thermometer and hid it beneath his bunk to keep us from growing discouraged. He need not have worried. Even though we have abundant snowdrifts, our spirits are high. Our piles of white pine at the riverbank look most impressive, and everyone is anxious for the weather to turn, so we can send the logs downriver and receive a bounty for our hard labours.

Katrina is a fun companion, and we keep busy by planning the circus she shall have someday. She invented a game where each day she adds a new act to her future show. Last night, she was very excited about the idea of you being an acrobat. Yes, indeed, I can easily imagine you on a trapeze!

The baby squirrel we saved is doing wonderfully. Right now, I am watching Katrina as she patiently trains him, trying to coax him to jump over a shoelace that she has strung between two chair legs. She calls him Pickles, and when he is not running all around the bunkhouse, he sleeps peacefully in her apron pocket.

I fear this will be my last letter because if I send more beyond this point, you probably won't receive them. My letter would pass

you while you're on your way here! I really cannot wait to see you,
Arthur. What fun we shall have! I wish you and your father a safe
passage.

Love,
Adara

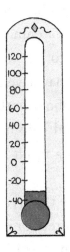

TOMMY

The kitchen was completely silent — and that was saying a lot, given that it held all of Tommy's brothers. After a suspenseful moment, Tommy asked cautiously, "So what happened, Papuza?"

She looked like she was remembering something from long ago. With a wistful smile, she said, "It seems like only yesterday when I was watching Katrina with that tiny squirrel. I was so excited to see Arthur. Truly, I couldn't wait until spring. I'm afraid I may have driven Katrina a bit crazy with my endless chatter about Arthur this, and Arthur that. Yet she bore it kindly, and I do believe she grew to have a fondness for him too, as a result of all the stories I shared with her.

"Spring came very late that year. And as the men waited for the river to thaw, I waited for my cousin. Arthur was due to arrive in early April, but April came and went. It grew harder and harder for me to remain patient.

"On the day before the men planned to float our logs down the river, some voyageurs from Fort Snelling stopped at our camp, bearing letters from the fort. In those days, mail was so rare it seemed like a present at Christmas time. Anxiously, we always longed for news from our homes.

"There was a letter for Father from Gran. Eagerly he began to read it. Then he stopped short. It held the most dreadful news that one can imagine. The ship bearing Arthur and his father had met with a disastrous storm. The authorities said there were no survivors.

"Father and I were stricken with despair. He had lost his brother, and I had lost my cousin. Katrina and the others tried to help as best they could, but a loss like that is a heavy burden to carry.

"Katrina's father also received a letter that day — a letter of quite a different nature. Cookie's eccentric uncle had perished and left him a small fortune, which he needed to go east and claim. When I heard this news, I realized I would soon be losing Katrina too. I was inconsolable. My life had changed overnight.

"Before those fateful letters arrived, we had planned that Katrina and Cookie and I would stay at the lumber camp while the men rode the logs down the river. We would wait for their return.

"But now that Katrina and Cookie were leaving, I would be at the camp all alone, which made my father uneasy. Thus it was decided that I would travel to Fort Snelling with Katrina and her father. They would look for a safe place to leave me at the fort, and my father would meet up with me when he came back upriver.

"So the next morning, Cookie and Katrina and I set our meager belongings in the wagon and watched the men start to float downriver on the logs. They waved farewell to us and called out heartfelt good wishes.

"Several days later, I said goodbye to Katrina and her father at Fort Snelling. On parting, she gave me a picture she had drawn of her future circus. She had written 'The Kirkkomaki Circus' across the top, and underneath, there was an image of her standing on top of a horse, waving. She drew me placing a bandage on the horse's leg. And high above the trapeze, she had drawn a picture of a boy who had wings and a halo. It was Arthur as an angel. It was truly the most touching gift I have ever received. That was the last time I ever saw or heard from her."

The kitchen was so quiet Tommy could hear Bess neighing far out in the barn.

He half-expected Papuza to look sadder than she did. Yet for some reason, she broke into a smile. She continued, "But now, the most astonishing thing has happened. A few days ago, as I was waiting in Mackey's for them to fill my order of flour, I chanced upon a newspaper. A customer must have left it behind, for it was sitting on the checkerboard table by the peanut barrel. I glanced at the paper, and an advertisement jumped right off the page at me!"

She reached into one of her many, many pockets and retrieved a small bundle of papers. Taking a scrap of newspaper from the pile, she unfolded it and laid it on the table. All the Dooleys pushed back their chairs and hurried to crowd around Papuza. The advertisement said:

THE KIRKKOMAKI CIRCUS
Prepare to be Enchanted
Three Nights of Spectacles in Beautiful St. Paul
From Acrobats to Zebras and Everything in between
Don't miss this Great and Glorious Show!
June 10th through 12th, 2 p.m. and 7 p.m.

"I assure you, I was stunned!" said Papuza. "I knew it had to be Katrina, or at least someone in her family, so I sent a telegram to the circus in St. Paul. Finally, this very afternoon, I received a response." She unfolded a telegram and read it out loud:

Hello, old friend. How wonderful to hear from you! My circus will be in Red Wing in a few days. Could we meet? You have been on my mind because a detective asked about you a few weeks ago. He left me his card, and it is somewhere here in my messy wagon. I was sorry I had to tell him I didn't know your whereabouts. He said someone is looking for you — a Mister Arthur Mundy! How can that be? I thought he perished at sea.

Anxiously awaiting you,
Katrina

"He's alive!?!" The Dooley clan cried in unison.

ESME

Esme asked, "But where in the world has he been all these years?" Jeepers, this was a real-life mystery! In her imagination, she was wearing a sleuth's hat and peering through a magnifying glass like Sherlock Holmes.

"In truth, I have no idea," said Grandma. "I was not expecting any news of Arthur. I was simply reaching out to find Katrina, and I received so much more!" She laughed with joy. "The possibility that Arthur might be alive astonishes me."

Grover Cleveland gave a low whistle. "Well, if that don't beat all!"

"Lost for sixty-six years." Uncle William shook his head in amazement.

"Wait a minute," Tommy almost had to shout to be heard above the hubbub. "Does this mean what I think it means?"

Everyone turned to him expectantly, waiting for him to finish.

"Does this mean . . . " His voice dropped to a whisper, as if he didn't dare to hope. ". . . we're going to the circus?"

Images of color and noise and animals leaped into Esme's mind. Oh, jiminy! Would it be like the circus in her book *Toby Tyler?*

"Esme and Tommy and I will leave tomorrow," said Grandma. "I responded to the telegram, telling Katrina to look for me in Red Wing."

"Can we go? Can we go?" Tommy's twin brothers jumped up and down, begging for an invitation.

"I talked with Papuza about this earlier," William told his eager sons. "Now is the worst time for us to pack up and leave. What with cutting hay and settling into this new place — well, I need all the help I can get."

"No fair," John Adams blurted out. "We've never gotten to go to the circus."

William held up his hand. "Papuza might only be with the circus for a short spell. Who knows where her search for Arthur will lead? She and I have agreed that we'll all go to the circus as a family, later in the summer. There should be a lull in the work in a couple of weeks. We could even take a train to see the show. How does that sound?"

With mumblings and grumblings, Tommy's brothers finally gave their grudging assent to this plan. Esme could tell that Tommy was trying to hide his excitement, so his brothers wouldn't feel bad. Yet he was about as successful at this as she was — or in other words, not successful at all.

"Esme and Tommy," said Grandma, taking them aside, "it might be a good idea if you packed tonight, for we're leaving bright and early in the morning."

They didn't have to be told twice.

Esme's heart beat fast as she and Tommy rushed up the stairs. *A journey,* she thought happily. *And to the circus!*

She pondered what she needed to pack. Well, of course she'd take her journal, so she could write all about their adventures. And of course she'd take Mr. Wright because it just wouldn't be right to go on an adventure without him. And of course . . . BAMM! She tripped on the last stair at the top, banging her shin on the tread before she fell forward onto the landing.

Tommy was so close behind her on the stairs that he didn't have time to stop, so he tripped right over her and somersaulted down the hallway!

Esme felt relieved when he stood up and adjusted his new glasses, and she felt even more relieved when he gave her a happy grin. She asked him, "Are you all right?"

He laughed. "I reckon we couldn't do that again, even if we tried a million times!"

Phew, she thought. *Thank goodness he's not mad at me.* She wouldn't want to start their journey that way. She was sure there would be plenty of chances in the days ahead for him to tell her she was trouble.

Tommy ran to his room, and she hurried to her room, which she shared with Grandma. The sun was setting, and darkness crept down over the inn. Esme dashed to where they kept the matches, so she could light the kerosene lantern.

She hopped up on a chair by the window, grabbed a match from the holder on the wall, and struck the match. Before she could even lift the glass chimney off the lantern, she caught sight of something outside her window. It was a wagon, rolling slowly by the inn.

Who can that be? A moment later, her curiosity turned to dread as an all-too-familiar figure rose from the wagon seat.

Holy mackerel, it was Hatch! And she held a rifle!

As Billy Groggs pulled up the reins, Hatch pointed the rifle at Esme's window. *She's aiming right at me,* thought Esme. *How in the world do you forgive a person when they keep trying to kill you?* Paralyzed with fear, Esme stood frozen while the lit match burned dangerously close to her fingers.

A moment later, the match singed her fingertips, so she dropped it to the floor. As she bent her head to look at her hand, Tommy barged into her room, asking, "Esme, have you seen my . . ."

He stopped in his tracks when KRAK! A bullet shattered the window.

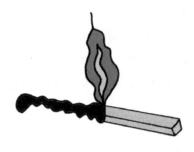

TOMMY

Holy smoke! The bullet nicked Tommy's ear before it lodged inside the wall. As his hand flew up to cover his poor, stinging ear, he thought, *We're lucky to be alive.*

"Duck down!" cried Esme. "Hatch is shooting!"

Well, thought Tommy, *thanks for warning me after the fact.* Not for the first time, he told himself that being around Esme could be mighty dangerous. A fellow really took his life in his hands just by being her best friend.

He rubbed his ear. He felt lucky it was still attached to his head, but jeepers, it hurt! Protectively, he covered it with his hand again. On the bright side, at least his ear wasn't lying on the floor.

"Oh, Tommy, are you all right?" Esme cried, clutching her lucky locket.

"I ain't sure, Esme. What about you?"

She jumped down from the chair and ran to his side. Her green eyes were wide, and he could tell she was shocked. "Let

me see," she said, trying to pull his hand away from his ear. Before Esme succeeded, Papuza came running up the stairs with her black braids flying. Right behind her were Tommy's pa and brothers, and they all jabbered at once, crying things like, "Are you okay?" and "It sounded like gunshots!" and "What happened?"

Papuza lit the lantern and gave Esme a big hug and a good looking-over, while Pa placed his hand on Tommy's shoulder and asked if he was all right.

"It was Hatch and Groggs," said Esme, drawing an anxious breath. "I'm worried that Tommy got hurt."

Gravely, Tommy said, "They shot me."

Of course that caused a gigantic commotion amongst his brothers, and they crowded around him to inspect his wound. Esme wormed her way into the middle of the huddle and stood on her tiptoes. Tommy didn't really want to remove his hand from his ear. *For gosh sakes,* he thought, *what if my ear falls off?* Yet there was no getting around it, so slowly, reluctantly, he dropped his hand.

His brothers leaned in to take a good look.

Almost immediately, their excitement faded, and they started complaining. Andrew Jackson groaned, "For crying out loud, it ain't even bleeding!"

"Yep," the rest of them grumbled regretfully. Tommy hated to be such a disappointment to them.

"But your ears sure are dirty!" George Washington passed judgment.

"I'm so glad you're okay," Esme said, squeezing Tommy's arm.

"Where's the bullet?" Millard Fillmore asked. It wasn't long before the brothers found it lodged in the wall. They started to bicker about who could keep it, once it was dug out of the plaster. Gee whiz, Tommy wondered if they'd be wrangling like this if the bullet had lodged in his head.

Pa told him, "It looks like you'll be fine, Thomas Jefferson." He patted Tommy's shoulder. Then he turned to the oldest boy, Zachary Taylor, and said, "Take George, John, James, Andrew, and Millard and go out to Groggs' place to keep an eye on them. Franklin, Abraham, Chester, and Grover, come with me to track down the sheriff. Ulysses and Rutherford, you stay here and board up that window."

"What about Esme and Tommy?" complained one of the twins. "Don't they have to help?"

"I think they ought to start their journey tonight," said Pa. "The sooner they're safely out of here, the better." Firmly he told Papuza, "Don't worry, we'll take care of Hatch."

She only hesitated a moment. Then she nodded at Esme and Tommy. "Be quick, my dears. Pack as swiftly as you can."

So Esme skedaddled to pack, and Tommy hurried back to his room. The prospect of the trip almost made him forget his throbbing ear. He threw some clean underwear and socks into his empty pillowcase. He couldn't find his comb, but that didn't matter because his hair had a mind of its own. It had never yielded to any comb that had crossed its path. In fact, the only thing it had ever heeded was a pair of scissors in Esme's hands!

Tommy felt in his pocket for the jackknife Papuza had given him. Yep, he had it, even though the twins had tried to spirit it away. All his gol-darn brothers could beat him at knife throwing, but he reckoned he'd surprise them. He planned to practice his throwing the whole time he was gone.

He was ready. He wasn't sure where he was going, or who he would meet, or how long he'd be gone, but he knew he was ready!

Goodbyes were said all around, with a fair amount of hugging, and handshakes, and slaps on the back. Papuza promised to send Pa a telegram soon, and he agreed to write back to her.

"Don't forget to write everything down, Esme," said James Monroe. "We sure enjoyed reading about your last trip."

By the time Tommy had tied Bess to the side of the gypsy wagon, and his brothers had left to track down Hatch and Groggs, and he'd placed the stuffed pillowcases and Mr. Wright inside the wagon, night had fallen in earnest.

"Come on, Zinjiber. Come on, Joe," Papuza coaxed her horses. They gradually picked up speed, and the gypsy wagon swayed slowly away from home.

Tommy took a last look behind him. As much as he liked their new place, it felt good to get back on the road, especially since Hatch was stirring up trouble again. He heard wagon wheels on the night wind, and he wondered if they might be hers.

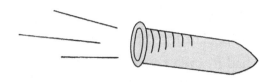

VILLAIN

The stormy weather lent itself perfectly to my plans. No one saw me by the animal pens. No one possibly could. Between my black garments and the ebony shadows of the evening, I was a mere ghost.

I slide silently through the tent flaps, for I have one more task to complete.

ESME

Even though Esme longed to reach the circus, Joe and Zinjiber had each lost a horseshoe, so Grandma decided to make camp for the day near a quiet hamlet called Hay Creek.

The late afternoon sun hung low in the sky. The gentle humming of cicadas accompanied the croak of tree frogs, creating a soothing chorus while Esme and Tommy worked. They were gathering stinging nettles for Grandma along the banks of the creek. Oh, jiminy, what a beautiful spot!

Thinking about their trip so far, Esme wondered if they'd pestered Grandma too much with all their questions about Arthur, even though she had answered good-naturedly. They had tried to unearth new tidbits of information that she might have forgotten to tell them.

The only thing they'd discovered, which was quite accidental and had nothing to do with Arthur, was that Grandma had learned how to belly dance while she roamed the deserts of North Africa with a Bedouin tribe. This bit of news surprised Esme, and she had a hard time forgetting the image of Grandma swirling around in scarves and bangles and bracelets.

And they'd talked about adopting again. Esme kept wondering if they'd run into someone on their journey who needed a loving home. The thought of her future sibling just waiting to be found was thrilling. Why, the very next child they bumped into could be her new sister!

Yes, it had been a jim-dandy day, and tomorrow they'd reach the circus. As Esme and Tommy took a break from gathering nettles, they rested on the creek's bank and surveyed the results of their work. "Grandma will be happy when she sees how much we gathered for her remedies," said Esme.

"I can't wait to tell my brothers about the cure for these miserable nettles." After a pause, Tommy smiled. "On second thought, maybe I won't tell them."

Esme laughed. "Who would have guessed that the cure grows right beside it?" For Grandma had shown them how to stop the burning by using the juice of the jewelweed, which grew next to the nettles.

A slight breeze blew — so slight it stirred only one lone bell on the gypsy wagon nearby. Esme felt pretty sure that she and Tommy thought the same thing at the same time, for they were true friends who knew each other well. Tommy said it for them. "I wonder when Papuza will be back?"

Grandma had gone to the Hay Creek General Store to see if there was anyone around who could shoe her horses. She'd been away for a while, and evening had arrived. A splendid idea hit Esme, so she jumped to her feet. "Let's surprise Grandma by having supper ready."

Tommy peered at her doubtfully. He had never known her to cook anything in her entire life. More than once, he had said he had grave doubts about her abilities in the kitchen. "Maybe I'd eat some beans," he said cautiously. "But shucks, I'd better not make any promises."

He followed Esme into the gypsy wagon to see what she would do. Searching under the dry sink, she found a kettle she could use, but it was much too heavy for her. "Can you help me carry this?" she asked Tommy.

He lifted the cast-iron pot by its handle and set it on the table. "Now what?" he asked.

"Do you think I can cook in this?" Her dress was awfully dirty, and she wondered if she should put on some kind of apron.

"Naw, I think you should cook in the pot," he said seriously.

She rolled her eyes, but she couldn't help but giggle. "Oh, go get the fire started."

After Tommy left the wagon, Esme shut the door behind him.

And locked it.

Mr. Wright sprawled on one of the benches, just waking up from a nap. As Esme stroked his fur, he yawned. She whispered to him, "We can do better than plain old bread and beans. Let's make something with some razzle-dazzle!"

She thought for a moment. Then she went to work. First she opened some cans of beans and emptied them into the pot. Even though she'd never cooked before, she felt supremely confident because she'd watched Grandma cook many times. All she had to do was to copy Grandma's technique, which was to add a little bit of this, and a little bit of that. Of course all the ingredients would be things that Esme loved.

She added fresh strawberries to the beans for a dash of color. And then she dropped in a chopped apple. Next she cut up some cheese and added dried mustard and two palms of sugar. With a handful of salt and some ground horseradish, she felt absolutely sure she was making a masterpiece. It would be so scrumptious that the great chefs of Europe would beg for her secret recipe. Even Mr. Wright seemed curious, paying close attention. If his actions were any indication, Esme was creating a whopping success.

"What's taking so long?" Tommy called warily from the back stoop.

"Just a little longer, Tommy," she sang happily. "You can't rush a masterpiece!"

"A masterpiece," she heard him grumble.

His obvious doubt made her more determined. *Just wait,* she thought. *You'll be scraping your plate clean, begging for seconds. Maybe even thirds!*

As she stirred the ingredients together, her brow furrowed. What was missing? *Perhaps some meat.* So she opened two cans of tuna fish and stirred them into the mix. She left the empty cans for Mr. Wright, so he could lick them out.

Now, surely some spices. She glanced up at the dried spices hanging from the ceiling. Then she crawled up on the table to smell the different bundles. She liked the aroma of one in particular, which she'd seen Grandma put in stews. *Oregano? Is that its name?* Well, anyway, she knew it was safe to eat, and it smelled delicious. She broke off some leaves, crumbling them into her concoction.

Esme had never dreamed that cooking could be so easy, which was a pretty good sign she had a natural talent for it. Maybe she would be a matchmaker AND a writer AND a cook when she grew up. *Maybe I'll write romantic cookbooks — or even better, a book of love potions.* That could really help her success as a matchmaker. Yes, her future looked bright, with many possibilities.

Then her brow furrowed because there was one thing for certain that she'd never be able to become — and that was a barber!

She placed the lid on the pot and finally unlocked the door to let Tommy in. She teased him, "You just can't wait to try my cooking, can you?"

"What did you make, Esme?" His voice was full of misgivings. He tried to lift the lid. Swiftly, she placed her hands on top.

"It's a surprise! I know you're going to love it."

"Hmm." He didn't sound at all convinced.

Together they carried the pot outside and hung it from the tripod above the fire. As Tommy tethered Bess close to the wagon, Esme found herself listening for the sound of hooves that would announce Grandma's return.

They lingered by the campfire as darkness crowded in. Tommy poked the flames with a stick, and firelight reflected off his eyeglasses. Esme heard his stomach grumble.

"Hello, my dears," said Grandma. It seemed as if she'd materialized out of nowhere. Esme and Tommy ran to her side as she tethered Joe and Zinjiber. Nodding towards the pot, Grandma asked, "And what do we have here?"

Bursting with excitement, Esme said, "I made supper. Do you want to eat?"

TOMMY

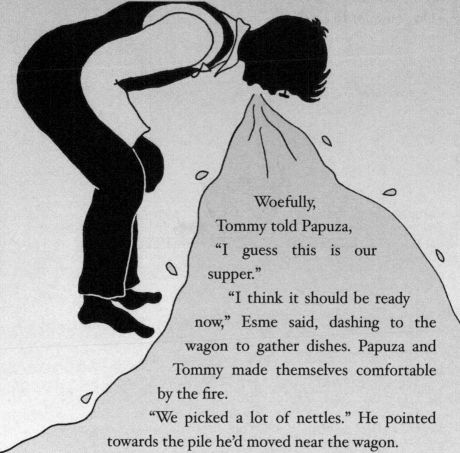

Woefully, Tommy told Papuza, "I guess this is our supper."

"I think it should be ready now," Esme said, dashing to the wagon to gather dishes. Papuza and Tommy made themselves comfortable by the fire.

"We picked a lot of nettles." He pointed towards the pile he'd moved near the wagon.

"So I see," Papuza said with a smile. "Well done! That will certainly keep us in stock for a while."

Esme returned and handed out bowls and spoons. Using a dishtowel to protect her small hands against the heat, she lifted the lid of the kettle. Tommy's curiosity got the better of him, so he leaned over and took a deep whiff of her concoction. "What in tarnation . . . ," he began.

"Just try it," Esme begged. "It might be the best thing you've ever tasted."

But it wasn't.

In fact, sure as shooting, thought Tommy, *it's the worst thing I've ever tasted.* He spat it out and began to gag.

Papuza took a bite and said gently, "Oh, my. What did you put in this, dear?"

Esme took a bite to try it.

Immediately she had to spit it out.

Tommy couldn't help but feel sorry for her. "Oh, it ain't so bad," he lied, before he fled away from the fire and vomited behind a tree.

Crestfallen, Esme mumbled, "I guess I won't end up being a cook after all."

"Don't believe any such thing," said Papuza. "Cooking simply takes practice — like many skills in life — and creativity, which I know you have. Are you all right, Tommy?"

"Yep, I reckon I feel better now."

"Shall we see what we can find for food?" asked Papuza.

Esme followed her to the wagon while Tommy headed off to dump the contents of the pot.

He toted it a ways from the wagon, so they wouldn't be able to smell it. By gum, he had to shudder. He sure felt sorry for Esme's future husband. The poor, unsuspecting feller would end up as skinny as a scarecrow, with only a few tufts of hair on his head. Tommy gagged again as he scraped the poisonous concoction out of the pot.

By the time he returned to the fire, Esme and Papuza had already placed comforters around the flames and were snacking on sandwiches. Esme handed a sandwich to Tommy, but then he needed to chase after Mr. Wright. The baby raccoon was heading towards the remains of Esme's "I-guess-you-could-call-it-food." Tommy caught him in time and whispered that he was only trying to keep him alive.

They all shared an enjoyable evening, drinking cocoa and talking of many things. Mostly they wondered what tomorrow would bring. Had Katrina found the detective's card? Had she already contacted him? Was there a chance that Arthur was at the circus?

"Do you think you'll recognize Arthur when you see him?" Tommy asked Papuza.

"I do hope so," she said softly. An expression of doubt crossed her face momentarily, only to be replaced by a smile. "He was a fetching lad when he was young. And more than a little bit mischievous." She laughed.

"Oh, did he do anything naughty?" Esme's bright eyes widened with interest.

Puffing her pipe, Papuza nodded. "Oh, heavens yes," she admitted. "Shortly before I sailed for America, Arthur took revenge on a cruel boy named Bram Brice. Bram had beaten one of Arthur's dogs — almost beaten it to death, just for the sport of it." Papuza's brows drew together in disgust.

"So Arthur dropped a small grass snake down the back of Bram's pants while they were singing in the church choir. Gracious, Bram certainly hopped up and down!" Papuza chuckled. "He looked as if he were possessed. He threw his hymnal in the air, and it accidentally landed on the organist's hands, ending the music for that day. Bram tore off his trousers and ran like blue blazes out of the church!"

Papuza paused and wiped a tear of laughter from her eye.

"Oh, Arthur was a feisty one. Yes, indeed. Yet he was a good soul too." She sighed. "I've thought about him all these years. It seems like a miracle that I might be seeing him again."

Esme slipped to her grandmother's side and gave her a hug. "You deserve a miracle, Grandma!"

"That's for sure," Tommy agreed, scooting closer to Papuza too.

Papuza hugged them both tightly and said, "Tomorrow cannot come soon enough."

And with that, they all said good night.

As Tommy snuggled down into his blankets, he heard a rustling in the forest. Nervously, he asked Esme, "Did you hear that?"

"It's just your imagination, Tommy, running away from you again."

Well, that was a bit rich, given that *she* was the one with the powerful imagination. And even though his ears might be dirty, and one had been grazed by a bullet, they sure weren't lacking in listening ability.

He kept one eye open for a good, long while.

esme

It took Esme forever to fall asleep. Images of the circus swirled through her mind, making slumber impossible. Finally, after knotting and unknotting herself in her blankets several dozen times, she dozed off.

Much later, in the dead of night, she woke up. She really, really, really wished she had a chamber pot. The fire had died down to mere embers, yet it gave off enough light for her to see. The night had grown chilly, so she shivered as she left the warmth of her comforter.

She slipped away from their campsite to do her duty as quickly as possible. Apparently she had ended up by her ruined supper, for she could smell that terrible concoction. It made her wrinkle her nose.

When she was ready to leave, she heard the very faintest sound. She told herself it was probably Mr. Wright, yet the skin on the back of her neck began to prickle. She turned around, and there, not five yards away, a deadly tiger crouched.

Holy Christmas! The tiger looked massive in the moonlight. Esme clutched her lucky locket, stiffening in shock. The cat stood motionless also — except for its eyes. They glinted in the darkness, sizing Esme up.

Esme longed to run, yet her instincts told her to remain still. This was a cat-and-mouse game, and she was definitely the mouse. Drops of sweat trickled from her brow, and she wondered how long she'd been trapped here, caught in the tiger's gaze. Ten seconds? Twenty? Thirty? It seemed like an eternity.

The horses were tethered on the other side of the wagon, and they must have picked up the cat's scent, for they began to snort and stomp their hooves. Maybe they would distract the beast. *Please,* thought Esme. *Please leap back in the forest and forget you ever saw me.*

But the tiger didn't move.

What would Mowgli from *The Jungle Book* do? He would know how to handle jungle-type emergencies. And then Esme's mind flashed to Grandma, who had faced that savage wolf near the lumber camp, so many years ago. Now Esme knew the terror that Grandma must have felt.

Esme tried *not* to imagine how it would feel when the cat sunk its sharp teeth into her flesh. Blood would gush out. And then the tiger would rip her open, slashing her sinews, snapping her bones, and sucking out her very marrow.

TOMMY

Meanwhile, Tommy was dreaming, although it wasn't a very fun dream. In fact, it was more like a nightmare, if you came right down to it. He and Mr. Wright were tied to dining room chairs, sitting before a table completely covered with pie tins. Dishes were stacked precariously in front of him, teetering this way and that, with food overflowing and nearly engulfing him.

Suddenly a tiny chef popped up at his side. It was Esme! She wore a baker's hat that was too big and slipped down over her eyes, and she held out a pie. Setting the pie in front of him, she sang, "I know how much you love my cooking!" She adjusted her hat and disappeared.

Tommy looked down at the pie. Gosh-almighty! It was filled with that poisonous concoction she had cooked last night. Right then and there, he knew they were in trouble, and it was only going to get worse because all the dishes on the table were filled with the very same thing.

Well, the food — if anyone could call it that — began to ooze towards him and Mr. Wright, filling the room. Tommy bobbed along in his chair, feeling mighty uneasy. He longed to call out for help, yet he didn't dare open his mouth. The grub was too dangerously near.

Mr. Wright, on the other hand, was floating (chair and all) on his back and singing hymns at the top of his little raccoon lungs.

Then, in that crazy way of dreams, their chairs became a boat, and they were heading down the Mississippi in a paddle wheeler, looking for a restaurant where a feller could find a decent meal.

Mr. Wright led Tommy to the riverboat's dining room, where they both felt mighty relieved that Esme was nowhere in sight. But then suddenly, she busted in, holding out a pie filled with her terrible, inedible stuff. "You can't get enough of this, can you?"

"No! No! No!" he cried out loud in his sleep.

ESME

Esme heard Tommy crying out, "No! No! No!"

The tiger flinched. For the first time, it broke its deadly gaze. *Is Tommy behind me? Is the cat afraid of Tommy?*

A burst of confidence surged through her. "No!" she screamed as loudly as she could, mimicking her cousin. The tiger took a cautious step back, making her feel even stronger.

"No! No! No!" Esme shouted so forcefully that it made her throat burn. "No!" she screamed, waving her arms, trying to look as big as possible.

Miraculously, the tiger bounded off into the woods. Catching her breath, Esme fell to her knees. Oh, good gravy, she didn't think she'd ever been so frightened, and that included all the times when Hatch had tried to kill her.

Her arms and legs had turned to jelly. She didn't even have the strength to lift her head. A hand touched her shoulder, and she flinched.

"What happened, dear?" Esme's screaming must have awakened Grandma, who knelt beside her and began to rub Esme's back. Still shaking, Esme gave Grandma a tight hug.

"A tiger!" Esme cried. "Right over there!" She pointed to the spot where the tiger had stood, just moments before. "I thought for sure it would eat me."

Joining them, Tommy asked doubtfully, "A tiger?"

Esme squeezed his hand and told him, "If it hadn't been for your screaming, I probably wouldn't be here right now."

"What are you talking about?" he asked in a puzzled tone. "I was sound asleep!"

"Ah, I imagine you were talking in your sleep," Grandma explained. "Perhaps you were dreaming."

"Yes," Tommy said slowly. His eyebrows crinkled in concentration. "I was having a nightmare about Esme's cooking."

Esme would have laughed, if she hadn't felt so shaken. "Tommy must have dumped my supper around here because I can smell it."

Grandma suggested, "Maybe that's what attracted the tiger."

"Maybe that's what scared it away," Tommy mumbled under his breath.

"Thank goodness it all turned out well!" Grandma gave Esme's shoulder a loving squeeze. "I daresay the creature must belong to the circus. We'll have to tell Katrina all about this."

"I still think you must have been dreaming," Tommy told Esme. "There ain't no tigers around here." He had barely finished speaking when a very real roar broke through the forest. Tommy was the first of them to skedaddle back to the dying campfire.

Esme and Grandma followed. Quickly they picked up Mr. Wright and their bedding and moved inside the gypsy wagon.

TOMMY

Tommy was all in favor of avoiding a wild, roaming, and no-doubt-starving tiger, so he hadn't argued when Papuza had suggested that they sleep inside the gypsy wagon. She had slept up in the bedchamber, Esme had taken one bench along the table, and Tommy had taken the other bench.

When he woke up the following morning, he opened his eyes and thought he must be seeing things. It sort of looked like an ostrich was peering down at him through the window.

Holy smoke! He shot straight up and grabbed his glasses. *Nope, I ain't seeing things.* A real, live, honest-to-goodness ostrich was peeking back at him. The strange thing (as if seeing a bird like that upon waking wasn't strange

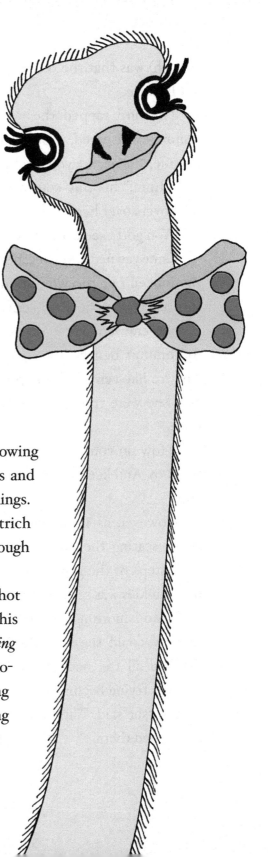

enough) was that the ostrich was wearing an orange polka-dot bow tie.

The bird tapped the window with its beak. "Esme," Tommy whispered, not wanting to scare the creature outside, "Esme, are you awake?"

"Hmm," his tiny cousin murmured lazily, as she pulled the covers over her head.

"You gotta see this," he whispered. "Wake up!"

Esme yawned and stretched, slowly coming to life. When she looked out the window, her dark eyelashes flew up in surprise. "An ostrich!" she cried.

She crawled across the top of the table and slid down to Tommy's bench. "Oh, she's beautiful! Look at her eyes! They're like velvet." Esme pressed her hand to the window as if she were trying to touch the bird's beak through the pane.

"How do you know it's a girl?" asked Tommy. "It could be a boy. And keep your voice down, so you won't scare him away."

However, as it turned out, they didn't need to worry about scaring the bird away. When they raced down the back steps of the gypsy wagon, they found that one of the bird's ankles was securely tied to a wagon wheel.

"Good morning, my dears!" Papuza sang out happily. Tommy could see that she'd been busy. She had already distilled all the nettles they'd picked yesterday, and now she was frying bacon over the fire. "I trust you noticed our visitor," she said. With a laugh, she set down the frying pan and joined them.

"I do believe she has a gentle nature," said Papuza. "I've met a few ostriches in my travels, and I have a healthy respect for their tempers, but this young lady has a pleasant disposition." Papuza stroked the bird lovingly, so Esme and Tommy reached out and stroked her too.

"How do you know it's a girl?" asked Tommy.

"Well," said Papuza, "the males of the species have black feathers whereas the females have gray and brown plumage, like our visitor here."

"I knew she was a girl," said Esme. "I could tell by her eyes." It took all of Tommy's willpower to keep from rolling *his* eyes.

"I suggest we take her to Katrina today," said Papuza. "I daresay I'm curious about the circus. Something may be amiss, for why would these exotic and rather expensive animals be roaming the countryside? I assure you, I have been keeping a keen eye out for that tiger." Her eyes twinkled as she added, "I am delighted to report I have seen neither hide nor hair of him."

She went back to cooking breakfast while Esme and Tommy grew acquainted with the ostrich. Mr. Wright kept his distance from the tall bird and stayed close to Papuza.

"Let's name her 'Pansy,'" said Esme.

"Shucks, Esme. We can't give her a name. She ain't ours! And why would you pick 'Pansy' anyhow?"

"Because the petals of a pansy are soft, like crushed velvet. Just like her velvety eyes." The bird bent down her long neck, and Esme stroked her head. "I wish I could keep her. I'd take such good care of her, and I'd ride her to school, just like you ride Bess."

"For gosh sakes," said Tommy, "you can't ride an ostrich!"

"Oh, but you can. You can!" Esme said eagerly. "I read all about it in *The Swiss Family Robinson*."

"Well, you can't believe everything you read," he said.

"Aye, very true, my dear," Papuza said kindly. "Although I must say that in Africa, I once saw grown men riding ostriches in a race."

"May I try to ride her?" Esme pleaded. "Please, please, please?"

So before breakfast, Esme and Tommy practiced riding Pansy. And then after breakfast, they rode again, whenever there was a free moment, as they helped Papuza pack up camp. Esme enjoyed it a lot more than Tommy did, and he thought, *I best be sticking with Bess.*

As they left their campsite, Papuza drove the gypsy wagon, Tommy rode Bess, and Esme rode Pansy. In the distance, they glimpsed deer grazing, and two woodpeckers were tapping a duet on a tree trunk. The noise may have startled Pansy because suddenly, she took off like she was in an ostrich race. Shrieking, Esme could barely hang on.

Tommy sighed and called after her, "Esme! You're going the wrong way!"

ESME

After Esme managed to turn
Pansy in the right direction, their
travels went smoothly. As the cousins rode in front
of the gypsy wagon, Esme began to daydream. If she didn't
look at Tommy riding Bess beside her, and if she pretended
she was traveling all by her lonesome on Pansy, she could
imagine being in a faraway land. Pansy was such a foreign
creature that she made Esme feel exotic too. Pansy's plumes
did a dance with the wind, and Esme could picture herself
wearing a headdress made from feathers that Pansy had
shed. Esme would be the Ostrich Queen and offer kindly
advice on dusting with ostrich feathers and cooking omelets
with ostrich eggs.

Yes, she was the ruler of a faraway land that was very clean. *Especially if I can get Tommy to pick up all the empty eggshells.*

Tommy interrupted her daydream. "All my life, I've wanted to go to the circus." Absently, he petted Mr. Wright, who nestled in the bib of his overalls. "The only thing that could make this day better would be if all my brothers were with us."

"But Grandma and your pa promised to take us all later this summer, so don't be sad."

He shook his head. "That's almost harder to believe than anything. My brothers ain't never been nowhere — except in trouble! They've never taken a train or left the valley."

His words brought the Orphan Train back to Esme's mind. *Will we meet any orphans in our travels?* They hadn't crossed paths with any orphans in Hay Creek, but maybe they would at the circus.

Esme and Tommy continued to ride side-by-side, for Pansy and Bess were well suited in their strides. As Esme tried to decide whether to ask her cousin a thorny question, she watched daisies bend and sway along the edge of the road. Finches fluttered through the flowers. "Tommy," she eventually asked, "if you had to choose between adopting a girl or a boy, which one would you want?"

He mulled it over for a while. Finally he said, "Probably a boy. I think a boy would fit in better with my brothers. A girl might feel overwhelmed."

Esme figured that was a well-thought-out answer. And there was something that had been worrying her a little about adopting a girl. She asked Tommy, "If we did adopt a girl, what if you ended up liking her better than me?"

"Well, that wouldn't be hard," he said.

"Tommy!" And then Esme saw that he was giving her a mischievous grin. She thought, *I can't wait to have a sister, so we can gang up and tease Tommy.*

They'd been climbing a hill, and now they reached the crest, in the tender sunshine. The sky was big and blue with cottony clouds, and the sights of Red Wing had opened below them. The circus was easy to spot, set on the edge of town, with colorful flags flying from striped tents. A faint calliope melody drifted up to them on the breeze.

Grandma pulled up beside them in the gypsy wagon, and they paused for a moment, taking it all in. My gosh, even from this distance, Esme felt the energy flowing from the circus. Her heart began to beat faster as she imagined the fun they were about to have — not to mention meeting Katrina and possibly Arthur. "Oh, Grandma," she confessed. "I can't wait! I think I need to gallop."

Grandma laughed. "Well, get going then. But do wait for me by the gates."

And with that, they were off. Tommy spurred Bess to run, but Pansy had no trouble passing Bess. The wind blew back Esme's bangs as she sped down the hill. She threw her head back and laughed, bubbling over with joy.

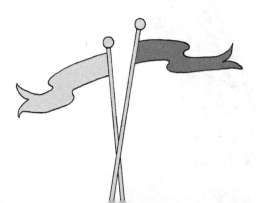

TOMMY

Tommy tried mighty hard to listen to Esme and Papuza, but jeepers, it wasn't easy! Things had a way of distracting him — like that lively band playing "A Bicycle Built for Two" or that troupe of Russian Cossacks in colorful silk costumes who were leading a bear by a rope. Mr. Wright cautiously peeked his nose out of the bib of Tommy's overalls to sniff the air. When he saw the bear, he immediately dove back down.

Not far away stood a gigantic tent. Red and blue flags flew high on its peaks, and hordes of people gathered outside. Hundreds and hundreds of them! How would they ever find Katrina in such a crowd? Tommy reckoned it would be easier to stumble on a snowflake in a fire.

It sounded like Papuza was telling Esme they should split up.

"But I want to meet Katrina," said Esme, "and find out about Arthur!"

"And so do I, dear. So do I." Around her wrist, Papuza wound Pansy's rope a little tighter to keep the bird closer. "But mind you, I have to find Katrina first, and that will take some time. Wouldn't you rather be exploring?"

Esme and Tommy exchanged a look, and it was absolutely clear that they both felt exactly the same way. *Yep, we are dying to go exploring!*

With a twinkle in her eye, Papuza said, "Meet me at the entrance of the big top when the show starts." Rummaging through her many, many pockets, she found a handful of coins, which she divided between the cousins. "Now, off you go, and have some fun!" She gave each of them a hug before she strolled away with Pansy.

"Come on," Tommy told Esme, steering her towards a fairway where merchants sold food, and crowds of spectators milled about. The cousins wove their way through a throng of men in seersucker suits, and women with silk parasols, and children with President Roosevelt buttons.

In one lane, a sign that said, "Fairy Floss" caught Tommy's attention because their friend, Leah Marne, had gone to the State Fair last summer, and she had tried to bring back some of the pink spun sugar, so Esme and Tommy could try it. But it had gotten stuck in Leah's hair before she got home. They didn't really want to eat it after that.

Now, Esme and Tommy stared at the fluffy pink treat. "Oh," gasped Esme, "so that's how it's supposed to look! It sure seems a lot better without hair in it."

Tommy agreed, and there was no doubt at all that they were going to have to try the spun sugar. Swiftly, Esme pulled a few pennies out of her pocket and bought two cones. She passed one to Tommy while he handed her Mr. Wright.

Esme cradled the raccoon in her free arm. As soon as he settled in, he reached over and stole a portion of her fairy floss. He quickly devoured it, much to their amusement. Tommy took a bite from his cone, and it tasted just as pink and fluffy as it looked. Delicious!

Across the way, there was a tent with a huge sign of a mermaid. Tommy looked away fast because he didn't think she was completely dressed. *Not that I know what mermaids wear,* he thought. Shucks, maybe she was fine, as mermaids go. Yet something told him that all his brothers would blush a little if Pa caught them looking at that sign.

"Step right up and be amazed!" cried a man outside the mermaid's tent. Above and below his armbands, his long sleeves puffed out a little. On his head, he wore a straw boater hat, and occasionally he whacked the mermaid sign with his cane. "Just a nickel. Only a nickel!"

"Oh, Tommy! Do you think she's real?" Esme was already searching her pockets for a nickel. While she was distracted, Mr. Wright seized the moment to steal another gob of fairy floss.

"One of the Wonders of the World!" cried the barker. He tipped down his boater, and Esme put in a nickel. Wondering if he was doing something wicked, Tommy dropped in a nickel too. Without pausing his pitch, the man scooped out their nickels, rolled the hat back up his sleeve, and set it on his head. "Yes, siree, folks, you won't be sorry!"

Using the curved top of his cane, he pulled back the flap of the mermaid's tent.

They stepped inside.

ESME

Once the tent flap closed behind Esme, she felt as if she'd walked into a completely different world. The barker's voice and the hubbub of the crowd outside faded away. The only sound inside the tent was the whirr of an engine.

It was dark, except for an eerie, green glow that shone from a huge fish tank that took up the length of the tent. Esme blinked several times, stepping closer.

The tank was filled with water and illuminated somehow by an unnatural green light. Bubbles bubbled to the top from different places in the watery room. For that's what it was — an underwater bedroom for a mermaid.

There was an enormous hinged shell that held a soft, luxurious bed. A vanity table made from smaller shells had a mirror that was framed in coral. Seaweed swayed in front of an elegant folding screen, and sparkling jewels spilled out of an open treasure chest.

But where was the mermaid? Esme stepped closer, utterly oblivious of the fact that Mr. Wright had finished off her fairy floss.

"Wow!" Tommy whispered next to her in the dark. They stood motionless, and Esme was mesmerized. Surely this was the very room of *The Little Mermaid,* her favorite Hans Christian Andersen fairy tale.

From behind the folding screen, a mermaid suddenly darted. Esme jumped, hugging Mr. Wright.

The fish girl stopped abruptly, which made her long hair float up and down in a ghostly fashion. She gazed directly at Esme and Tommy.

Goose bumps rose on the back of Esme's neck.

Slowly the mermaid swished her tail back and forth, studying the cousins. Her tail looked real to Esme, who was very curious to touch it. The mermaid wore shells on her chest and a pearl choker around her neck. Her pale coloring and the dark circles around her eyes drew attention to the haunted expression on her face.

She was small — not as small as Esme, but smaller than Tommy. She seemed so real that Esme looked for gills on her neck but didn't see any. Esme stepped closer, spellbound. *How is she breathing?* For she couldn't really be a mermaid, could she? Even though Esme's eyes were telling her that the mermaid really was real?

Is she a nice sort of mermaid or a mean sort? If Esme had been a betting kind of gal, she would have laid her money on the side that said this was one of

the mean ones — the type that lures sailors to their deaths and feasts upon them. Or were those sirens? Esme's brow furrowed as she concentrated on this otherworldly being.

Unexpectedly, the mermaid lunged at Esme and Tommy! Esme screamed, frightening Mr. Wright, who leaped from her arms and fled.

"Mr. Wright!" she cried, racing after him.

Instead of scurrying towards the entrance, Mr. Wright decided upon a different route. He bolted to the side of the tent and crawled beneath it. Esme scrambled after him.

Before she left the tent, she turned around and called, "Tommy!" She had expected him to help her, but he was so mesmerized by the mermaid that he hadn't even noticed she was gone. "Tommy!" she yelled again, but he didn't move. *Hmm,* thought Esme. *And he claims he doesn't like girls.* She didn't dare wait for him any longer, or she would surely lose Mr. Wright.

She crawled under the tent just in time. If she'd been one second later, she wouldn't have seen Mr. Wright scurry into a different tent across the way. She followed him, and when she stood up inside the second tent, she realized she'd stumbled into another exhibit. The air smelled of incense, and colorful lanterns hung around a small stage.

Crumbs! Mr. Wright was on that stage! Melodious music flowed from bagpipes that were being played by a burly man wearing a plaid turban. At his feet, a hissing snake stretched up, poised to strike Mr. Wright!

ESME

Esme's hands flew up and covered her mouth. Jumping Jehoshaphat! A mere three feet separated her from the stage where Mr. Wright stood frozen. She could tell that their baby raccoon was leery of this strange creature that swayed hypnotically in front of him.

Esme knew exactly how he felt. The memory of that tiger last night was still vivid in her mind. Poor Mr. Wright! He was so helpless! *I have to do something — and fast.*

There was no time to run and get Tommy. There was no time for anything, really, because every precious second that slipped by could be Mr. Wright's last. Esme looked up at the snake charmer. Good golly, his eyes were closed. It looked as if he'd hypnotized himself with his haunting music.

Esme glanced back at the death dance between the hissing snake and poor Mr. Wright. She realized the stage was littered with woven rugs — rugs that reminded her of Persia, although they weren't the flying-carpet kind. They were small ones scattered about the stage.

Quickly, before she lost her nerve, she jumped up on the stage. Grabbing a rug, she didn't pause to think about the danger to herself. Instead she threw the rug over the snake!

A gasp went up from the crowd.

Esme swooped Mr. Wright into her arms, and even though her knees shook, she jumped down lickety-split from the stage. The audience burst into applause and cried, "Bravo!"

Esme dashed to the exit. As she fled, she took one last look over her shoulder and saw the snake charmer leaping from the stage, coming after her!

Jiminy! Her legs wobbled, and her heart pounded so loudly that she barely heard him cry, "Stop, stop! Come back, wee lassie!"

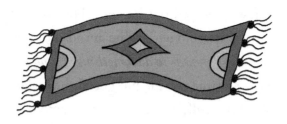

PAPUZA

Wending her way with the ostrich through the crowded chaos, Papuza headed behind the big top, searching for the circus wagons where the performers would live. She kept an eagle eye out for anyone who might have resembled Katrina. And Arthur!

As she neared the "behind the scenes" area of the show, she spotted Katrina in the distance. Even though more than sixty years had passed, Papuza knew, without a doubt, that she'd found her long-lost friend.

Katrina was engaged in a conversation, and Papuza studied her face for signs of the girl she had known so many years ago. *Yes, there are traces of my old friend.* Katrina still had a hopeful shine in her eyes. Laugh lines along her mouth suggested she had never lost her sense of humor. Sporting gray-blonde curls, Katrina towered over a man who was ranting on and on. He was dressed like a ringmaster, in a red jacket with gold buttons. He held a black top hat.

"A disaster! A complete disaster!" he cried, wiping his brow with his

handkerchief. His thinning hair lay plastered in strands across the top of his head. The portly gentleman seemed so distressed that Papuza felt sorry for him.

"Settle down, Samuel," Katrina said calmly. "It could have been much, much worse. We've recovered all the animals." Her voice faded as she added, "Except for my ostrich. And my poor tiger, Tasha."

"Tasha!" The ringmaster groaned. "A Siberian tiger on the loose, and you tell me to settle down! We'll get sued! She'll eat some poor, innocent farmer, and that will be the end of us!"

"You know Tasha wouldn't hurt a flea. She has no teeth left! She's old and defenseless, and she's the gentlest of my kittens. I worry that someone will hurt *her,* poor thing."

A loud, exasperated sigh came from the ringmaster. "This is no accident, and you know it!"

"Samuel, go check on your daughter." Katrina patted his shoulder. "But don't let your misgivings show. She has enough to worry about right now. You know how she loves all our animals."

The ringmaster stormed off. Katrina started to leave too, but then she noticed Papuza and broke into a huge grin. "Adara, it's you, isn't it?" She rushed towards Papuza and gave her a great, big bear hug. "I'd have known you anywhere!" She leaned back to examine Papuza's face. "I've been expecting you today, but I didn't think you'd show up with my ostrich! How are you, my dear, old friend?"

Laughing, Papuza hugged her back. "How wonderful to see you! I can hardly believe it, after all these years."

"That's exactly how I feel," said Katrina, as she tethered the ostrich to her wagon. "And where did you find my bird? Samuel, my son-in-law will be very relieved that she's back. And he'd be even happier if we could find my tiger!"

"I daresay we met your tiger last night. We were camping outside Hay Creek, a few miles from here."

"Oh, thank goodness she's still alive! I'll send a search party in that direction. Was she okay?"

"I must confess I didn't see her, but my granddaughter did! Your tiger leaped off into the forest. If her roar is any indication, she is absolutely fine. You can tell your son-in-law that she did us no harm. That might reassure him."

"Oh, nothing can reassure Samuel anymore." Katrina sighed. "When my daughter married him, he was a pleasant sort of fellow. But she died five years ago, and Samuel has changed, utterly changed. You would need to travel far and wide to find a more unhappy soul. Sometimes I wish he would leave the show, but then his daughter — my sweet granddaughter — might leave too. She is the apple of my eye." Katrina raised her arms and then dropped them, in resignation.

Gradually, her tense face relaxed, and she grabbed Papuza's hand. "Let's not talk of such things now. I'm just happy you're here."

"I'm glad of it too! Now, may I ask if there's any news of Arthur?"

Katrina said she hadn't found the detective's calling card yet, but she was still searching. Papuza tried to hide her disappointment, but her old friend saw her expression and read it well.

"We will find him, Adara, don't you worry. In case the card doesn't turn up, I've placed a 'Looking for Missing Persons' ad in the St. Paul newspaper plus a dozen other papers in the Midwest. That detective is *bound* to see that we're hunting for him and Arthur. Maybe Arthur will notice the ad too." She squeezed Papuza's hand. "We will find him. I promise."

Papuza's heart swelled with gratitude. "Thank you, Katrina."

And thus they entered Katrina's wagon, which was a jumbled mess of clothing and costumes and boas and hats and makeup. Circus posters covered all the walls. With a laugh, Katrina said, "After the show, if you help me look, there might be some hope of finding that card!"

They chatted and asked each other questions while Katrina got ready for the show. Quickly she did her hair and makeup before putting on her costume. They laughed about old times, and it seemed as if they'd only been apart for sixty minutes, instead of more than sixty years.

A pounding on the door interrupted them. Katrina opened it to find a small clown in distress. "Missus, missus," he panted, trying to catch his breath. "Come quick. Mr. Samuel's been attacked by spiders!"

ESME

Springing out of the tent with Mr. Wright in her arms and the snake charmer at her heels, Esme had only two thoughts: One — she needed to get away, and Two — she had to find Tommy. With Thought Number One being the most pressing, she slipped between two tents and kept running.

Making her way between the expanses of striped canvas, she began to worry. What if she'd hurt the snake? It wasn't exactly her favorite species, but still, she hoped she hadn't injured it. What if she'd broken its back? Can a snake be put in a body cast? How would it be able to move? Pondering these mysteries, she tripped over a tent stake.

As she fell on the ground, Mr. Wright leaped from her arms, landing a few feet away from her. As soon as *he* hit the ground, he scrambled under a nearby tent. *Oh no! Not again!*

Esme crawled after him as fast as she could. Expecting another chase, she was surprised when she wriggled under the canvas and saw Mr. Wright directly in front of her. She grabbed him.

She had every intention of creeping back to where she'd come from, but when she saw what she'd stumbled upon, she couldn't move.

Beneath a banner that said, "Maxwell the Magnificent," a broad-shouldered man in a black, velvet cape stood squarely in the center of the stage. He held out a top hat, from which doves poured forth. *Oh, it's so beautiful,* thought Esme, catching her breath.

When the last bird had flown above the soft spotlights, the man donned his hat and bowed deeply, making his cape swirl gracefully around him. The crowd broke into a thunderous applause, and Esme was about to do the same, when she realized she couldn't because she was holding Mr. Wright.

The applause died down, and a delicate woman emerged from behind the curtains, pushing a tall box on wheels. She had blonde hair and wore a striking gown of green velvet. Esme thought she looked absolutely lovely. The magician introduced her as his assistant, Emmeline.

Maxwell the Magnificent showed the audience that there was nothing inside the box before he helped Emmeline into it and closed the door. As he spun the box around and around, he smiled cheerfully to himself. Finally he stopped the box and opened the door.

The crowd gasped because Emmeline was gone!

Esme remarked to herself that the magician didn't seem at all worried about Emmeline.

Maxwell called for volunteers from the audience to step forward and try out his reappearing box. Esme suspected he'd have more volunteers if Emmeline had survived the ordeal. *Where in the world (or universe) did she go?*

Esme wondered if she could learn how to disappear like Emmeline. There had been times when she would have given anything to melt away from Hatch. And right now, she wouldn't mind slipping away from that snake charmer. So when Maxwell asked again for another victim, Esme shot up her free arm, jumping up and down to catch the magician's attention. "Me, me. Please, sir, me!"

But it was too late. The magician had his sights on somebody else. "You there, young sir!" Maxwell pointed to someone on the other side of the crowd. "You. The young man in the overalls and glasses."

Esme gasped. *That sounds a lot like Tommy!* She tried to see above the crowd, but of course her attempts were useless, so she wove around people to get closer to the stage.

"N-N-No, sir," she heard Tommy say, although for the life of her, she still hadn't caught a glimpse of him.

"Now, don't be shy," the magician encouraged Tommy. "I need a strapping, young lad to enter the box and rescue the fair Miss Emmeline. Fellows, help him up to the stage."

Esme could finally see Tommy. He was being guided up to the stage, even though he kept protesting.

Well, at least she now knew where he was. Although maybe she wouldn't know for very long, if *he* disappeared too! Esme was very excited and more than a little proud of her cousin. Even though he was not the most eager volunteer she'd ever seen, he was still showing some real daring. Esme wormed her way closer to the stage, not wanting to miss one teeny-weeny detail.

The magician shook Tommy's hand. "Thank you for being brave enough to assist, young man. Where do you hail from?"

Tommy cleared his throat. "Z-Z-Zumbro Falls, sir."

Esme shouted, "Yay, Zumbro Falls! Yay, Tommy!" She hopped up and down, holding Mr. Wright in one arm while waving her other arm in the air. She sure hoped Tommy saw her.

He did! She had caught his attention, and he gave her a shy smile.

Maxwell the Magnificent opened the door to the box where Emmeline had disappeared. Tommy looked downright reluctant to step inside. *Oh, poor Tommy*! He believed in spooks and superstitions, and Esme knew he felt afraid to step into that magic box. She wished she could change places with him. Why had the magician tried so hard to get Tommy to volunteer?

After some hesitation, Tommy stepped in and turned around to face the audience. He looked like he was heading to his doom. He gave Esme a mournful wave, as Maxwell shut the door.

TOMMY

Well, even before Tommy had stepped into the box, he'd had mighty grave doubts, and those doubts turned into absolute certainties after the door closed. Holy smoke, what was he doing? He felt like he was caught in a wooden coffin.

What was that gosh-awful smell? Some stinky perfume? It made him gag, and it stuck inside his nose like the reeking scent that Hatch sprayed all over herself whenever she gussied up.

If he ever got out, at least he'd be able to brag about this to his brothers. Not that disappearing was all that much fun.

So far, it was just the same as being trapped in a dark, smelly box.

His situation grew worse when the box started spinning. Tarnation! He thought he was going to throw up! Between the whirling box and the stinking perfume, he didn't think he'd be able to keep all that fairy floss down. To top it all off, Esme's cooking unfortunately came to mind, and now he was mighty close to being sick.

To steady himself, he stretched out his arms to press his hands against the sides of his rotating coffin. As soon as he did, he heard a woman's voice, very nearby. He couldn't say she sounded very nice. In fact, she sneered, "Let go, you idiot! I need to swing this around!"

He figured the speaker was probably the magician's assistant, and he remembered that the owner of this box of torture had called her Emmeline. Right away, Tommy dropped his arms, trying not to topple forward, and more importantly, trying not to throw up.

A mighty shove behind him spun him around to a secret hiding compartment, and at the same time, it moved Emmeline into the spot where Tommy had just been standing. "As soon as I get out," she hissed meanly, "spin yourself around."

Suddenly the box spun and stopped. He heard applause. He reckoned Emmeline had stepped out of the door and was now bowing to the crowd.

To his horror, the box started to spin again, taking him by surprise. *Gosh almighty, I can't help it.* Right then and there, he threw up the fairy floss.

When the box stopped spinning, he was still retching, and he hadn't had time to obey Emmeline. By now, he could see exactly how the box worked, and he knew he should have spun himself into the other compartment.

But it was too late.

He heard a huge gasp from the crowd, probably because the door had opened, and he wasn't there.

He'd ruined the magician's trick, and he didn't want the crowd to know he'd been sick. Embarrassed as all get out, he wanted to hide in this secret place until everyone left. *Shucks, maybe I should hide here forever.* He'd made such a mess. *How will I ever be able to face the magician?* His brothers would tease him for ages, if they ever found out about this.

Just when he thought things couldn't get any worse, the box began to spin again.

PAPUZA

Papuza stood in Samuel's circus wagon, and she could hear the fear in his voice as he cried, "This is proof. Someone is out to destroy me!"

As Katrina consoled her son-in-law, Papuza studied the jar on the table. It held the wriggling spiders they had removed from Samuel's hatbox.

In truth, they appeared to be common wolf spiders. To Papuza's knowledge, they were harmless, although finding a dozen of them inside a hatbox was somewhat suspicious. Someone must have gathered them and placed them there — someone who knew that Samuel was afraid of spiders.

Setting the jar aside, Papuza began to investigate Samuel's hatbox. "I could have been killed," he carried on angrily.

"Now, Samuel, settle down," Katrina said soothingly. "The spiders might have found their own way into your box. This doesn't mean someone put them there."

Yet Samuel disagreed. When he'd donned his best top hat for the show, he'd found this "vehicle of my own death," as he put it. He was utterly positive that someone wished him ill.

Papuza picked up his hat and tipped it upside down. Peering inside, she stopped short. Not wanting to cause undue alarm, she remained quiet while she casually searched her many, many pockets. Once she found her glasses, she put them on and looked inside the hat again.

Even though it had been many years since she'd encountered the sign, she knew what she was seeing.

Someone had scratched a hex sign inside the top of the ringmaster's hat.

Samuel is right, she thought. *Someone **is** out to hurt him.*

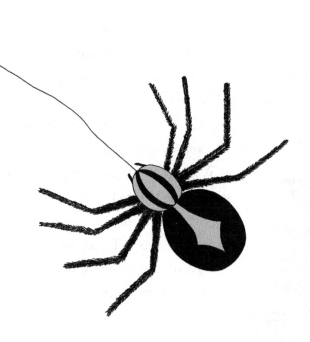

ESME

After Emmeline stepped out of the box, Esme couldn't wait to see Tommy's expression when he came out too.

But when Maxwell the Magnificent opened the door, Esme gasped. Tommy had disappeared!

Where had Tommy gone? Esme held her breath.

Watching.

Waiting.

The magician's expression provided no clues. He smiled at the crowd as he shut the door and spun the box again. Maybe it was just part of the act. Maybe he was trying to build suspense. Nevertheless, Esme unconsciously gripped Mr. Wright so tightly that she was on the verge of choking him.

When the reappearing box finally stopped, Maxwell the Magnificent opened the door with a great flourish.

But it was still empty.

Esme panicked. This couldn't be right. *Oh, good golly, where is Tommy?*

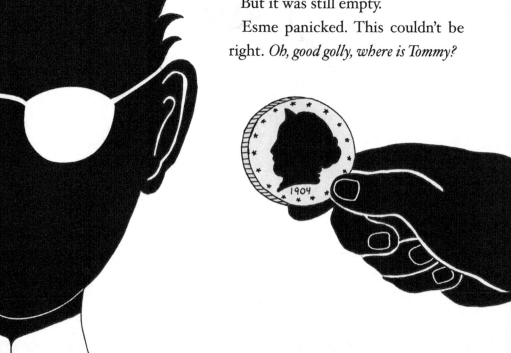

The audience remained quiet, waiting to see what would happen. Meanwhile, the beautiful assistant rolled her eyes and left the stage. At that awkward moment, the calliope began to play, announcing the start of the afternoon show in the big top.

With embarrassed coughing and harrumphing, the crowd shuffled out of the magician's sideshow tent, confused about what they had just seen.

Everyone left.

Everyone except Esme.

"Be sure to stop back after the show," the magician called out to his departing audience. "See the conclusion to this great mystery!"

Esme climbed onto the stage, determined to find Tommy. The magician had his back to her, so she tugged on his velvet cape to get his attention. "Please, sir, can you tell me what happened to the boy? He's my cousin."

As he turned around and looked down at her, she studied his face for clues. He seemed to be deciding on how to answer her question. Finally, bending down to her level, he petted Mr. Wright's head. "A good magician never reveals his secrets. But as you can see, I'm not a very good magician. I guess I can tell you. He's still in the box." Suddenly he put his hand behind Esme's ear and pulled out a small, red ball.

She laughed. "Oh, that was good!"

"Not really. It was supposed to be a flower," he admitted. "You see, my magic tricks never turn out they way I think they will. Honestly, at some of my shows, I'm even more surprised than the audience." He laughed a most marvelous laugh.

Rising to his feet again, he chuckled. "Maybe it's time to retire this trick. This is not the first time it's failed. If I don't find a volunteer who's within a few pounds of Emmeline's weight, the mechanism won't work." He winked at her and added, "On second thought, maybe it's time to retire Emmeline. She despises my bumbling ways! Well, anyway, that's why I wanted your cousin to volunteer, even though he clearly didn't want to."

"He sure was brave," Esme said, speaking up for Tommy. "Please, sir, may I see him?"

Maxwell pushed against the back wall of his reappearing box, and Esme was surprised to see it move like a revolving door. As the wall spun, it revealed a secret compartment — and, oh good gracious, there was Tommy!

Wobbly-legged, a shaky and pale Tommy stumbled from the box. "I'm sorry! I was sick as a dog."

"Are you okay?" Esme asked, squeezing his arm.

Tommy seemed grateful to be free. "I feel a little better now." And he *did* look better than he had a few seconds ago. He wasn't as pale, and his coloring was starting to return to normal. "I'm sorry, sir," he apologized again to Maxwell.

"No, son, it is I who am sorry. It was never my intention to make you sick." Maxwell patted Tommy's shoulder. "It's good to have you back amongst the living."

Instantly Esme liked the magician. He could have yelled at Tommy and been very upset, but he wasn't. He was as nice as nice could be. And he was funny. He might not have been the world's greatest magician, but she thought his surprises made his show even more interesting. "Mr. Maxwell," she said, "thank you for not being mad at my cousin. And by the way, I thought the doves in your act were wonderful!"

Maxwell bent down to her height and whispered, "They were supposed to be rabbits!" Then he burst out laughing, which made her giggle.

But not Tommy. He looked about as far away from happy as a person could be. "I need to clean up my mess!" he mumbled, truly embarrassed. Esme offered to help too.

"No, no, don't worry," Maxwell told them. "I'm more qualified than most people to clean up messes like this." For the first time, he looked serious, as if he were musing over memories. "I used to work in a hospital. Even during surgery, I never met a mess I couldn't handle!"

Esme asked, "If I may ask, sir, how did you become a magician?"

Maxwell sat down on the edge of the stage and made himself comfortable. "Well, a few years back, I had an interesting patient, who was Hungarian. He was a talented, young magician. I don't suppose you've ever heard the name Houdini?"

Esme and Tommy both shook their heads.

"Well, you will in time. I predict he will be famous someday." Maxwell smiled. "Anyway, he was my patient, and during his stay at the hospital, he entertained the other patients with his sleight-of-hand tricks. Thanks to him, I became interested in magic and decided to quit the medical field. It was a choice between making people smile by doing magic tricks, or making them cry by giving them diagnoses. So abracadabra! Here I am!"

Esme liked this doctor-magician even more.

"So please don't worry about the mess. I'll clean it up," said Maxwell. He reached behind Tommy's ear and pulled out a silver dollar.

"Wow!" Tommy whistled. "That's great!"

"Not really," Maxwell confessed. "It was supposed to be a nickel." Laughing at his mistake, he insisted that Tommy keep the dollar to make up for being stuck in the box. "I know what it's like in there. Sometimes Emmeline puts *me* in the box, and *I'm* supposed to disappear. I think she likes to turn the tables on me."

"Why?" asked Esme.

Maxwell explained, "Something's been bothering her lately, and she can't seem to ignore my magic mistakes. Yesterday, I told her that a forgiving nature is a magnet for attracting good. But I think she somehow missed my point because she grabbed the magnets from my hat trick and hurled them into the river." Maxwell chuckled, which made Esme smile. She stole a glance at Tommy and felt thankful for *his* forgiving nature. She shuddered as she remembered that unfortunate haircut.

At that point, the calliope music in the background ended. "The show's about to start," cried Maxwell. "Go on, enjoy it!"

So Esme and Tommy dashed out of the tent while Maxwell called after them, "Stop back later, and I'll show you some magic tricks. Maybe next time they'll work."

ESME

Esme and Tommy ran as fast as they could. No people remained in the fairway. Everyone must have been in the big top, waiting for the show to start. Esme longed to tell Tommy about the snake charmer, but she couldn't because they were racing so hard. Tommy held Mr. Wright as he dashed, jiggling the baby raccoon.

Esme saw Grandma standing outside the main entrance, waiting for them. Grandma was alone, so Esme suspected she hadn't found Arthur yet. "Ah, there you are, my dears," Grandma said with a gentle smile. "Come along now, it's about to start."

Panting, Esme asked, "Did you find Katrina?"

"Yes, dear, but no Arthur yet. I'll tell you all about it after the show." She escorted them inside, where she'd saved seats for them in the front row of the bleachers. Esme was happy they weren't sitting further back, where it would have been hard for her to see over the hats of the buzzing crowd — especially the ladies' hats that were trimmed with feathers and ribbons and silk roses.

Soon after they sat down, a man sauntered by with a tray of roasted peanuts. They smelled delicious! They made Esme's mouth water, and Grandma must have read her mind because she bought three bags, one for each of them.

Esme had just cracked the first salty peanut between her teeth when the ringmaster strode into the tent, holding a baton and pumping his arm up and down, in time to the music. He was followed by a band of musicians in red and gold uniforms. The tuba and trumpets were so loud and close they made Esme's heart throb!

An elephant followed the musicians, and it was so enormous it took Esme's breath away. She had seen pictures of elephants in books, of course, but nothing had prepared her for its astonishing size. Perched on top of the elephant's neck was a woman wearing a yellow, sparkly costume, complete with a feathered headdress.

Things were almost moving too fast for Esme! Bedecked and bedazzled horses pranced behind the elephant, and zebras and clowns followed the horses. *Oh, there's Pansy!* Esme was so enthralled that she forgot all about her peanuts.

"Look!" Tommy nudged her, pointing up above. Acrobats were warming up overhead. A bare-chested man in tights stood on a small platform, pushing the trapeze bar back and forth. A woman in an orange leotard climbed the ladder to the platform, and when she reached her destination, Esme clapped. *Oh, how I would love to be up there!*

Her envy grew as she watched the woman fly through the air so effortlessly, so beautifully, ignoring gravity. "Oh, Tommy," sighed Esme, "look at them!" She was so captivated by the acrobats that she didn't even notice that the three rings on the ground were filling up with acts.

The ringmaster bellowed through a megaphone, bringing Esme's attention back down to earth. She caught her breath as a lady bareback rider sped by. The black horse cantered, while the dark-haired young woman stood on her hands on the horse's back, earning "ooh"s and "aah"s from the crowd. Then she did a graceful backbend, ending up standing on the horse's rump and waving to her admirers.

Esme jumped up waving. The bareback rider saw her and waved back. "Oh, Tommy!" Esme grabbed his arm. "She waved at me!"

Grandma pointed towards the center ring, where a tall, blonde woman worked fearlessly with lions and tigers, as if they were merely kittens. "That's my old friend, Katrina," said Grandma. Excited, Esme watched Katrina, imagining the girl she used to be, at the lumber camp so long ago.

As the circus performances continued, each act was more breathtaking and dare-defying than the last. Lions leaped through flaming hoops, making Esme squeeze her fists together in fear. Clowns made her laugh so hard she spilled her remaining peanuts. She lost all track of time and felt as if she'd been transported to another world.

This is magical.

When the ringmaster announced the end of the show and thanked the crowd for coming, Esme's heart dropped. *It can't be over,* she agonized. It had gone by far too fast.

To finish off the show, the bareback rider returned. This time, hoops were placed around the ring. As Esme watched the rider intently, she only half-noticed the clown who set down a box near the rings. Esme figured it must be part of the act.

As the black horse gained speed, and the rider prepared to hop through the first hoop, the clown removed the top of the box.

Doves poured out.

The timing was dastardly. As the birds scattered, they frightened the horse, which reared up in alarm.

Everything happened so quickly that there was no time to help. Oh, mercy! Esme watched in horror, as the horse trampled the ringmaster, and the beautiful trick rider flew through the air and crashed to the ground!

PAPUZA

Papuza leaped from her seat to rush to the fallen trick rider, and Esme and Tommy came running too. The dark-haired girl lay on her side, very still. *Too still,* Papuza worried.

She knelt on the ground and placed her fingers on the girl's neck, feeling for a pulse. Within seconds, a nervous mob gathered around them, pushing them from all sides. Papuza and the children were in danger of getting trampled.

"Make way!" a woman shouted. Papuza recognized the voice of Katrina. "Move back now. The show is over!" Her old friend successfully squeezed through the throng of people and knelt beside them.

Katrina cried, "Is she alive?" Mournfully she added, "This is Maria. My granddaughter. My baby." She reached out to hold her granddaughter's hand.

"She's alive," Papuza reassured Katrina. "But she's stunned. I won't know the extent of her injuries until I can look her over."

The dazed ringmaster broke through the crowd of people. The spooked horse that had trampled him didn't seem to have caused him serious harm, although his jacket was torn, and his cheek was bleeding. "People, move back, please," he pleaded. "The show is over." He joined his mother-in-law, who knelt on the ground beside his unresponsive daughter.

"We might be able to revive her with smelling salts," Papuza said, as she stroked Maria's forehead. "I have some in my wagon."

"Let's move her there," said Katrina. Effortlessly the large woman scooped up her granddaughter. She and Samuel forced their way through the mass of people, while Papuza and Esme and Tommy followed.

They reached the gypsy wagon, and once they were inside, Katrina gently placed her listless granddaughter on one of the benches. Meanwhile Esme and Tommy joined Mr. Wright up in Papuza's bedchamber, where they were out of the way but could still see everything. Papuza noticed that they watched intently, and she heard Tommy tell Esme to get her journal.

Esme slid down and grabbed her journal off the table. Then she crawled back up and settled beside Tommy.

Papuza pulled a vial of smelling salts from one of her many, many drawers. As everyone watched anxiously, she uncorked it and placed it under Maria's nose.

The lovely girl fluttered her eyelashes, and soon she opened her piercing blue eyes. She groaned. When she tried to sit up, she cried out in pain.

Gently Papuza held her down. "I'm afraid you've had a bad fall, dear. Where does it hurt?"

"My arm," she exclaimed. "Something is wrong with my arm."

Papuza searched her many, many pockets and pulled out a pair of scissors. With great care, she cut along the sleeve's seam, revealing Maria's limb. It was plain enough to Papuza that Maria's arm was broken. When Papuza touched it gingerly, Maria gasped.

"By all means, I've seen worse," Papuza said, trying to comfort Maria. "It should be easy to set, and in no time, you'll be as right as rain. Does anything else ache?"

Maria bolted up and asked anxiously, "Oh! How is Arabella? Did she get hurt?"

"Arabella is fine. Absolutely fine," Katrina answered.

"Arabella?" asked Papuza.

"Her horse," Katrina explained. "Maria worries more about her horses than herself."

"Hmm. Well, I believe she's lucky to have come out of this with only a broken arm," said Papuza. "To be sure, I'll check her over closely. Do you have a doctor that travels with your show? Someone else you could consult?"

"No doctor." Katrina sighed. "Our magician used to be in the medical field, but he's told me many times that his doctoring days are over. Thank goodness you're here."

For the first time, Katrina noticed the children up in the bedchamber, so Papuza introduced them. "This is my granddaughter Esme and her cousin Tommy."

"Oh, my," Katrina chuckled. "Esme, you're the spitting image of your grandmother when she was a little girl!"

Esme lifted her head high in pride.

"I am honored to make your acquaintance," Katrina said, shaking the children's hands. They already seemed to like her, which pleased Papuza immensely.

Then Katrina turned to her son-in-law. "Are you all right, Samuel?" She placed her hand on his cheek.

"I'm fine, I'm fine. I want to talk with the clowns to see if they know who set down that box of doves by the ring. It was a malicious act of sabotage!" And with that, he stomped from the wagon.

As he left, a handsome trapeze artist rushed in and knelt by Maria's side. "Thank goodness, you are alive!" he said, burying his face in her dark, scented hair.

From his accent, Papuza guessed that he might be from Italy. *He must be her sweetheart,* she thought. *Or perhaps her husband.* Maria suffered from a broken bone. *But not — I daresay — a broken heart.*

Passionately, the man kissed Maria's lips, making Tommy wrinkle his nose and turn away in embarrassment. Yet Esme watched with great interest, which made Papuza smile.

"Come, children, roll up your sleeves," she said. "We have a bone to set!"

VILLAIN

She lives. What a pity she didn't break her pretty, little neck.

And all the animals except the tiger found their way back or were returned. So that failed also.

And that buffoon Samuel is still around. The spiders didn't scare him to death.

Nothing has gone according to plan.

Nothing.

Who is this black-braided meddler who has shown up at this most inconvenient time and helped Maria? Already I despise her. I don't like that boy and girl either.

They'd better leave soon, or I'll have to eliminate them.

TOMMY

Having twelve older brothers had made Tommy an expert at recognizing broken bones, so he wasn't at all surprised when Papuza said the stunt rider had a broken arm.

Papuza asked all the visitors to leave the wagon, so she could concentrate on setting Maria's broken bone. It sure wasn't easy to get that kissing guy to leave. Tommy told himself, *I ain't ever going to act like **that** over a girl!*

He watched Papuza give Maria a glassful of mandragora potion to help her sleep. After Maria drank the rosy-red liquid, she shut her eyes and began to relax. The medicine started to take effect.

As Maria fell into a deep slumber, Papuza showed Esme and Tommy how to rip a sheet into two-inch strips. Tommy had torn sheets accidentally before but never on purpose, so this felt a mite unusual.

As they were ripping, Esme asked, "Did you hear anything about Arthur, Grandma?"

"No, darling. Not a glimmer." Papuza's voice sounded a smidgen

disappointed, and that was unusual too. The cousins looked up at her.

"Don't give up hope, Grandma." Esme stroked Papuza's hand in encouragement. "Does that mean Katrina hasn't found the detective's card yet?"

"Yes, my dear. I quite understand, now that I've seen her wagon. I'll help her search, and perhaps the card will turn up. Bless her, she placed advertisements in a number of newspapers, looking for both the detective and Arthur." Papuza bent down to examine the strips the cousins were ripping, and they must have been doing a good job because she continued, "I only wish I had thought of the ads myself, for it might have saved us some time. Right now, all we can do is wait."

"Wait?" Tommy asked. He thought, *Does this mean we'll be lucky enough to stay here a spell?*

Esme must have thought the same thing. Breathless with excitement, she asked, "So we're going to stay with the circus for a while? Can we? Will we?"

Papuza chuckled. "I suspected you wouldn't mind." She laid a finger on her lips to quiet the cousins, so they wouldn't hoot and holler and wake Maria.

"That's enough strips, my dears." Papuza stepped over to her utensil drawer and pulled out three wooden spoons. "We're ready to begin."

She explained that although Maria had broken her arm, the young lady was very lucky it hadn't been a "compound fracture" because then her broken bone would be sticking out through her skin. Instead Maria had a simpler injury that should mend more easily.

Without taking away from Maria's problems, Tommy could honestly say he'd seen worse breaks in his own family.

Papuza asked Esme and Tommy to hold the wooden spoons to the broken arm, using them as splints while Papuza wrapped cotton strips all around the spoons and Maria's arm. "It would be most unwise to bind it so tightly it cuts off her circulation," said Papuza. "Yet it mustn't be too loose, or the bone won't set. It has to be just right — nice and snug." Papuza was teaching them while she did her doctoring.

"Can she feel this?" asked Esme.

"Not now. Not while she's sleeping," said Papuza.

Tommy remembered when his twin brothers, Ulysses and Rutherford, had set his eyebrows on fire while he was sleeping. If he'd had a glass of mandragora he might have snored through the whole ordeal, but as it turned out, he'd woken up mighty quick. Not quick enough, though! His eyebrows looked downright awful until they grew back.

When Papuza finished binding the spoons into place, she said she needed to leave and give Katrina an update. She asked Esme and Tommy to stay in the wagon and watch over Maria.

As soon as Papuza left, Esme and Tommy started chattering about the circus. "I feel like the luckiest kid alive!" said Tommy. "My brothers will be green with envy!"

"I know!" Esme exclaimed. "I can't wait to start exploring. But we can't go just yet." She studied the slumbering invalid, wondering how to help her. "Maybe I can make her broken arm a little prettier." So Esme pulled the red ribbon from the end of her braid and tied it around Maria's wrist. "I feel so sorry for her. What if she won't be able to ride again?"

"Well, I trust your grandma. She knows what she's doing."

"Yes, she does," Esme said proudly. "I'll need to know what I'm doing too, if I'm ever to become a doctor."

Tommy could tell from the look in her eye that she was getting one of her big ideas. Most of them were dangerous — at least to him. Even though he should have been used to them by now, he still was a little surprised when she said, "Let me practice on you with these leftover strips."

Tarnation! Firmly he declared, "I ain't got nothing broken."

"Not yet," she said with a grin. "No, seriously, Tommy. Let's pretend your arm is broken, and I'll fix it."

Her idea didn't sound like fun to him at all, although he couldn't imagine her doing as much damage with strips of cloth as she had done with a pair of scissors. "I'll tell you what," he said. "Why don't you practice on Mr. Wright?" He was joking, but Esme took him seriously. Poor Mr. Wright looked at her innocently, unaware of what the future held. Tommy thought, *I reckon he's gonna look like a wrapped mummy.*

"That's a brilliant idea!" cried Esme. Excited, she climbed to the drawer where Papuza kept her tongue depressors. Esme pulled out a few and asked Tommy to snap them in half while she ripped some of the cotton strips into even smaller pieces.

"I was only joshing, Esme."

But she was absolutely convinced that this would further her medical experience. *When she gets like this, there ain't no use arguing with her.* Tommy decided to leave her be, while he contemplated sneaking out and exploring the circus. Shucks, it didn't take two people to watch a sleeping patient.

He glanced out the window just as a colorful wagon of black-and-white zebras rolled by.

"I want to go see that elephant," Esme confided. As she "doctored," she talked to Tommy just like Papuza had spoken while she had worked. But unlike Papuza, Esme didn't talk medically about what she was doing. *That's because she don't know what she's doing,* thought Tommy.

She told him about saving Mr. Wright from a snake.

"A snake? Were you crazy?" He figured her battle with a killer snake outshone his tribulations in the reappearing box.

"Well, if you had been there, I'm sure you would have done exactly the same thing." She had now wrapped their pet's front two legs and was starting to put splints on his back legs. "How is that, Mr. Wright?" she cooed in a honey voice. "Do you feel all right?"

Tommy rolled his eyes.

Still pondering her story, he asked, "Did you hurt the snake?"

"Oh, I hope not," she said with a sigh. She bound up the raccoon's fourth leg and looked her patient over. "But I was so afraid that the snake charmer would be mad, and —"

A knock on the gypsy wagon door interrupted her. Tommy stuck his head out the window to peek at the back stoop.

"Who is it?" asked Esme.

"A big man with a red mustache, wearing a turban."

"Oh, no!" she whispered, clasping her hands nervously. "It's the snake charmer."

PAPUZA

Meanwhile, Papuza had found Katrina. She was in the big top, gathering the hoops from her tiger act. Papuza told her the encouraging news that her granddaughter Maria was now resting comfortably.

"What would we have done without you? You're a blessing, a true blessing." Katrina gave Papuza a grateful hug. "Thank goodness you're staying longer. We need you. My granddaughter needs you. I need you!"

Papuza told her sincerely, "I'm delighted to help, my old friend."

Tears sprang to Katrina's eyes. As she brushed them away, her face brightened. "I know Samuel will be happy to hear about Maria. Well, maybe not happy, for I fear happiness is beyond his grasp these days. He has so many worries. Right now, he's anxious about the next town on our schedule because we often run into stormy weather there."

"What town is that?"

"Lake City," Katrina answered. "Now, let me go make arrangements for loading your wagon onto our circus train. We're leaving at five this evening."

"May I hope to find a telegraph office at the station? I need to send a message to Tommy's father."

"Oh, yes. They have one. I used it last year." Katrina bent over and picked up the empty box that had held the doves.

It was a pink-and-gold striped hatbox with flowers on its lid. "This is mine," Katrina said in surprise. "I wondered why I couldn't find it the other day. I just figured my wagon was too messy." She bit her lip in dismay. "I do believe my suspicious son-in-law might be right. It does seem like the doves were part of a calculated plan."

Papuza asked, "Have you any idea who would do such a thing?"

"I can't imagine anyone in the circus doing this," said Katrina. "We're family."

Yet it was clear enough to Papuza that at least one member of the family was unhappy. She took the hatbox and dusted it off. *Such a beautiful box used for such evil intentions.* Papuza placed her hand on her friend's shoulder to reassure her. "I promise we'll get to the bottom of this, Katrina."

They parted ways, and Papuza headed back to the gypsy wagon. As she drew near the back stoop, she saw a man in a plaid turban. He was knocking on the wagon's door, so she asked, "May I help you?"

ESME

"Don't answer it," Esme whispered to Tommy. She figured the snake charmer wanted to give her a comeuppance. Maybe he'd fling her in a snake pit, full of wriggling asps. Or maybe he'd toss an Oriental rug on her, just as she'd thrown on his pet. Whatever he decided, it wouldn't be good.

"But Esme," said Tommy, "don't you want to find out if you killed his snake? You'll have to face the music sometime."

Before Esme could make up her mind, Grandma opened the door from the outside and let in the snake charmer! Oh, how Esme wished she could hide! Yet Tommy was right. She needed to face up to it. At least she'd learn what had happened to the snake.

Esme set Mr. Wright on the table, where he wobbled with his four bandaged legs. With a sinking heart, she turned to meet her punishment. She looked up at the snake charmer, and he offered her a smile, which gave her a small bit of hope that he wasn't so very angry. Timidly she smiled back.

He was a sturdy man, wearing a plaid kilt with a matching plaid turban. He had a large, red mustache and even larger red muttonchops. Esme could plainly see his startling eyes, which were crowned by bushy eyebrows that shifted up or down, depending on his expression. *By jingo,* she thought, *his eyebrows look like dueling caterpillars!*

The man knelt down to her height. With an accent that sounded a little like Grandma's, he said, "I'm glad I found you." At that point, Esme thought, *I'm not!* He continued, "One of the clowns told me that the woman who doctored Maria travels with a wee lass and a raccoon."

He noticed the slumbering Maria and asked how she was doing. Esme glanced at Grandma, who chimed in to say Maria had been fortunate, and they all hoped for a speedy recovery.

Then the snake charmer's eyes fell upon the splinted-and-bandaged Mr. Wright. "Och," he groaned. "Creampuff could not have possibly done *that!*"

"Creampuff?" asked Esme. She was starting to warm up to the man. There was something about him that was very likable.

"My snake, Creampuff. She's just a bairn — a wriggly, gentle baby. And she's not the slightest bit venomous." He laid his hand over his heart, and Esme believed him. "But

I should have introduced myself. I'm Angus McDuff." He extended a strong hand to her.

"Esme Dooley," she replied, shaking his hand as she gave him a small curtsy.

Angus bowed his turbaned head in response. Grandma offered him a seat on the bench, so he plopped down amongst the silk and velvet cushions.

He seemed to be gathering his thoughts. Pressing the tips of his fingers of one hand against the tips of his fingers of his other hand, he formed a steeple. Finally he asked Esme, "Could you in any way — any way at all — be persuaded to repeat your performance? I have never had such a response from an audience."

Astonished, she stared at him.

Grandma chuckled and asked her, "What on earth did you do, my dear?"

So Esme told Grandma all about her adventure, glancing occasionally at Angus. Near the end of her tale, Esme explained to him, "I thought Mr. Wright would die, so I threw a rug over your snake and ran. I'm so sorry. Did I hurt your snake?"

Angus reassured her, "Nay, lassie. 'Tis a bold thing you did. I sincerely hope you will join my act."

The thought of it was utterly thrilling! Esme fantasized about telling all her friends back home that she'd been in a genuine circus act. "Could I?" She peered at Grandma hopefully. "Would that be all right? May I?"

Grandma laughed at her excitement. "Very well, my dear. I don't know how long we'll be traveling with the circus, but while we're here, I see no problem."

Esme clapped enthusiastically, Angus clapped heartily, and Tommy clapped cautiously. "Let's start tomorrow afternoon," said Angus. "I believe we'll be in Lake City. Drop by my act five minutes before showtime."

"Five minutes?" Esme worried. "Won't I need some time to practice?"

"Nay! I want it exactly as you did today. It was perfect. Don't forget to bring your raccoon."

"Oh, thank you, Mr. McDuff!"

"Thank *you*, Miss Esme." His expressive eyebrows crawled upwards as he gave her a kindly smile.

Happily, Esme turned to Tommy — only to find that he looked uncomfortable. He was chewing on his lip and fidgeting uneasily. Esme knew he tried to avoid snakes at all costs, but still, she hoped he would come to watch her and Mr. Wright as they stepped upon the timeless stage.

Grandma asked Angus, "If I may be so bold, am I hearing a Scottish accent?"

His face lit up. "Aye, ma'am. I was born and raised just outside of Edinburgh."

"Oh, I've had the pleasure of exploring Edinburgh," Grandma exclaimed. "What a delightful place!"

"Aye, that it is, that it is." Angus beamed with pride.

Immediately, Esme promised herself that she would visit Scotland someday. She asked Angus, "How did you end up in a circus in America?"

"Now that's a strange but true tale." Instantly Esme and Tommy were all ears. Angus went on, "Several years ago, I was visiting relatives in the Ohio River Valley. One evening I was taking a stroll on the outskirts of town, playing my bagpipes because that helps my digestion, when I wandered into the back of a circus. A knotty board lay in the grass, and I started tapping my foot upon it, using it as a drum to go along with my pipes. Apparently I created inviting vibrations because half a dozen snakes from the circus slithered towards me. Behind them came a woman.

"It was Katrina." He chuckled. "She said she'd never heard such haunting music . . ."

"Oooh!" Esme butted in. "You're like the Pied Piper! Except with snakes instead of rats!"

Angus laughed. "Aye, you could say that. Anyhow, Katrina needed a replacement for her snake act, and she liked the sound of my bagpipes ever so much better than the old charmer's screechy oboe. You could say she charmed *me* into joining her show."

He added, "And now I'm expanding my act! I'm pleased, Miss Esme, that you have no fear of snakes."

"No, not like Tommy." Esme nodded toward her cousin. "He's terrified of them!" Tommy blushed, and she realized she'd embarrassed him. *Oh, no!* Right away she told him, "I'm sorry." She scuffed the toe of her shoe against his boot, trying to make amends.

With a thoughtful squint, Angus had been studying Tommy. "Fear of snakes is a common phobia. I've cured hundreds of people of it." He tipped his turban towards Tommy before he removed it.

Christopher Columbus! Creampuff was coiled on top of Angus' head.

Esme spun around to her cousin to warn him, but there was no time. Creampuff rose up, as if she was going to strike Tommy!

TOMMY

Tommy hadn't stuck around to become acquainted with Creampuff. No, siree. He'd fled the wagon and put plenty of distance between himself and that sneaky snake before he finally slowed down.

He swore that if they measured that snake, it would be taller than Esme. She'd better not tease him about it. *Some folks are snake-lovers, and some folks ain't.* His family was mighty divided on the matter. In fact, his brother Rutherford loved to scare his own twin, Ulysses, by hiding snakes in his boots.

And now Esme got to be in a show with that snake charmer. It made Tommy want to practice his knife throwing even more, so maybe *he* could be in some kind of act. Well, he supposed he had been in that magician's act. But not in any way he could brag about.

All this passed through his mind as he and Esme strolled along the circus fairway. The circus folks were getting ready to travel to the next town, so they were packing their rainbow-colored wagons and taking down their striped tents.

It was amazing to observe the collapse of the big top. Tommy wanted to watch the workers longer, but music rollicked in the distance, coaxing Esme to mosey on. They rounded a corner, and suddenly they were face-to-face with a wagon of fearsome lions.

The cousins froze.

Tommy had a powerful hankering to step a little closer to the lions to see them better.

*But not **too** close.*

He decided to simply clean his glasses, and then he should be able to see the lions better. Shucks, there was no need to step any closer to them.

Esme pulled her journal from her satchel and started to write in it rapidly. Every few seconds, she stopped to examine the lions before she scribbled again with enormous concentration.

"Was the tiger you saw last night this big?" Tommy asked.

"She was twice this size." Esme was utterly serious.

"Is that so?" He had to smile because that meant her tiger would have been about as big as an elephant. But since she had kindly refrained from saying anything about his flight from the snake, he reckoned he wouldn't call her on her whopper.

One of the lions roared angrily, making the cousins jump. And then they jumped again because a girl had appeared at their side, almost as if she'd materialized out of thin air.

She looked mighty familiar, yet Tommy couldn't place where he'd seen her before. She was shorter than he was, yet taller than Esme. He figured she was about their age. Her golden hair was pulled back in a bow, and her eyes were red, as if she'd been crying. When she opened her mouth to speak, he finally realized who she was. Holy mackerel! It was the mermaid!

Gee whiz, he couldn't help it. He had to look down to see if she was walking on a tail. But no, she was standing on two feet and wearing awfully normal shoes and stockings. Tommy reckoned that deep down, he'd always known she'd just been wearing a costume. But jeepers, she had seemed so real that he'd wanted to believe in her. Now he felt a little foolish for ever thinking she might have been part of the fish family.

Esme had been studying the girl too, and suddenly she burst out with, "Oh, my gosh, you're the mermaid!"

"My name is Annie," said the girl. "Sorry I scared you earlier. They want me to look and act scary, so they'll sell more tickets."

"You didn't scare me," Tommy declared. "By the way, this is Esme, and I'm Tommy. I'm itching to know something. How did you hold your breath for so long?"

Annie the Mermaid giggled, and then she looked around cautiously. "I'd probably get in trouble for telling you this, but there are air tubes hidden all over the tank. Didn't you see the bubbles in the ferns? Whenever I need some air, I just turn my back to the crowd and take a quick breath."

"How does it work, exactly?" asked Tommy. Maybe he could use the same idea at their swimming hole this summer.

"Didn't you hear the noise behind the tank? There's a steam engine out there that powers the whole circus. It's connected to an air compressor that pumps air into my tank."

Tommy realized Esme was watching the mermaid as closely as he was. Esme smiled at Annie in a friendly way and asked, "Where are you from?"

"From the circus," said Annie. "Where are *you* from?"

Esme said, "We're from Zumbro Falls. But how can you be from the circus? Where is your home?"

Tommy thought, *Hopefully not in the fish tank.* Even Pa, who could sleep through just about anything, couldn't sleep underwater.

"I think I was born in Texas," said Annie, "but I'm not sure. The circus has always been my home."

"Wow!" Tommy was completely filled with envy. "So you get to travel around all the time, and you never have to go to school?"

"And your family travels with the circus too?" asked Esme.

"In a way, everyone who works here is my family." Glancing in the direction of the mermaid tent, she added, "But my only blood relative here is my uncle. He runs the mermaid tank. My parents used to be part of the circus, but they passed away. I guess I'm really an orphan."

Tommy wondered how they had died, but he wasn't sure it would be polite to ask. He felt awfully sorry for her.

He peeked at Esme, who was staring at Annie with a moonstruck expression. "I'm an orphan too!" said Esme. She reached out and grabbed Annie's hand, giving it a squeeze. A half smile crossed Annie's face.

Tommy ventured, "Hey, we're going to be traveling with the circus for a while. Do you think you could give us a tour?"

Annie perked up right away. "All the kids I meet leave right after the show. I never get to have friends for more than an hour. It's the worst part of traveling." Her face beamed with excitement. "Sure, I'll show you around. Let's start by going in the lion cage!"

ESME

As soon as Esme heard that Annie was an orphan, you could imagine what she thought. *She's the one!*

Even though Annie said the circus was her family (and it would be pretty grand to spend one's life traveling with the show), Esme still had the tingly feeling that Annie could be her new sister. Of course there was always the big question of what Annie would want.

But Esme couldn't mull it over just then because there was too much to see and absorb on their tour from Annie the Mermaid. It was absolutely jim-dandy! Esme and Tommy were truly in the thick of things, exploring the circus while it packed up. Performers and crew rushed this way and that, and Esme needed to stay alert, so she wouldn't get trampled. The big top lay collapsed on the ground, and workers struggled to roll up the massive canvases. *Everything looks different now,* she thought. *Completely different.*

They didn't actually go inside the lion cage because Annie had only been kidding. But they did get to pet the sleek zebras. And Esme was momentarily reunited with Pansy! The tall bird preened in a pen with another ostrich. Esme imagined that Pansy was telling her companion all about her grand adventure and her race with Bess, but Esme didn't speak Ostrich, so she'd never really know!

Annie introduced Esme and Tommy to a group of clowns behind the circus, not far from the banks of the Mississippi River. Some of them still wore the tops or pants of their flamboyant costumes. They were developing a new act, and they tossed balls to Tommy to teach him how to juggle. After a few minutes, he began to catch on, and everyone clapped.

But then he dropped all the balls, and everyone laughed.

They met a man on stilts, who was actually pretty short when he only stood on his own two legs. And then they ran into the trapeze artist who had kissed Maria in their gypsy wagon. His name was Bernardo, and they learned that he was also a knife thrower for the circus.

Bernardo let them watch him practice his knife-throwing act, and Tommy was mesmerized! As he observed the act, Esme just *knew* he was imagining himself as a Master Knife Thrower. At one point in the practice, a wild toss made her flinch, and she had to look away.

And that was when Esme saw the elephant. She was tethered to a tree on the riverbank, and jeepers, she was huge!

She was the largest animal Esme had ever seen. She was a majestic creature, and if truth be told, Esme was both in awe of her and a little terrified.

Annie must have noticed how Esme was staring at the elephant because she asked, "Do you want to ride her?"

"Oh, do I! Could I? Are you sure? Oh, I'd love to!"

"Well, of course you can."

So the three of them walked over to the elephant. As Annie untethered her, Esme noticed a hooked pole leaning against the tree. Anxiously, Esme asked, "Does anyone hurt the elephant with that?"

"Heavens no!" Annie said firmly. "Mama Kat would never let anyone mistreat her animals."

"Mama Kat?" asked Tommy.

"She's the owner of the circus. Well, she and her son-in-law own it. He's the ringmaster."

"You mean Katrina!" said Esme. "She's one of my grandma's oldest friends." She looked at the elephant again and whispered in awe, "She's magnificent!"

Annie gently introduced them to the elephant, which was named Buttercup. Tentatively, Esme touched Buttercup's trunk, and to her surprise, the elephant wrapped her trunk around Esme's arm. Esme giggled with delight.

Then Annie told Buttercup, "Down, girl." And just like that, Buttercup knelt before them.

While Buttercup's head was close to the ground, Esme looked into her eyes. They were brown, and lustrous, and

highly intelligent. *She has the longest eyelashes!* Esme smiled at her.

And she swore, Buttercup smiled back.

Esme very much wanted to show her how she felt, so she leaned over and kissed the elephant's cheek.

Instantly Buttercup's trunk rose right up to Esme's face, and the tip of her trunk stroked the tiny girl's cheek.

Annie said, "She likes you," which made Esme sigh happily.

Then Annie told them that if they'd like a ride, they'd need to crawl up behind Buttercup's head. So of course Esme scrambled right up! Tommy followed, a little more hesitantly.

Annie helped them get situated, and soon Esme sat in front of Tommy on Buttercup's neck. "Are you ready?" asked Annie. After they said yes, Annie told Buttercup, "Up, girl."

Slowly the elephant rose to her feet while Esme's stomach churned with fear and anticipation. For a moment, it felt like they were sliding off Buttercup's neck, but they caught hold quickly, as she began to walk.

It was thrilling! Esme thought, *I'm on top of the world!* She imagined she was in the deepest corner of Africa, crossing a plain on her way to an important tribal meeting to discuss important tribal secrets. As she approached the circle of great chieftains, they greeted her, and she invited them to Zumbro Falls, where they all had a wonderful time. The chieftains led them in tribal dances . . .

"Esme!" Tommy cried. She'd been so engrossed in her daydream that she hadn't noticed that Buttercup was moving faster.

Then Tommy screamed, "Esme!"

Buttercup was definitely gaining speed. Trotting, one might say. Esme looked back and saw the clowns chuckling, but right now, this didn't feel very funny. In fact, it felt downright terrifying! Buttercup charged away from the circus, moving towards the Mississippi.

They approached the water at an alarming rate, and Esme could tell that Tommy was panicking because he was squeezing her tightly around her waist. *What should we do?*

At the water's edge, the elephant came to a sudden stop, and they slid forward. Then Buttercup shocked them by reaching her trunk behind her head, wrapping it around them, and lifting them in the air.

Esme screamed!

TOMMY

Tommy didn't know how this would end. It wasn't every day that a feller was held hostage by an elephant.

Buttercup held them in midair, with her trunk wrapped tightly around their waists. Esme was screaming so loudly that Tommy felt sure she'd puncture his eardrums.

And then WHOOSH! Buttercup flung them into the river! They tumbled into the muddy Mississippi, in the shallow water along the riverbank. Behind them, Tommy heard roars of laughter from the circus clowns.

Quickly Esme stood up and gave Tommy a hand to pull him out of the muddy water. She had mud all over her dress, and all over her hands, and all over everything. Tommy had a hard time standing up because it felt like he had twisted his

ankle. Pain shot through him. He mumbled, "Gosh-almighty, that hurts."

Before they could free themselves from the mud, Buttercup sprayed them with a snoutful of water. The laughter started again, and Tommy felt himself blushing.

Then Esme started to laugh, so Tommy begrudgingly smiled. He had to admit, it must have looked sort of funny. He reckoned nothing was really hurt, except maybe his pride.

Standing on the riverbank, Annie extended her hands to both of them. Her beaming face told Tommy she had also enjoyed the elephant's prank. "Buttercup is very playful," she admitted, as she helped them ashore. With a giggle, she added, "But honestly, I didn't know she was going to do *that*."

Tommy wasn't sure he believed her. What if she'd set them up? What if Buttercup did this to everyone who rode her?

A clown hurried up to them with a towel. "No hard feelings, I hope," he said good-naturedly.

"Can we do it again?" chirped Esme. "That was the most exciting thing ever!"

Leave it to his cousin to actually enjoy a near-death experience. *She'd probably love to be chased by a stampeding herd of buffalo.* Esme wiped her face with the towel and then handed it to Tommy, so he could use it too.

The cousins needed clean clothes, so Tommy started limping back to the gypsy wagon while Esme and Annie lagged behind, chatting a mile a minute. It turned out that Annie loved to read books as much as Esme did. And Annie dreamed of being a writer too. And Annie would love to learn about plants from Papuza, just like Esme and Tommy were. It seemed like Annie was the perfect match for Esme. They chatted and giggled and laughed, and Tommy couldn't stop himself from muttering, "Girls."

On the way back to their gypsy wagon, he saw circus wagons on the move. Some of the wagons were cages, which held wild animals. Other wagons had solid walls, and Tommy reckoned the circus performers lived in those ones. All the wagons were painted bold, cheerful colors, and they were a sight to behold.

He felt like a mighty lucky fellow to be traveling with this fascinating group. So what if today had brought him a little vomiting in a box? And a quick dunking from an elephant? And a tiny bit of ankle pain? All in all, he had nothing to complain about, and his brothers would have told him the same thing.

At the gypsy wagon, Papuza was hooking Joe and Zinjiber into their harnesses, so Tommy went over to lend her a hand. When he told her about their elephant escapade, she laughed. *Shucks,* he thought, *doesn't anyone think we could have been in a heap of trouble?*

Papuza must have sensed how he felt because she said, "I hope you're not the worse for it, Thomas." She put her hand on his shoulder. "Shortly we shall leave for the depot, to load up with the circus. Have you ever traveled by train?"

He shook his head no.

"Well, then, you're in for a real treat!"

By now, Esme and Annie had arrived. Esme introduced her new friend to Papuza before they dashed up the back steps of the wagon, so Esme could change clothes. As soon as the girls entered the wagon, Tommy could hear them starting to coo over Mr. Wright.

Papuza and Tommy waited outside, watching the circus as it packed up to leave. They were both quiet, lost in their own thoughts. Finally he asked, "Did they ever learn who set out that box of doves?"

"Not that I'm aware of," Papuza replied. "But I'll be speaking with Katrina shortly."

Just then, an elegant, blonde lady dressed in green velvet strutted by. Tarnation, it was the magician's assistant. *Emmeline.* Tommy ducked his head because he was afraid she'd recognize him. However, she merely nodded to them and kept walking.

Something fluttered to the ground as she passed by. Tommy bent down to pick it up and examine it. It was a downy, white feather.

From a dove.

ESME

The train was speeding down the track, clickety-clack, clickety-clack. It felt like a song in Esme's head, and she loved it. She wondered if she should be a train conductor when she grew up. Because honestly, she'd never get tired of traveling this way. Maybe she should add train conductor to her long list of future professions.

That made her think of the Orphan Train. She felt a pang of guilt because she was enjoying this ride so much, and maybe those poor orphans didn't have very much fun on their train rides.

Her mind skipped to Annie, and she got excited. *I wonder if we'll be able to adopt her?* Esme wasn't going to tell Tommy or Grandma about her hopes just yet. First she had to find out how Annie felt. Yet Esme couldn't help but think that Annie would feel exactly as she did. They had so much in common! Esme had even gotten Grandma to help her change her hairstyle, so it looked just like Annie's.

Right now, Esme sat inside the gypsy wagon with Tommy, Grandma, and Mr. Wright. The wagon was perched inside a train car, which was sashaying down the tracks, along with the other circus train cars.

Esme was wrapping Tommy's ankle, even though he didn't really want her to work on it. He'd said he was afraid she'd wrap it too tightly, and she'd cut off the circulation in his foot, and his foot would fall off. Esme had to pester him and pester him before he finally wore down and let her doctor him.

In the back of her mind, Esme kept wondering what it would be like if his foot really did fall off. She had a sneaking suspicion that it would be harder to attach a limb than to take one off. What if she put Tommy's foot on backwards? She suspected he'd probably make a big deal out of something like that. Since it had taken eight days for him to speak to her again after a bad haircut, how long would he stay mad at her if she put his foot on backwards?

Mr. Wright was now splint-free, and Tommy teased him with a string while Esme practiced her doctoring. When Grandma cleared her throat, they all looked up.

In her lilting voice, Grandma said, "There are things I'd like to tell you."

Esme tied her last knot, and Tommy put aside his string, so they could give Grandma their full attention.

"I wanted to let you know that I sent a telegram to Tommy's father to give him an update on our situation.

I asked him to send his response to the Lake City office, where I'll check for it tomorrow.

"I also wanted to tell you about the talks I've had with Katrina. It appears there is someone who wishes to harm the circus. No one knows who it is, or why it's happening."

"Someone definitely knows," said Esme.

"And who is that?" asked Tommy.

"The person who is doing it!" said Esme.

Tommy rolled his eyes, but Grandma laughed. "You're right, my dear. The problem is that nobody *else* knows who's doing it. I'd like you two to keep your eyes and ears open over the next few days to see if you detect anything suspicious. Your observations could be extremely helpful."

"You know who else could be helpful?" Esme asked. "Annie."

Tommy nodded. "You bet. She knows everyone in the entire circus. She said they're her family."

"No doubt you're right that she could be very helpful," said Grandma. "But I think you should keep the secret from her also. She might innocently reveal your activities to the wrong person, and you could end up in danger."

Then Grandma told them everything she knew about the animals leaving, and the spiders, and the hex sign, and finally the box of doves. Samuel's efforts to learn who had set the box by the ring had not been fruitful. He had only determined that the guilty party was not one of the regular clowns. It must have been someone who had dressed up as a clown, as a disguise.

Esme mulled this over. Jiminy, it was time to put on her sleuth's hat! She'd always thought it would be rollicking fun to be a detective. Her list of possible future careers was growing so long that she'd need to live to be two hundred years old, if she hoped to accomplish everything.

She thought of all the Sherlock Holmes books she'd read. The guilty person could be someone you least expected. She glanced at Tommy. Well, she knew he couldn't be the culprit. That would be like Sherlock Holmes accusing Dr. Watson.

Then she examined Mr. Wright. The dark rings around his eyes did give him a rather shady appearance. Esme knew no one was supposed to be above suspicion, but she thought this might be going a little too far.

Tommy blurted, "I bet it's that magician's assistant, Emmeline. Remember how a dove's feather drifted to the ground when she passed us?"

"But that might not mean anything," said Esme. "She works with doves in her act." If she had to put Emmeline in her "Yes" or "Maybe" or "No" columns of suspects, she'd probably fall into the "No" column. Esme couldn't imagine that someone who looked like a beautiful princess would do villainous, dastardly acts.

"She ain't nice. Nope, she ain't nice at all." Tommy told them how Emmeline had hissed at him during his reappearing box fiasco.

"Perhaps we just need to get to know her better," Papuza murmured, as she headed towards her wooden shelves. There she chose a slim volume. She set it on the table and flipped through its pages. "This is an old book on symbols. I vaguely recognized the hex sign inside Samuel's hat. I know it represents evil, but I don't know much more than that."

Esme climbed on the bench to view the pages better. "What did the hex sign look like, Grandma?"

Grandma searched her many, many pockets and unearthed a pencil. She drew a symbol in the book's margin, for them to see.

Tommy asked, "Do hex signs really work?" Esme thought she heard an edge of fear in his voice. He'd never fully overcome his worries about ghosts and curses.

"Heavens no," said Grandma. "I would call them mere humbug, but nevertheless, some people do believe in them."

She stopped flipping through the pages. Esme asked, "Did you find what you were looking for, Grandma?"

"No, it's not here." As she closed the book and returned it to the shelf, they realized the train was beginning to slow down. "I suspect we're nearing Lake City. Remember, my dears, to keep all of this a secret."

Before Esme could promise that her lips were sealed, the train came to a screeching halt, throwing them from their seats.

ESME

The train had needed to make an emergency stop because a tree had fallen on the tracks. While a circus crew removed the tree, Esme and Tommy watched through an open train door. Both of them longed to join in the commotion, but Grandma told them it was probably better if they stayed out of the way.

They arrived in Lake City just in time for a breathtaking sunset on Lake Pepin. The sun's orange rays turned the lake a golden hue, making it shimmer. Their gypsy wagon followed the circus wagons off the train, and they all parked in a spot with a stunning lakeside view. Esme thought the circus had picked the very best place for its next performance.

Later, Esme and Tommy and Annie sprawled on the grass and watched another crew set up for the next day's show. Buttercup was helping them. She maneuvered the big top's tent poles, and her strength made the work seem like child's play. Esme couldn't wait to ride her again. *Because somehow, some way,* thought Esme, *I just have to ride her again!* She sighed in contentment. "It's lovely here."

Annie said, "When we were here last year, I heard an old legend. The local people say that when this region came into being, it was so beautiful that the angels looked down upon it and wept. Their tears created Lake Pepin."

They were all quiet for a moment.

Then Tommy said, "Maybe that's how the Zumbro River was made too. It's mighty pretty around our valley." He fiddled with his jackknife, pausing now and then to select a sweet gumdrop from the bag that Annie was sharing with them.

It had been very hard for Esme to keep secrets from Annie because Esme already felt a warm bond with her. And she had so many questions to ask Annie! But Esme hadn't forgotten Grandma's reminder to stay silent.

Suddenly Esme recalled her exciting prospect of working with Angus, the snake charmer, and she shared the news with Annie.

To Esme's surprise, an unexpected cloud settled on Annie's face. "Oh, I wouldn't do that. I don't really trust him."

Esme was shocked. "Why not? He seems so nice." She noticed that Tommy had stopped throwing his jackknife and had moved a little closer to them — probably to hear better. Ever since Creampuff had emerged from the turban, Tommy hadn't trusted Angus either.

"To be honest," said Annie, "I think he's the one who put that box of doves by the ring. I think he wanted to hurt Maria."

"But why?" Esme cried in disbelief.

"Everyone in the circus knows he proposed to Maria. She turned him down, and he can't stand to see her with Bernardo. If you ask me, Angus is as sneaky as his snakes."

Esme felt flabbergasted. Good gravy, this was a startling revelation! She and Tommy exchanged a thoughtful look. She couldn't shake the feeling that Angus was a nice guy, but then again, she didn't know him very well. Annie's worrisome news only made her want to work with Angus all the more. What better way was there for her to gather clues?

While she weighed the chances that Angus might be the villain, she spotted a purple wagon in the distance, parked near the others. It was fancy, with elaborate decorations and mystical symbols. The back door displayed a poster that said, *"Madame Sage, Fortune-teller."* Esme wondered if this Madame Sage happened to know anything about hex signs.

"Annie, do you know who owns that wagon?" Esme pointed to the purple, showy one.

Annie finished chewing a gumdrop before she said, "Madame Sage?"

Eagerly Esme asked, "Do you think we could meet her?"

"Sure," said Annie.

Excitement flared through Esme, and she jumped to her feet. Annie stood up too, but Tommy stayed on the ground. Eyeing Esme suspiciously, he asked, "Why do you want to visit a fortune-teller?"

"Oh, come on, Tommy. It'll be fun!" He didn't seem to believe her, so she grabbed his sleeve and pulled him up from the ground. Playfully, Annie tugged on his other sleeve, and together, the two girls marched him in the direction of the purple wagon.

As they walked, Esme asked Annie, "What's she like?"

"Madame Sage? It's hard for me to say," Annie confided. "She's only been with the circus for a few weeks."

As they drew closer, it was easier to see the wagon's mysterious paintings of stars, and palms, and crescents, and other signs that Esme didn't recognize. She searched for an image of the hex sign that Grandma had drawn for them, but she didn't find one.

Annie knocked on the back door. "Madame Sage, are you home? It's me, Annie."

An ancient-sounding voice muttered, "Come in."

They entered the dimly lit caravan, where candles cast flickering shadows. A crystal ball glowed on the table, and charts that encompassed moons and planets covered the walls. A grim raven that would have rattled Edgar Allan Poe perched on a skull, tilting a sullen eye at them.

Yet the most interesting thing of all was Madame Sage.

She faced them, sitting behind the table. She was a tiny woman with white, wild hair that was interwoven with twigs and ribbons. Her nose was large, and her eyes were even larger. Power blazed in those black and brilliant eyes, and Esme gasped as she stared into them. Holy smoke, Madame Sage looked exactly like a witch! Well, in truth, Esme had never met a witch, but if she ever did, this is what she'd look like.

Madame Sage broke her gaze with Esme and returned to rolling dice with the morbid raven. The bird cawed, picked up a die with its beak, and cast it down again. "Good roll, Mordecai," the old crone cackled.

Tommy whispered, "I-I-I reckon I'll wait outside." Esme grabbed his wrist and pulled him closer to the table.

"Good evening, Madame Sage," said Annie. "I want you to meet my friends." After Annie introduced them, there was a lengthy pause. Madame Sage studied them again, even more closely. Her gaze was so severe that Esme felt as if it pierced her very soul. She heard Tommy gulp.

"Sit down," said the fortune-teller. "Mordecai and I are just finishing up."

They obeyed immediately, dropping onto chairs across the table from the soothsayer. As she tossed the dice, she made casual conversation. "Bad weather tonight. Batten down the hatches." Esme thought she sounded like a pirate in *Treasure Island*. Gloomily the crone added, "No moon to see by. No stars to guide you."

"Oh, there's always a storm when we stop in Lake City!" Annie shuddered. "I still remember the thunder and lightning from last year." Madame Sage tilted her head, well . . . sagely.

Esme was fascinated (and maybe just a little bit spooked) by the fortune-teller. She wondered if the woman could tell her what the hex sign meant, and Esme was dying to ask Madame Sage to read her fortune. As Esme worked up her courage, Annie asked the fortune-teller, "Did you hear about

Maria's accident? She broke her arm, but it could have been much worse. I was so worried she might die!"

"Oh, no, no, no." Madame Sage shook her head, dislodging a dead leaf as she did so. "Maria will have a long life, with many horses."

A tingle ran up the back of Esme's neck. *Can she really see into the future?* She decided to ask one of her many questions. "Excuse me, Madame Sage, but could you tell me what a certain symbol stands for?"

"What symbol?" the woman croaked.

Esme leaned forward and used her finger to trace the hex sign on the tablecloth. She waited to see Madame Sage's reaction.

There was a flicker of interest in the crone's eyes, but other than that, her face betrayed nothing. "Where did you see this?"

Esme remembered Grandma's warning, so she didn't want to mention that someone had drawn the hex sign inside Samuel's hat. Yet at the same time, she didn't dare to lie to Madame Sage. Esme thought the woman would know if she told her a lie. So truthfully, she just said, "My grandma showed it to me."

Madame Sage muttered, "Well, since you ask, it's a hex sign for evil. The person who receives it will suffer misfortune."

Nervously, Tommy cleared his throat. "D-D-Does it work?"

The fortune-teller let out a hoarse, cackling laugh. A moment later, the sinister raven hopped on Tommy's head and gave him a hard peck. "Ouch!" he cried, shooing

Mordecai away. He jumped up to leave, but Esme tugged on his overalls to make him sit back down.

The crone scooped up the dice from the table and handed them to Tommy. "Go ahead and roll," she coaxed. "Let me tell your fortune." Firmly he shook his head no, absolutely refusing to have his fortune told.

So Madame Sage handed the dice to Esme. "Do you have a question, tiny one?"

Esme chewed on her lip, thinking hard. Her problem was that she had *too* many questions. Would they find Arthur? Would they solve the mystery of the circus? Would Annie want to come live with them? And would Hatch *ever* stop trying to kill her? Esme tried to think of a way to combine all her questions. She ended up asking, "Will we find the answers we're seeking?"

Madame Sage commanded, "Roll the dice."

Esme shook the dice in her hands. Then she dropped them and watched them roll to a stop.

She had a one and a six.

Madame Sage leaned over to peer at the dice. With a cackle, she rasped, "Things are not always what they seem."

TOMMY

"It's her, I tell you. It has to be. I can feel it in my bones!" Tommy was plumb sure that Madame Sage was the villain behind all the troubles. He still got the willies whenever he remembered how she'd stared at him. And that raven of hers — tarnation! It had practically pecked a hole though his skull, which still hurt like the dickens. *But I don't dare say anything,* he thought, *because Esme will try to bandage up my head, which would probably suffocate me.*

Esme and Tommy were both sitting on one bench in the gypsy wagon, while Papuza was on the other. They were in for the night, chatting about their day. When Tommy described their visit to "that spooky villain of a fortune-teller," Papuza chuckled. She said she was intrigued and would pay a visit to Madame Sage tomorrow.

"Don't go!" Tommy pleaded. "I don't trust her at all."

"Well, Annie says the one we shouldn't trust is Angus," said Esme. So they talked over their impressions of the snake charmer. Esme and Papuza thought he was a mighty courteous gentleman. Tommy, on the other hand, was having a hard time forgetting the surprise of Creampuff.

Next, the cousins told Papuza about meeting Maxwell the Magnificent earlier that day. Tommy didn't see any need to mention his troubles in the reappearing box, so he kept quiet about that part. He ended with, "Both Esme and I think Maxwell is too nice a guy to be the guilty person."

"Besides," Esme giggled, "he wouldn't be able to pull anything off because he'd get it all mumbled-jumbled."

"I still think it's Emmeline. Or that Madame Sage..." Tommy didn't finish because lightning flashed by their windows. A cracking boom of thunder followed, a moment later.

"That's her," he whispered. "I reckon it's Madame Sage, using her mystic powers. She probably heard me complaining about her."

Papuza laughed. "You mustn't let your imagination run away with you, Tommy. Although Katrina and I could certainly use your creative help in finding the detective's card! We searched for an hour this evening, to no avail."

Another clap of thunder shook the heavens. Rain started pelting the roof with hard, angry drops that sounded like hail. A roaring gust of wind blasted the wagon so hard it swayed.

"This came on quickly," murmured Papuza. "When I visited Maria tonight to check her arm, Katrina told me they suffered through a violent storm here last year. Funnel clouds touched down around Lake Pepin, and lightning killed one of Maria's horses."

Lightning struck again. And again. Thunder rumbled right behind it. "I know you're big children," said Papuza, "but would you like to join me over here?"

Well, she didn't need to ask twice. Esme and Tommy scooted across to the other bench and huddled near Papuza. She wrapped a soft blanket around them and put her arms around their shoulders. They listened to the storm, counting the seconds between the lighting and the thunder.

Tommy peeked out the window, hoping to spot his pony Bess. She was huddled between Papuza's two large horses, as if they were trying to keep her warm. They were tethered to a tree branch, which thrashed in the wind. "Bess is afraid of storms," said Tommy. "Jeepers, I wish I could bring her in here with us somehow."

"I know just how you feel," said Papuza. "Joe and Zinjiber don't care for storms either. I wish I could bring them all inside, but there's no room."

"I'm worried about Buttercup," Esme said in a soft, sad voice.

Another bolt of lightning struck, and they watched a huge cottonwood split and crash to the ground. It shook the earth around their wagon, making all their dishes and bottles and silverware clatter. Mr. Wright scurried up into the bedchamber and buried himself beneath the blankets.

Branches swirled by. Some hit the wagon with loud thuds while others lashed and scratched the roof before they sailed away. When the next stroke of lightning lit the dark skies, Tommy thought it looked as if it were snowing leaves outside! Millions of leaves whipped around in the wind, and some of them plastered themselves to the wagon's windows.

For gosh sakes, Tommy had never seen a storm like this. He was starting to believe the wagon itself might blow away. *Or that Bess will whirl away.* Fear welled up from his stomach. He cried, "I think it's a hurricane!"

Another streak lit up the sky, and through the window, they saw an ominous sight. Bouncing off the bluffs, spiraling towards them, was a funnel cloud!

"It's not a hurricane, Thomas," Papuza said gravely. "It's a tornado."

VILLAIN

This wicked weather is perfect. It's as if I conjured it up myself, for my own purposes. It will cause all kinds of trouble for the circus. I hope it will harm our meddlesome visitors too.

It's almost a pity that everyone will clean up tomorrow after the storm. After all, in just a few days, the circus will be ruined.

Even this rain can't drench my fantasy of flames.

ESME

Sheer fright swept through Esme. She began to tremble, waiting for the tornado to strike. She was not yet ready to die, but she didn't seem to have much choice in the matter. Huddling as close as she could to Grandma and Tommy, she clutched her lucky locket and closed her eyes.

If she had to go, at least she was with her two favorite people. Not that that made her feel much better. It was bad enough that she might perish. *I don't want Grandma and Tommy to die too.*

She thought of Arthur and of how sad it would be if Grandma got killed before she could reunite with her beloved cousin. The wagon began to shake violently, and dishes crashed to the floor. Esme hugged her loved ones tighter, waiting for their wagon to be smashed to smithereens.

She heard a roar as loud as a locomotive, and then it became louder and louder until it was deafening. Tommy was mumbling — maybe praying — although Esme couldn't hear him well enough to tell.

Just when she thought this would be her last second left on Earth, the sound was gone.

She stayed hunched close to Grandma, waiting to see if the sound would return. When Grandma released a deep sigh, Esme lifted her head. "Is it over?" She swallowed hard.

"Let's hope it is, my dear." Grandma stroked the top of Esme's head. Then she lit a kerosene lantern and handed it to Tommy to carry. Cautiously, they opened the back door of the wagon and peeked outside. The rain had stopped. Everything was still.

Stepping outside, they heard voices and saw flickering lantern-lights. They hurried to where the horses were tethered. "Thank goodness," Grandma said with a sigh. Joe, Zinjiber, and Bess had survived the storm.

Softly Esme said, "I hope Buttercup's okay."

"Well, let's go find out, dear. And I want to check on Katrina." So Grandma and Esme and Tommy left the gypsy wagon to learn what damage had been done.

Oh, mercy! It seemed like a dreadful nightmare, with people in their pajamas slipping in the mud and crying out for help. Branches were strewn everywhere. Some wagons had tipped over. Shock and panic filled the dismal atmosphere.

Spotting Annie, Esme ran to her, and they hugged like long-lost friends. "Are you okay?" cried Annie, "I was so worried about you!"

"We're all fine — " Esme was interrupted by howls of anguish in the darkness.

One voice could be heard above the rest, and his angry curses filled the night air. Esme and Annie rushed ahead of Grandma and Tommy, racing to see what had happened. It was the ringmaster, Samuel.

He was a powerful sight. With his head bent back, he shook his fist in the air, bellowing obscenities at Mother Nature.

He had set his lantern on the ground. In its orange light, Esme could now see more. With a startled gasp, she froze, wishing she could erase what she'd just seen.

It was Buttercup.

The elephant lay on her side, struggling to breathe, and her eyes were clamped shut in pain. A large branch pierced her side, and blood gushed from the wound. Esme ran to her, throwing herself down near Buttercup's head and hugging her trunk. Esme felt like her heart was breaking.

ESME

Tommy and Grandma had caught up with Esme and Annie, and they were all at Buttercup's side. "Grandma, can you save her? Oh, please, can you help her?" It felt like a cold fist was squeezing Esme's heart.

Tommy and Annie tried to reassure her. Tommy said, "If anyone can save her, it's Papuza." Esme knew he was right, yet what if the elephant's nasty wound was even too much for Grandma?

We have to save Buttercup. We must.

Katrina arrived with her granddaughter, Maria, who wore a sling for her broken arm. Maria was Buttercup's trainer, and when she saw the condition of her beloved animal, her face glazed with shock.

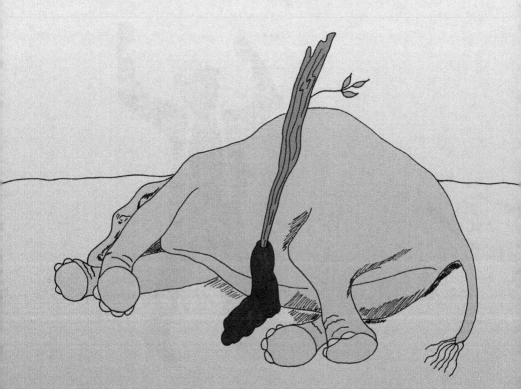

Katrina knelt down beside them. Her expression was grim, yet her voice was steady. "Will she survive?"

"I'm afraid I haven't worked with elephants," Grandma admitted. "But perhaps with Maria's help . . ." Her voice died away.

Grandma sent Tommy, Annie, and Katrina back to the gypsy wagon to retrieve supplies — clean sheets, a bottle of whiskey, and all the mandragora potion under the dry sink. "Hurry!" she urged. "Every second counts."

As soon as they left, Grandma began doctoring. As she and Maria tugged gently on the branch in Buttercup's side, Esme cringed. She stroked the elephant's forehead and comforted her lovingly, as she watched them remove the spear.

It came out cleanly, which was good because Grandma said there was always a risk of leaving remnants inside, which could be quite dangerous. The wound wasn't as deep as they had feared, which also gave them hope. The branch had penetrated perhaps a foot into Buttercup's side.

But had it punctured any internal organs? That was Grandma's biggest concern, for she was unfamiliar with elephant anatomy. Maria said the branch had entered Buttercup below the ribs, so the lungs should be okay. If they were lucky, it might have slipped past her digestive tract without piercing anything. Yet how could they know for sure? They'd just have to wait.

Jiminy. Esme was terrible at waiting.

Tommy and the others returned with the supplies, and Grandma doused the wound generously with whiskey. Then she wadded up a sheet, pressed it directly on the wound, and applied pressure. As she worked, she muttered, "We *must* get this bleeding under control."

She asked Tommy to uncap a bottle of mandragora potion and to hand it to Maria. "It should help Buttercup sleep," she explained. "Although I daresay I don't know how much an elephant can consume."

"Probably a lot," Maria said glumly. Kneeling, she coaxed Buttercup's mouth open and poured the potion inside.

For the first time, Buttercup opened her eyes.

"She likes the taste," Maria said, as a tear trickled down her cheek. "Hang in there, old girl," she whispered, stroking Buttercup's trunk.

Miserable, Esme felt sorry for both of them.

When the bottle was empty, Tommy handed Maria another one. Buttercup drank it, and eventually five more. Finally, with a soft groan, she shut her eyes. Esme feared it might be for the very last time.

"I believe she's breathing a little easier," Papuza murmured gently. "Tommy, could you please take my place for a minute?" Tommy hurried to where Papuza knelt, and he took over her job of putting pressure on Buttercup's wound. Papuza stood up and raised her arms to stretch. Then she told them, "I daresay her bleeding has almost stopped, which is a very good sign. I've done all that I can. Now we must simply wait."

More waiting.

Katrina said a fire should be built nearby, for Buttercup's comfort and for the people who would stay with the elephant through the night. However, due to the storm, dry wood was scarce. Esme and Annie were proud to find some usable branches, which Maria splashed with kerosene. A glowing fire was soon underway.

Esme settled down by Buttercup, stroking her head and talking to her in soothing tones. She wouldn't leave Buttercup's side, not even when Grandma suggested she should try to get some sleep. They discussed plans, and in the end, they decided that Maria and Grandma and Esme would keep watch through the night.

People started to leave the scene. Katrina wanted to check on the rest of the circus folks, Annie declared that she'd better get home, and Tommy decided to go back to the gypsy wagon and sleep. Before he left, Esme hugged him and thanked him for his help.

A little embarrassed, he mumbled, "Shucks, Esme. I didn't do anything." Yet truly he had.

He was gone for a few minutes. Then he surprised Esme by coming back with blankets from the gypsy wagon, which she and Maria and Grandma wrapped gratefully around themselves. Then Tommy said his final good night.

As the evening wore on, they kept the fire going. Leaning lightly against Buttercup, Esme was aware of every breath the elephant took. Buttercup wound her trunk around Esme, snuggling her close. The gesture nearly tore Esme's heart out. Buttercup was the one who was injured, yet she was comforting Esme.

To keep awake, they talked about the circus. Gently Grandma asked Maria, "Have you any idea, dear, who might have left those doves by the ring? Is there someone who wishes you ill?"

Esme sat up with interest, watching Maria's puzzled face in the firelight. "No," Maria sighed, "not that I know of. Although there used to be a boy here at the circus who truly hated me."

"Who was that?" Esme asked, very curious. *How could anyone hate Maria? She's so sweet.*

"His name was Eddie," Maria continued. "I caught him whipping my horse, Arabella, so I asked him to leave the circus. I still see those brutal scars on Arabella every day, and I have never been able to forgive him. But Eddie left a year ago."

Grandma thought this over. "Could he possibly be back, seeking revenge?"

"Well, I haven't seen any sign of him," said Maria. "But I did think of him when Father found spiders in his hatbox. Eddie used to plant spiders in the wagon of Jessamina, our Bearded Lady. Poor Jessamina! She faints dead away at the sight of the smallest spider."

A bearded lady! I haven't met her yet, thought Esme. She asked, "What did Eddie look like?"

Maria shut her eyes as she tried to recall him. "He was stoop-shouldered and gangly, but he might have filled out since then. And he had a large, red birthmark. Right here." She patted her cheek.

Jeepers, he wouldn't be hard to spot, thought Esme. Maybe if they found him, they'd solve the mystery, and the circus could be happy again.

Next they talked about Buttercup. Maria claimed she'd never known an elephant that loved to play pranks as much as Buttercup did. Buttercup's love of teasing was remarkable!

Esme nodded wholeheartedly, remembering how Buttercup had doused them in the river.

Then Maria told them about some of Buttercup's favorite tricks. Apparently she liked to drench an unsuspecting person with a trunkful of water. All you had to do was point at someone and say, "Thirsty," and Buttercup would hose him or her down.

Esme smiled to herself. She couldn't wait to try this trick on Tommy! Of course Buttercup would have to recover first. And Esme had a feeling that she *would* recover. Esme leaned her head against Buttercup's trunk and closed her eyes . . .

Despite her best efforts, Esme's head began to nod. As dawn broke, painting the sky pink, exhaustion overtook her.

TOMMY

Tommy woke with a start. His first thought was that he must have dreamed about a tornado, but then he looked out the window and realized it had only been too real. He was all by his lonesome in the gypsy wagon, except for Mr. Wright. Tommy scooped up the raccoon and headed towards the door.

Esme and Papuza were probably still with Buttercup. Or Esme might be with Annie, which didn't exactly thrill Tommy because he half-blamed their new friend for the drenching they'd received yesterday. At least his ankle felt better this morning, and he wasn't limping any more. His head hurt, though, where that danged raven had tried to peck through his skull.

When Tommy stepped outdoors, it was clear and sunny. He wouldn't have believed there had been a storm last night if he hadn't seen all the branches strewn around. It looked like an ornery giant had jumped up and down on a forest and smashed all the trees to kindling.

As Tommy headed towards the river, where he'd no doubt find Esme and Papuza and Buttercup, people greeted him with "Good morning" and "Top o' the day." He saw workers filling up the aquarium for Annie's act, and she waved at him as he passed by. Other performers were repairing wagons and canvases, and no one seemed terribly out of sorts. In fact, they seemed just the opposite, like they were fighting back against misfortune.

Scanning the horizon, Tommy was surprised to see Buttercup standing by the river! As he drew near the spot where she'd been struck down — the place where he'd feared she'd be buried — he shook his head in amazement. *It's an elephantine miracle,* he thought. *Yes, siree, that's exactly what it is.*

Esme didn't see him coming because she was gazing up, admiring Buttercup. "Hey," he greeted her.

She spun around. "Oh, Tommy! She's going to be okay!" Esme bubbled with happiness, and the warmth of her smile echoed in her voice.

Papuza climbed down from a ladder, where she'd just finished tying strips around Buttercup to bind up her belly. "Say, Papuza," Tommy told her, "she looks great!" Papuza gave him a gentle smile as she wiped her hands on her top skirt.

"And Tommy, there's been a flood of good news!" added Esme. "People have been stopping by all morning, telling us that things are not as bad as they'd feared. The canvas for the big top just needs some small repairs, and no other animals were injured, and the wagons that tipped over will be okay — well, except for some broken windows — but it could have been a lot worse!" she finished breathlessly.

It was impossible to not return her enthusiasm. "Jeepers, Esme, that *is* good news!"

"Excuse me, dears. While there's a smidgen of free time, I'm off to the telegraph office." Papuza patted each of them on the shoulder and hurried away with her skirts billowing behind her.

Esme grabbed Tommy's hand and pulled him forward. "We have so much to do! Everybody needs help. And we'll be able to work on the mystery as we help people because that will be the perfect time to ask questions. But first let me show you something. Stay right here."

Esme stepped back by Buttercup, who was drinking water from the river. "Buttercup," Esme sang out.

The elephant stopped drinking, and her eyes searched Esme's face.

"Buttercup," Esme said again. "Thirsty." Then Esme pointed at Tommy.

Well, before Tommy knew it, that elephant shot a stream of water at him from her trunk, and if he hadn't jumped aside, he would have been drenched. Astonished, he stared at Esme. Then he burst out laughing. "Holey buckets! How did you get her to do that?"

Esme stopped giggling long enough to say, "Maria taught me." She clasped her small hands in delight.

Tommy reckoned it would be mighty handy to have Buttercup on his side during a water fight with his brothers.

"Come on," Esme urged. "You don't want to miss the breakfast tent. The circus cooks have been up since dawn. And then there's all the food the town folks brought. Everyone in Lake City has been so nice. It's a regular feast!"

His tiny cousin was so talkative this morning that he wondered if she'd been drinking coffee — cups and cups of coffee.

When they reached the food tent, he couldn't believe his eyes. In fact, to be sure, he took off his glasses and rubbed them on his sleeve to clean them. *By gum, Esme had not been exaggerating!* She grabbed a plate and piled it high with sausage, eggs, biscuits, marmalade, and toast. Tommy just filled his plate with sausage and flapjacks — lots and lots and lots of flapjacks.

They looked around for a place to sit. The tent was nearly full, and conversations were mighty loud. "There," Esme said, spotting Annie. They headed to the table where Annie was sitting, and when they reached it, they plopped down. Suddenly Tommy realized they'd chosen a perilous place! Emmeline, his partner in the reappearing box of torture, sat right across from him. On the bright side, at least

there were no traces of spooky Madame Sage and Mordecai, the raven that acted like a woodpecker.

Annie told everyone the story of how they'd run to get sheets and whiskey and sleeping potions, and how Papuza and Maria had worked on Buttercup and saved her life.

"How powerful is the sleeping potion?" asked Emmeline.

Annie laughed and said it was powerful enough to knock out an elephant.

As Tommy listened, he took a bite of sausage, and it was probably the best he'd ever tasted. In fact, it was so good he shut his eyes and wondered if he'd gone to heaven.

When he opened his eyes, for gosh sakes, the obviously evil Madame Sage and her raven were taking the seat next to him. Tommy gasped!

And that was the worst thing he could have done because the piece of sausage got stuck in his throat.

He couldn't get it out! Was he choking? Panic like he'd never known before hit him. He looked at Esme, and she smiled at him. Didn't she realize he was in trouble? He needed help! *Does a feller have to die before he gets noticed?*

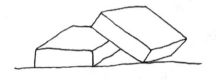

ESME

Esme wished she had a picture of Tommy's face when he opened his eyes and saw Madame Sage sitting down beside him. He was so surprised that his eyes just got bigger and bigger and bigger.

Annie said, "I think the cat's got Tommy's tongue."

He shot Annie a murderous glance, and Esme noticed that his face was red and seemed to be growing even redder.

Madame Sage patted Tommy's hand and croaked, "How kind of you to save me a seat."

Her words startled Tommy so much that he coughed in disbelief. Suddenly a piece of sausage flew right out of his mouth and bounced across the table. Everybody stopped and stared. *Poor Tommy!* How embarrassing! He turned an even deeper shade of red.

Mr. Wright bolted out of Tommy's bib to grab the sausage, but Mordecai the Raven swooped in to claim it too. The baby raccoon hissed while the raven flapped his wings and let out a deafening caw.

The normally easygoing Mr. Wright swiped his paw at Mordecai! Were they getting into a fight? Would Esme see fur and feathers flying any second now? Good gravy, it was a regular animal showdown! The two contenders circled each other warily, so Esme quickly set her plate on her lap, beneath the table. She didn't particularly want *either* feathers or fur in her scrambled eggs this morning.

Greedily, Mordecai snatched the sausage. He preened, gloating, leaving Mr. Wright dejected and defeated. The bird swallowed the sausage. Then he hopped over and pecked Tommy's hand.

Hard.

"Ouch!" Tommy cried.

Mordecai flew back to his owner's shoulder, and his laughing caw matched the current, loud cackling of Madame Sage. Tommy grabbed Mr. Wright and put him in his bib.

"Let me see your hand," Esme told Tommy. "Would you like me to wrap it for you?"

He gave her a black look but didn't get a chance to say anything because Katrina had chosen that moment to make a brief announcement. Calmly she told everyone, "Obviously, there won't be a show today. But tomorrow, the show will go on!" Even though her gray-blonde hair was in curlers, and she wore a bathrobe, she still commanded the room — which in this case happened to be a tent.

Maria joined them, and her blue eyes flashed with merriment. She was in much better spirits today than yesterday, and Esme noticed she still wore the red ribbon around her wrist. Nearly everyone made a fuss over Maria, asking about her arm and her elephant. Only Emmeline, the magician's assistant, remained silent. She didn't look happy at all, and within minutes, she left the table.

Hmm, this made Esme wonder. She whispered to Annie, "Emmeline doesn't seem to like Maria very much."

"She hates her!" Annie whispered back. "Maria stole her boyfriend."

Well, that might make a person want to kill someone. At least it did in the detective novels Esme had read. Love was almost always a motive. A crime of passion, that's what they called it. She had to admit that she'd never really understood this. *But then again, I've never been in love, so how would I know?* Anyway, Emmeline instantly became Esme's prime suspect and the first one to fall into her "Maybe" column. Esme was eager to share her keen deduction with Tommy.

Annie asked, "Do you want to go swimming in my fish tank this afternoon? You and Tommy? We could have so much fun!"

Right away, Esme said, "Oh, I'd love to!"

But then it hit her.

She felt herself blushing as she added, "Except that I don't know how to swim."

"Oh, that doesn't matter," Annie waved her hand, shooing away Esme's worries. "You can stay by the air tubes the whole time. I'll help you. It will be fun!"

"Okay, when?" Esme asked eagerly.

"Sometime after lunch." Annie swallowed a forkful of eggs. "And I have an old costume that should fit you." She gave Esme a wide, open smile.

Now here's a girl after my own heart, thought Esme. *A girl who loves costumes as much as I do.* That had to be a sure sign that their friendship was special.

"Okay, what's all the whispering about?" Tommy whispered to them.

"Whisper, whisper, tongue will blister!" sang Madame Sage. Her powerful, black eyes burned directly into Tommy.

He shuddered. Then he gave her a scathing look, which made her cackle. Annoyed, he grabbed his plate and stood up to get seconds, but as it turned out, he didn't even leave the table. An approaching lady had captured his attention.

She was a willowy woman with a long, full, auburn beard that would have made any Amish man envious. Esme thought, *This must be the Bearded Lady that Maria talked about last night.* The woman wore a lavender blouse and a violet skirt, and she carried a lace parasol. Esme thought her features were quite lovely, and somehow, the beard suited her face and added to her beauty.

Annie whispered to Esme, "That's Jessamina. She's French."

Esme had read books about elegant French ladies, and she had to agree that this one was utterly sophisticated.

Esme found herself wondering what her own face might look like with a beard. Unconsciously she touched her chin.

As Esme studied the Bearded Lady, she could tell that something was wrong. With an edge to her voice, the woman addressed Katrina. "A thief, he is here with us. My jewels, they have gone missing. I insist you find zee culprit!"

Everyone at the table fell silent, even Mordecai. A worried expression had spread across Katrina's face. "Are you sure, Jessamina?"

"But of course." She pulled up one of her long, white gloves. With a snap, she positioned it on her arm precisely.

Katrina asked, "Could your jewels have been misplaced somehow, during the storm?"

"Zee storm, it spared my wagon. I felt lucky to have so little of zee damage — until my jewel box went missing." Her beard quivered, and her voice began to tremble. "I store it under my bed. It was there an hour ago, but now it is gone. All my shining jewels from my admirers, they are gone too!"

Jeepers, this intrigued Esme. The lady had admirers *and* a beard! *Maybe my prospects of finding a beau won't be as hard as I'd thought.*

Jessamina's eyes darkened as she issued an angry warning. "You must search every inch of zee circus. If my jewels do not show up, I am going to zee police!"

Suddenly a small clown rushed up to Katrina in distress. "Missus, missus," he panted, trying to catch his breath. "Come quick! We found Angus, and he might be dead!"

PAPUZA

Stepping out of the telegraph office, Papuza admired the sky, which was a robin's egg blue. Gracious, what a lovely day! It was so cheerful it didn't seem to match the unwelcome tidings she'd just received from Tommy's father. And she felt disappointed that there wasn't any news from the detective or Arthur.

She sighed as she took in the beauty around her. The wild phlox were such a vibrant purple they made her blink. She hoped time would permit her to explore the woods around Lake Pepin, for this was the prime season for rooting.

But first she had to see whether she could provide any assistance to the circus performers, and she needed to check on Buttercup too. At some point, she would like to help Katrina rummage about for the detective's card again. Perhaps Esme and Tommy could help them search.

WESTERN UNION TELEGRAM

RECEIVED at
LAKE CITY MN

SENT FROM
ZUMBRO FALLS MN

ADDRESSED TO
PAPUZA DOBBS

MESSAGE:

As Papuza thought of the children, she smiled. *What delightful traveling companions!* She dearly wished she had better news for them. She read again the telegram from Tommy's father:

Glad you have reunited with your old friend Katrina. No sign of Hatch and Groggs at their home. No sign of them anywhere. Afraid they may have left the area. Be extra cautious. — *William*

TOMMY

Like many of the folks at the table, Tommy jumped up to follow that clown. The clown led them along a broken trail into the deep woods. After a while, they reached a handful of people who were standing around the body of Angus.

The Scottish snake charmer lay so still that Tommy feared the worst. Then he saw Angus' chest rising and falling faintly. *By gum, he's still breathing!* Even though Tommy hadn't liked how Angus had sprung Creampuff on him, that sure didn't mean he wished the fellow were dead.

Next to Angus' head lay a thick branch that was cracked in two. It looked as if he'd been struck with that branch and knocked plumb out. Tommy couldn't rightly tell if the branch had fallen naturally from a tree, or if someone had used it to whack the snake charmer. A nasty gash, caked with dry blood, sliced across the man's forehead, and his caterpillar eyebrows weren't moving. *Too bad he wasn't wearing his turban,* thought Tommy. It might have protected his head.

A lantern lay beside Angus, although its flame had long gone out. A woman in the group claimed she'd seen him searching for his snakes last night, after the tornado.

Now, some of the strongest men lifted the wounded snake charmer to carry him to his wagon. As they bore him away, Angus revived briefly and muttered gibberish. Over and over again, he groaned, "Must find Katrina! Must find Katrina!" Esme and Tommy exchanged a worried look as they watched them depart.

When they were finally alone, Tommy told Esme, "I wonder what that meant. Was he making a confession?"

"No, I don't think so. I think he knows who the villain is!"

"Hmm," Tommy mumbled gloomily. He was still a little annoyed that Esme and Annie hadn't even realized that he was choking at breakfast. "Well, one thing's for sure," he said. "Now we'll know if *Annie* is right that Angus is the guilty party."

"What do you mean?" asked Esme.

"If *Annie* is right, then all the bad things that have been happening will stop happening. Angus looks too injured to cause more shenanigans."

"Why do you say Annie's name that way?" Esme asked cautiously. "You never sound that snotty about anybody."

"I'm sorry, Esme, but you've only just met her, and now everything is 'Annie this and Annie that.'" Tommy paused, suddenly feeling a little embarrassed. "It's not like I'm jealous or anything," he added quickly. "But I still think she set us up, when Buttercup threw us in the river."

He realized he'd stunned Esme into silence. She strode away towards the circus grounds, and he ran to catch up with her. Hoping to reason with her, he said, "You know how you always rush into things."

After a moment, Esme said, "You're right, Tommy. I do rush into things, and I'm sorry if I hurt your feelings . . ."

To stop her from speaking, he held up his hand, just like Pa always did. He said, "I don't want this to be a big, girlish hullabaloo, where I have to talk about my feelings!" For whatever reason, Esme began to giggle.

Which made Tommy laugh.

And then it felt like everything was back to normal again.

"You know," said Esme, "Annie invited both of us to go swimming in her fish tank this afternoon. Maybe if you spent some time with her, you'd like her as much as I do!"

"But you're terrified of water! You don't even know how to swim."

"Annie promised I would be fine," Esme hurried to say. "There are air tubes all over the tank. It would be fun to try! Oh, please Tommy?" She got down on her knees, begging him.

He wasn't interested in getting to know Annie better. Yet someone needed to look after Esme, so he grumpily said, "Oh, all right."

"Yay!" she cried, hopping up from the ground. They started walking again. After a few minutes, Esme said, "You know, Tommy, I don't think Angus could have stolen the jewels."

"Why do you say that?"

"Because Jessamina saw her jewelry box this morning, and *then* it went missing. From the looks of his wound, Angus has been knocked out since last night." Excited about her theory, she started to speak rapidly. "And he wouldn't have been carrying a lantern after daybreak. That just goes to show that he got knocked out last night, which means he couldn't possibly have stolen the jewels."

Tommy could tell she was pleased with her deductions because she straightened up and stood tall. "Well, look at you." He felt proud of her too. "I reckon I'm going to have to call you 'Sherlock.'"

"Oh!" Sudden disappointment smacked Esme hard. "Now that Angus is hurt, he probably won't be able to do his show for a while. And that means I won't be a circus performer." Glumly, she kicked a rock. "Gosh-darn! My one and only chance at stardom, and I'm struck down before I even set foot onstage."

"That's probably for the best anyhow," he told her. "Because I sure wouldn't trust that snake Creampuff."

Suddenly Tommy stopped. Fear flickered through him. "It just hit me," he said gravely. "If all of Angus' snakes slithered away, where are they now?"

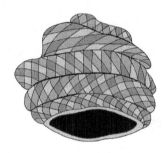

ESME

Esme sat on a hay bale, petting Mr. Wright and watching Tommy learn the finer points of knife throwing from Bernardo, the star of the "World's Best Knife Thrower" sideshow. Bernardo was also the trapeze artist who had bounded into their gypsy wagon and kissed Maria. Esme had learned that Bernardo came to America from Italy.

"The knife, it is held by you like this," he was now telling Tommy. Bernardo grasped the blade instead of the handle, which surprised Esme. Standing back from the target, Bernardo expertly threw the knife and hit the dead center of the bull's eye.

He's like a dancer, thought Esme. *A flamenco dancer, with his fashionable mustache and his dark hair slicked close to his head.*

Bernardo's lean body moved gracefully as he practiced his art. On second thought, he reminded Esme of a panther because he lunged when he released his knives, and he wore black clothing. His only splash of color was a red scarf around his neck.

"The throw, it is now for you to try." Bernardo encouraged Tommy, handing him a knife. "Remember to be snapping the wrist and following through."

Tommy studied the target for a few seconds before he threw the knife. It landed in the third ring from the center. Bernardo praised him, "Not bad, as they say. Try again."

As Esme waited through Tommy's lesson, her mind zipped around to a million different things. My stars! It had been quite a morning. Between the "almost fight" that Mr. Wright had with Mordecai the Raven at the breakfast table; and the discovery of the knocked-out Angus; and then another "almost fight" (this time between Tommy and herself about Annie); and the hours they'd spent gathering branches, twigs, sticks, and leaves to build a huge pile because the circus was planning a spectacular bonfire, which would be a regular, old party — well, yes, it had been quite a morning. And this afternoon, Esme would get to turn into a mermaid, for a while anyway.

She thought back to what Tommy had said about Annie. Esme realized she'd been rather exuberant about making friends with Annie. And yes, Tommy was right, she did rush into things. But jeepers, he was wrong to mistrust Annie. Even if Annie had known that Buttercup was going to toss them in the river — and that was a big "if" — that still didn't make her a bad person.

It was a good thing Esme hadn't told Tommy yet that she was hoping they'd adopt Annie. By gosh, that might have made his head spin around!

Her attention was drawn back to the knife-throwing lesson because Bernardo paused just long enough to let Emmeline, the magician's assistant, pass by safely. Esme would sure like to ask that woman a few non-nosy questions. She gave Emmeline a friendly wave. The woman hesitated a moment, and then she smiled and began to strut closer to Esme's hay bale.

Excitement stirred in Esme. *Here's my chance!* As she shifted Mr. Wright in her arms, she imagined donning her sleuth's hat and beginning her interrogation.

Emmeline, dressed in a fitted shirt and narrow skirt, looked thinner today, and Esme noticed dark circles under her eyes. Even so, she was a striking woman.

"Hello," Esme said as Emmeline reached out to pet Mr. Wright's shaggy head. The baby raccoon backed away from the stranger. "You're Maxwell's assistant, aren't you? I saw you in his show. Nice to meet you. My name is Esme."

"A pleasure to meet you too. My name is Emmeline." She sat down near Esme on the hay bales, keeping an eye on Bernardo, who wasn't paying any attention to her. She tried to pet the raccoon again, asking, "And who do we have here?"

"This is Mr. Wright." As Esme held up the squirmy raccoon, he made a screeching noise, which made Esme and Emmeline laugh.

Esme cleared her throat, preparing to start her questions. "Have you been with the circus long?"

"Long enough." Emmeline laughed again. "It's been about a year now. I used to teach elocution at a boarding school out east, but I wasn't very happy. I finally decided I wanted more excitement out of life, so I joined the circus." She rubbed her chin thoughtfully. "I can't say I've enjoyed being a magician's assistant, but I hope to switch to a new act soon. Bernardo and I have talked about pairing up. I might be his human target!" she ended dramatically.

Shocked, Esme took a sharp breath. "Holy Moses! You're going to have knives thrown at you?"

"Well, Bernardo is a skilled knife thrower. I feel safe with him. And I think my former students, with their spitballs and paper planes, prepared me well for this."

Esme laughed. She liked this Emmeline and couldn't imagine her harming anyone. She seemed very friendly and sweet. But then Esme remembered Madame Sage's warning that things are not always what they seem. Esme guessed she didn't know what a would-be murderer looked like — except for Hatch of course. Esme supposed killers could come in all sorts of disguises. At least they did in books.

Trying to avoid being swayed by her feelings, and aiming to run a strictly scientific investigation, Esme continued. "Are you happy here?"

Emmeline's expression changed and became unreadable. "What deep questions from such a tiny girl." She smiled bleakly. "Well, yes, I'd have to say that overall, I'm happy here. A life in the circus is just like life anywhere else, full of ups and downs."

Esme nodded.

"How about you?" Emmeline asked, still watching Bernardo. "Are you enjoying your time with us?"

"Oh, yes. Very much, thank you."

"How long will you be traveling with us?"

Uncertain, Esme shrugged her shoulders. "I don't know. I think Katrina wants my grandma to keep doctoring Maria's arm . . ." She paused, watching for a sign. Sure enough, Emmeline's eyes blazed with sudden anger. Now *this* seemed more like the woman that Tommy had talked about.

"Hmph." Emmeline snorted. "I don't have fond feelings for that uppity Maria." She stewed for several seconds.

Then her mood began to lighten. "Forgive me," she said, sounding utterly sincere. "I spoke out of place. Bad blood has passed between Maria and me, but it's over now. I'm very glad she wasn't seriously hurt in that fall yesterday."

Esme studied her face, and Emmeline did indeed look truthful. Hoping she sounded fairly innocent, Esme asked, "I wonder who would do such a terrible thing to Maria?" She was curious to see and hear Emmeline's response.

Emmeline leaned in close to Esme, acting very conspiratorial. "Well, everyone in the circus is talking about who it could be, and many people are suspicious of Madame Sage. She's new to the show, and strange things have been happening ever since she arrived." Emmeline paused to clap, as Bernardo hit another bull's-eye. "But you know, I've talked with her several times, and I think she's a sweet, old thing."

Then Emmeline nodded towards Tommy. "Wasn't he in Maxwell's ridiculous reappearing box yesterday? Is he your brother?" Slowly she stood up and stretched.

"No, he's my cousin." Esme hopped down from the hay bale, realizing their conversation was about to end, and she'd learned very little. In fact, if anything, she had even *more* questions. After Emmeline's angry response about Maria, she was still in Esme's "Maybe" column of suspects.

"Well, Esme, I should go. I need to talk with Mama Kat. Goodbye for now." As Emmeline strolled away, her glance slid to Bernardo.

Mr. Wright squirmed in Esme's arms, so she absentmindedly set him on the hay bale. Oh, no! In a flash, he dashed over and wove through Tommy's legs, just as Tommy was about to let go of his knife.

Tripped by Mr. Wright, Tommy slipped, which threw his knife off course. Horrified, Esme squealed, "Oh, mercy!" Tumbling end over end, the knife sailed right over the target to fly straight at a giant!

TOMMY

Great guns! Tommy watched in horror as his knife flew off in the wrong direction, soaring right at the tallest man he'd ever seen! "D-D-Duck," he screamed! The last thing Tommy wanted to do was to accidentally murder someone, and it didn't help when that someone was a giant.

The giant calmly grabbed the knife midair by the handle. Stepping closer to them, he handed the knife down to Tommy. "Just learning?" he boomed. "Or are you trying to tell me something?"

Tommy stared, dumbfounded, at the biggest man he'd ever seen. He must have been almost nine feet tall! Tommy would have been running in the opposite direction if the giant hadn't been smiling. He had a mighty kind face.

"No, sir," Tommy mumbled. If the giant lifted Tommy up to his face, the boy would be dangling high above the ground. Instead the giant bent down on one knee, so they could talk with each other better. As the man bent, he groaned ruefully, as if his knees hurt.

Esme, who had caught Mr. Wright, was only as tall as the giant's knee. "Sorry, sir!" She peered up at him, holding her hand to her brow as a visor. "That was my fault. I shouldn't have let go of Mr. Wright!"

Bernardo introduced them to Henry, who held out his hand to Tommy. "Holy mackerel!" Tommy muttered in awe, for Henry's hand was gigantic! Tommy was almost afraid to shake hands with him, for Henry could have crushed Tommy's bones in an instant. Yet when they did shake hands, the giant was gentle.

Esme reached out her hand, and it was only as big as Henry's thumb.

"I heard of a tiny girl who slept by Buttercup's side last night," Henry rumbled kindly. "That must have been you."

Blushing, Esme nodded. "I checked on her an hour ago, and she was eating like an elephant." She giggled.

Henry told the cousins, "And I understand you're Annie's new friends. She's a sweetheart. Since her parents died, she's been a little on the quiet side, so it's good to see her laughing with some young people."

Tommy wasn't sure he'd call Annie a friend. But when a grown-up stranger (who also happened to be a giant) said something nice like that, it wasn't easy to set him straight.

Bernardo left, but not before Tommy thanked him for his knife-throwing lesson. Bernardo told Tommy he could come back again, if he'd like to practice some more. His words practically made Tommy burst with happiness.

As Henry tried to straighten up, he groaned. Tommy felt

sorry for him because he realized the giant's pains were as big as he was. Esme must have seen it too because she asked Henry, "Are you okay?"

Henry had made it to an upright position. "I'm afraid there's nothing anyone can do for me. The doctors say it's my joints — a curse of my height."

"Well, maybe my grandma could help," Esme offered. "She saved Buttercup's life last night, and she knows all kinds of wonderful remedies, for all kinds of ailments."

"That's right," Tommy added. "She's gotta have something for you!"

Henry looked down on them wistfully, and Tommy really hoped Papuza could help him. Henry agreed to go with them to the gypsy wagon.

Tommy ran ahead to locate Papuza. She was inside the wagon, consulting an herbal book, as he burst up the back steps. "You have a patient," he cried. Although Tommy could have been wrong, he doubted she'd had many patients like this one.

"You're certainly excited," said Papuza, as she followed Tommy outside. Then she whispered, "My goodness," as she saw Esme and Henry approaching. "My goodness gracious."

Esme and Tommy introduced Henry to her, and Papuza was as much in awe of him as they were. He was too large to enter their wagon, so Papuza sent Tommy for some hay bales to make a temporary chair, so Henry could "rest his weary bones."

When Tommy returned, he wasn't alone, for some of the clowns were helping him haul bales to the wagon. "Anything for Henry the Eighth," a clown said playfully, bowing to Henry before he left.

Henry sat down, and a heavy sigh escaped his lips. "That feels much better." His voice swelled in contentment.

"Why did he call you Henry the Eighth?" Tommy asked, scooting close to him. Esme was already so close that she was practically leaning on Henry's knee.

"They like to tease me. I'm over eight feet tall, and I've been married a number of times. Not as many times as the real King Henry, but who's counting?" He laughed deeply and warmly.

And so the gentle giant told them the tale of his life. He was raised in Minnesota, and then he went east to study law. There, he grew to admire a good-natured lady, but she declared that doing his laundry would be a "gigantic" task, and any woman in her right mind should stay clear of him. So he learned how to do his own laundry (and cook as well), and she agreed to marry him. Unfortunately she died of diphtheria on their honeymoon. Later, he married again, but Wife Number Two ran off with his law partner. Henry thought Number Three might be a charm, so he married yet again. He told Papuza and the children that he felt lucky because even though his last wife poisoned him with arsenic, he survived.

"How awful!" said Papuza.

"Oh, I'm fine now," said Henry, "I was sad for a long time, but then I realized my heart needed to be as big as the rest of me. I forgave my last two wives, so I could find peace."

Here he paused, rubbing his neck as if it hurt. Watching him, Tommy thought, *That poor man.* He could very well be the bravest fellow Tommy had ever met, jumping into love three times! Henry's acts of forgiveness seemed gigantic — much, much greater than Tommy's own forgiveness of Esme's derelict haircut.

Papuza asked, "How long have you been with the circus, Henry?"

"Oh, about twenty years. In all those years, we've never had times like this."

After a glance at Esme and Tommy, Papuza asked Henry, "Are you referring to the recent troubles?"

"Yes, that's *exactly* what I mean. As much as it pains me to say it, the scoundrel has to be someone inside the circus — someone who is very familiar with the show."

Henry shifted his weight on the bales of hay. "You know, once you join a show, the people become your family — even closer than your family. No family is ever perfect, but someone here must be very, very angry." He sighed a gigantic sigh. "I've thought and thought about this over the past twenty-four hours. In fact, I haven't gotten much sleep. And it's not because of the storm."

He gazed into the distance as if he were musing over a memory. "Now, if this had happened a year ago, I would have felt sure it was a boy who used to be with the circus. He had a cruel streak, and I could imagine him doing this."

Esme exclaimed, "Maria mentioned a boy last night! She said his name was Eddie."

"Yes. That's the very one." Henry's face became grim.

"Well," Tommy said, "do you think he's come back? Could he be lurking around?"

"Trust me," said Henry, "I see everything that goes on in this place. With my height, I have a tremendous vantage point, and there's been no sign of Eddie whatsoever."

Then Papuza began to question Henry about his ailments. He said his joints caused him such grief that he found no reprieve from the pain, even when he was lying in bed. As he talked, Papuza felt his wrist and finger joints. Then she asked him to roll up his sleeve, so she could check his elbow.

After examining him, she went to her wagon and returned shortly with a bottle. "Now, this is distilled from ash leaves," she said. "I use it myself, for my arthritis, and I daresay it's the best cure I know. The normal dosage is three tablespoons a day, yet a man of your size could safely take six." She handed the bottle to Henry.

He offered payment, but Papuza shook her head. "You are very kind, sir, but let's see if it helps you first."

At that point, Henry said he'd better get going because he had to replace some broken windows. They'd all enjoyed meeting him so much that they hated to see him leave. Wistfully they watched, as he lumbered away.

They headed inside the gypsy wagon, where Esme declared, "I'm dying to write all about him!" Looking for her journal, she pulled the cushions off one of the benches and lifted the lid to the storage bin below. "Oh, my stars!" she gasped.

"What?" Tommy asked, walking over to her. When he peered down inside the compartment, he gasped too.

"What is it, my dears?" Papuza joined them.

There, in the bin, sparkling just as pretty as could be, sprawled a tangled mess of glittering jewelry!

ESME

Esme stared up at Grandma, who was blinking in bewilderment. Grandma muttered, "What in the world?"

"How did they get here?" asked Tommy. He sounded utterly baffled.

Esme's mind reeled in confusion. *What kind of tomfoolery is this?* She mumbled, "They must be Jessamina's jewels."

"Who is Jessamina?" asked Grandma. Esme and Tommy realized that since Grandma hadn't been at the breakfast table that morning, she hadn't encountered The Bearded Lady yet. So they told Grandma the story of the missing jewels, and then Tommy went on to describe the length and luxuriance of Jessamina's beard. Listening to Tommy's very detailed account of the lovely French lady, Esme had doubts again about whether he truly didn't like girls, as he always claimed.

Tommy touched a topaz ring as he studied the tangle of jewels. "How do you reckon they got here?"

"Well, Thomas," said Grandma, lighting her pipe. "I suspect someone planted them here to make it look as if we stole them."

"But we didn't, Grandma. I swear!" Esme's voice rose with frustration. "You have to believe us!"

"Of course I do, dear." She gave Esme a hug. "I *know* you would never do this. Someone has put them here to make us look like thieves."

Esme cried, "How could anyone be so mean?"

"Well, Hatch is this mean all the time," said Tommy.

"Yes, but how could anyone *else* be so mean?" For a moment, Esme wondered if Hatch might be at the circus.

"Now, now, my dears," Grandma said calmly. From one of her many pockets, she found a scarf and carefully laid the jewels upon it. Then she tied up the bundle with a knot. "I daresay we have a delivery to make, and the sooner the better."

So a few minutes later, Grandma and Esme and Tommy knocked on the door to Katrina's wagon.

Katrina unlatched the top half of her door, and Grandma handed her the knotted scarf. "I believe this is something of importance," said Grandma.

When Katrina untied the scarf and saw the jewels, she sighed, "Thank goodness!" She ushered them into her chaotic wagon, scooping up the costumes and curlers and headdresses that were strewn over her chairs. Even though

200

she tried to make room for everyone to sit down at the table, Esme still had to stand on her chair to see over the piles of letters, dirty coffee cups, perfume bottles, and hats that were stacked precariously in front of her. Good gravy! Esme wouldn't have been surprised if a few forgotten meals were buried in there somewhere.

"Jessamina was just here," said Katrina. "She's extremely upset. She threatened to shave off her beard and quit the show." Katrina set the jewels on the table. *Oh, dear,* thought Esme, *in this jumbled chaos, that puts them at serious risk of disappearing again.* Katrina added, "Jessamina will be so happy when I return these. Where did you find them?"

As Grandma described how they'd discovered them, Katrina listened closely, nodding occasionally. Grandma added that she had no idea if all the jewels had ended up in their wagon, or if they'd only received a portion of them.

When Grandma finished talking, Katrina remained silent for a moment, rubbing her forehead. Then she murmured regretfully, "Somebody wants you gone."

Thinking about that scheming somebody made Esme's stomach knot in anger. She clenched her fists. Earlier, the mystery of the circus had seemed like a game, but now she took it personally. Somebody had tried to make them look like thieves. And that same somebody wanted to cast black shadows not only on Tommy and herself but also on her sweet, innocent grandma. Determination swelled inside of her. *As sure as my name is Esme Dooley, I am going to find that villain.*

Katrina placed her hand over Grandma's. "In all my years with the circus, I've never seen times like these. Thank you for helping me, my old friend." She gave them all a kindly smile, and her face was full of strength.

Katrina unearthed a tin of sugar cookies and offered them to her guests. As Grandma and Katrina chatted, Esme bit into her cookie and glanced around the overwhelming wagon. It was fascinating, filled with circus posters from Katrina's travels. Esme started to realize how many places Katrina had visited. To Esme, the cities were only names in her geography primer, but Katrina had actually been to those faraway places, like Milwaukee, Chicago, Boston, and Buffalo — places that Esme imagined as very big, and very noisy, and very exciting!

The more she gazed around the cluttered wagon, the more she understood why no one had found the detective's card yet. She knew Grandma and Katrina had searched for it last night before the storm had struck, but they hadn't had any luck. So Esme began to review Katrina's collection of oddities with renewed interest. Maybe she could find the card! She nudged Tommy and whispered, "Help me look for that detective's card."

With a wry look, he whispered back, "That would be as hard as finding something good in Hatch." Nevertheless, Esme noticed that he was starting to glance around too.

Esme cleared her throat and asked Katrina if it would be all right if they hunted for the detective's card.

"By all means, please do!" she exclaimed. "I was looking this morning, with no success."

The search was on.

"I'll find it before you do," Esme teased Tommy.

"Is that so? We'll just have to see about that." He smiled, which made his blue eyes crinkle into half-moons.

Esme decided to begin with the small mountain right in front of her. She put letters in a pile on her right, and gloves in a pile on her left. Cups and saucers ended up in a stack in the middle.

Twenty minutes later, when Esme separated two saucers that were stuck together, she found the card! It had been resting between the saucers, and now it was curved and covered with brown coffee stains, but that didn't matter because they could still read it. "I found it!" crowed Esme.

Everyone gathered around her to study the card. It said...

Detective Joseph C. Krepfle
Finder of Lost Souls
Formerly of the Pinkerton Detective Agency
St. Paul, Minnesota
Telephone Number 16

Katrina sprang up. "There's a phone at the telegraph office." Excited, she told Grandma, "I'm taking you there right now!"

"Oh, Grandma!" Esme cried. "You're going to find Arthur!"

TOMMY

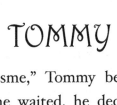

"Come on, Esme," Tommy begged impatiently. "She's fine." As he waited, he decided Esme looked mighty small when she stood next to that gigantic elephant. She was stroking Buttercup's trunk, talking to her in something that must have been Elephant language. Whatever it was, it was making Buttercup happy.

They were on their own, trying to solve the mystery while Papuza and Katrina were at the telegraph office. "I'll be right there, Tommy!" Esme chirped happily. "See you later, Buttercup." She said goodbye to the elephant and started down the fairway with her cousin.

Riding in the bib of Tommy's overalls, Mr. Wright sniffed the air. None of the food stands had opened since the storm, but it looked like he smelled something interesting. Esme reached over and scratched his furry head. "I wonder what Grandma is learning," she told Tommy. "How exciting to find someone you thought was dead! Can you imagine if I disappeared, and you didn't see me for sixty-six years? Wouldn't you miss me?"

"Maybe not for the first sixty-five years," he teased. "But seriously, Esme, where should we start investigating? Just think, we're like that detective that Papuza is trying to reach."

"Well, we have an hour before we go swimming." As Esme thought about swimming, she clapped her hands and started skipping. "I can't wait! In the meantime, I'm thinking of heading to the big top to question that sweetheart of Maria's. You know, the knife-throwing trapeze artist."

Confused, Tommy stared down at his little cousin. "Bernardo? He ain't the villain." *He can't be!* "Didn't you see with your own two eyes how he was smooching all over Maria? He wouldn't want to hurt her."

"Maybe he has an idea of who *might* want to hurt her."

"*I* reckon you just want to mess around on the trapeze."

"No!" she exclaimed, but then she giggled, making Tommy absolutely, positively sure that he'd guessed right about her trapeze aspirations. She begged, "Let's go see if they're practicing."

So they peeked through the flaps of the big top, where three rings had been laid out. The ground inside each ring was covered with sawdust, which men were raking smooth.

Up near the top of the tent, acrobats soared, practicing their acts. Of course the trapeze appealed to Esme, who had always had a hankering to fly. She gazed up longingly while Tommy looked up with dread. He thought, *No one will ever talk me into swinging from a trapeze.*

Tommy realized that somebody had come up and was standing by his side. It was Bernardo, his knife-throwing teacher, who was now dressed for trapeze practice. Bernardo had also waxed his handlebar mustache, which curled up on both sides like it was doing loop-de-loops of its own.

Tommy was amazed by Bernardo's muscles. His older brothers were strong from working on their farm, but they sure didn't have muscles like this guy. Tommy guessed that if your life depended on your muscles, you'd better have good ones. *A feller could do just about anything, if he were built like that.* Unconsciously, Tommy straightened his posture and stood a little taller.

"Maria's doing well," said Esme, smiling at Bernardo. "Before you know it, she'll be back on her horse."

Bernardo smiled back. "The hope, it fills me, little one."

"Say," Esme began carefully. "I was wondering if anyone ever found out who put that box of doves by the ring?"

Sudden anger lit Bernardo's eyes. "No one is knowing. But if I ever be finding it out . . ." His voice broke off in mid-sentence, and he struck his palm with his fist.

Tommy gulped. *I sure wouldn't want Bernardo mad at me!*

"Is anyone jealous of her?" Esme asked boldly. "Or does anyone want to hurt her?"

Tommy nudged Esme. She was asking mighty pointed questions, and Papuza had warned them against raising suspicions.

"No," Bernardo answered firmly. "Maria, she is loved by everyone. So kind and sweet, she is adored by all."

"I can see why," Tommy said quickly, to cut Esme off. She opened her mouth, and no doubt she was fixing to ask another nosy question, so he gave her another nudge. She nudged him right back.

Apparently deciding to change the subject, Esme asked Bernardo, "So, what's the weather like up there?" She nodded towards the top of the tent, where the trapeze was swinging.

Oh boy, here she goes. She was going to try to talk her way all the way up to the top of the tent. Tommy *knew* that's why she'd wanted to come here.

Yet it turned out Tommy was only partly right. Esme didn't have to talk at all because the look on her face said it for her. When Bernardo glanced at her, he asked, "The trapeze, is it something you are wanting to try?"

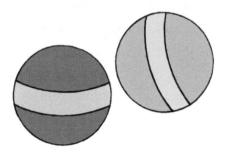

Esme

A warm glow flowed through Esme. "Do I!" she cried. "Oh, jeepers, yes!"

"And you?" Bernardo asked Tommy. "You are wanting to try the trapeze too?"

Tommy hesitated before he said, "That's mighty nice of you. But I should take care of this varmint." He pointed down at Mr. Wright in the bib of his overalls.

Esme stole a glance at his face. He was blushing, probably because he hadn't exactly told the whole story. Esme knew he was afraid of heights and would never, ever try the trapeze. She wouldn't embarrass him, though, by mentioning this in front of Bernardo.

"Okay, then, Miss Esme. Up you are going." Bernardo stepped away from the ladder to give her room to climb. "The nets, they are up, so do not worry."

Before Bernardo could change his mind, Esme started scrambling up the ladder. She was too small to climb more than one rung at a time, so she tried to make up for it by moving quickly. It reminded her of climbing to their tree house back home, except this ladder was considerably taller. My gosh, it stretched a long way up!

She finally reached a tiny platform and crawled upon it to stand upright. Clutching the big pole in the middle of the platform, she looked down.

It was so much higher than she had imagined. People down below looked tiny! They reminded her of the Lilliputians in *Gulliver's Travels*. Spotting Tommy, she whistled to get his attention. They waved to each other.

Bernardo had been climbing the ladder also, and now he stood beside her on the platform. Grabbing the trapeze bar, he gave it a mighty shove to create some momentum. As he pushed the bar back and forth, he instructed Esme on how to grip the trapeze, how to reach her toes to the bar, how to follow through with her body, and how to kick her legs to send the trapeze forward.

Another acrobat waited on the platform across from them. Bernardo told Esme, "His name, it is Kenneth. He will give to you the help, when you reach the other side." Bernardo whistled to catch Kenneth's attention. Kenneth waved in response.

Bernardo continued, "Now I shall lift you, so you will be ready." He hoisted Esme, and she stretched out her arms, ready to go. As he held her, waiting for the swinging bar to arrive, he said, "When it gets here, grab on. Do not have the worries about falling. The nets, they are there to catch you."

The bar came closer, and a thrill of excitement surged through her. "Now!" said Bernardo.

Esme grabbed the bar.

She thought of everything he'd told her, and she also pictured the acrobats she'd watched yesterday during the show.

Stars tingled in the pit of her stomach as she was lifted into flight. She stopped holding her breath and simply sailed through the air.

This is how I want to spend the rest of my life. Gliding just beneath the tent top, she felt completely at home. This must be how a bird feels when it soars into the great blue beyond — effortless, weightless, and free.

Much too quickly, it was over. As Esme neared the other platform, Kenneth reached out and pulled her to a stop. The acrobats applauded.

"Oh, may I do it again, please? I loved it! I absolutely loved it!"

And so she did it again.

And again after that.

And even more after that.

Esme beamed when Bernardo said she was a natural. Before her lesson ended, she even talked them into doing a release, where Kenneth met her halfway and caught her by her legs, as she let go of the bar.

It's magic!

Swinging upside down, she caught the barest glimpse of Madame Sage sprinting out of the tent entrance. How could an elderly woman possibly move that fast? *How strange!*

Things were *definitely* not what they seemed with Madame Sage.

PAPUZA

"He's been where?" Papuza spoke loudly into the dark mouthpiece of the telephone. The connection with the detective in St. Paul crackled, so she held the hand-piece even closer to her ear. As she waited for his answer, she watched the swirling dust specks in the sunlight.

"He's been shipwrecked, marooned on an uncharted island off the coast of South America. It's an amazing story," the detective rambled on. "And one that he's keen to share with you. He'll be happy to hear I've found you."

"Where is he?" asked Papuza.

"He's traveling at the moment. However he left me an itinerary of his plans." After more crackling and a slam of a desk drawer, the detective muttered, "Oh, yes, here they are. I *think* he's in Dubuque, but he might be in La Crosse by now. I'll try to track him down. Be sure to check the

telegraph office frequently, because given my client's desire to find you, I'm sure you'll be hearing from him shortly."

"Oh, thank you kindly, sir," she gushed. "Thank you so very much."

"He sounds like a very interesting . . ." The detective's words were lost in the crackling. ". . . I've never worked with royalty before . . ."

"What?" Papuza tried desperately to hear what he was saying, but the line went dead. Reluctantly, she hung up, setting the hand-piece back in its cradle.

Katrina drew near, eager to learn the news. Papuza told her, "With any luck, I could hear from him today!" She hugged her old friend in happiness. "I'll check back here throughout the day for a reply. It all seems so unbelievable. And I fear I'm confused because the connection was quite poor. It sounded as if the detective said something about royalty."

ESME

Esme decided that Tommy's hair looked perfectly normal underwater, floating straight up. Why, she never would have guessed that his hair hadn't needed a comb. It had just needed water! The thought of this made Esme giggle, and a bubble popped out of her nose.

They'd been in Annie's aquarium for half an hour now, having a jim-dandy time. Esme was in her sailor dress, but she also wore one of Annie's old mermaid tails. *It's kind of like wearing pants that only have one leg,* she thought. The tail was made of rubber, and it weighed her down a bit. At first this had scared her, for she'd sunk to the bottom, but right away, Annie had guided her over to an air tube.

Then Esme began finding her way from one air tube to the next. The steady hum of the air compressor vibrated constantly in her ears. She and Annie and Tommy couldn't speak with each other, so they pantomimed everything. Before long, they were holding their sides and laughing.

Soon Esme could take a deep breath and move across the entire tank. She grew less and less worried about not knowing how to swim because Annie and Tommy were at her side, and there were air tubes in the ferns, and the vanity, and the clam bed, and the folding screen, and the treasure chest, so the water didn't seem at all scary.

Right now, Esme was reclining on the clam bed. It was splendidly comfortable because the mattress was made of huge sponges that were gathered together in a fisherman's net. She felt thankful for the air tube by the bed, and she could imagine living in this fishy kingdom forever.

Strings of blue and green lights hung above the tank, casting sea hues through the water. Esme watched Tommy, who was on the other side of the tank. He was in his overalls but shirtless. Esme could see the farmer's tan on his arms, even under a green light. His bare feet, which she hardly ever saw, were so white and wrinkled that they seemed downright bashful. He held a trident in his hand, pumping it up and down playfully. Esme had to say he looked, for all the world, like King Neptune — if King Neptune had ever dressed up as a farmer.

Then Tommy got rambunctious and grabbed a crown from the open chest of jewels and pulled it onto his head. Laughing, Esme left the clam bed and floated over to him. The crown was too big for him, and it kept slipping down his forehead.

It covered his eyes, so Esme helped him tug it up. Then he pretended to charge Esme and Annie with his trident, so they swam away while he followed in hot pursuit.

Tommy and Annie were having such a fun time playing that Esme felt sure he'd think differently now. He'd realize he'd been all wrong about Annie, and that she really was the most wonderful girl.

They were floating behind the folding screen, having such a good time that it surprised Esme when Annie wanted to stop. Annie put her finger to her lips before she pointed through some rippling strands of seaweed that were taller than Esme. As Esme and Tommy peeked through the strands, they caught sight of someone entering the tent.

The tent flap was open, and light spilled inside. From Esme's location, the person was backlit, like a silhouette. Esme could tell that the person was a woman, from the outline of her skirt. It was not until the person drew nearer, and a green light brought the woman's features into focus, that Esme realized it was Madame Sage!

Then a man entered through the spillway of light, and Madame Sage spun around. To Esme's surprise, the fortune-teller ran towards him and threw herself into his arms. The man was not close enough for Esme to tell who it was, yet she could clearly see from his outline that he wore a cape. *Could it be Maxwell?* Esme also noticed that the man wore a top hat, which made her believe her suspicions were correct, and it was indeed the magician who was embracing Madame Sage.

Suddenly the two separated and seemed to be arguing. The man went down on his knee, and Madame Sage took his hands and pulled him to his feet. They embraced all over again.

What in the world was going on here? Were these two in any way guilty of the crimes against the circus? Madame Sage was so much older than Maxwell. *How could he be in love with her?* Maybe this is what the books meant when they said that love is blind.

It looked like the mysterious cape-man was going in for a kiss. This was so startling that Esme gasped and accidentally gulped some water. Hurrying to use an air tube, she noticed that the lights were growing dimmer, and Annie was not at her side. Quickly Esme glanced around the tank, but Annie wasn't there! *Where did she go?*

Tommy must have been thinking the same thing because he was looking everywhere too. As Esme met his eyes, a wave of panic washed over his face.

And then the air compressor stopped, and everything grew quiet.

And then the lights went out, and everything became dark.

And then the air tubes stopped working.

TOMMY

Tommy grabbed for Esme, so he wouldn't lose her in the dark. *But she ain't here!* Anxiously, he felt all around his body, but all he touched was water. There was nothing solid.

Maybe Esme knew enough to float to the top, but then again, maybe she didn't. She still didn't really know how to swim.

He lunged around in the dark with his trident, hoping to find her. That darn crown had fallen over his eyes again. He reached up to tug it off when WHOOSH!

What in tarnation was that? Could it be a spooky sea creature, with grasping tentacles that would choke the life out of him? Tommy's heart beat fast as he poked around blindly, fumbling and fighting unseeable foes. His lungs started to burn, and he couldn't remember how long he'd been holding his breath.

Something grabbed him under his arms and hoisted him upwards. Urgently! He broke the surface of the water and was released from the iron grip. He pulled off the crown, trying to make sense of what had just happened.

The first thing he realized was that the lights were back on. And the second thing he noticed was that Annie was smiling at him. But more importantly, she was holding Esme's arm to keep his cousin above the surface. Even though Esme tilted her head jauntily to one side, he noticed she was grasping her locket.

Laughing, Annie asked, "Were you trying to stab something with that trident of yours? When you couldn't see a thing?"

Esme giggled, which told him she had also seen his fumbling ways. He only hoped she had the good sense to keep this story away from his brothers. "What happened?" he gasped.

"Sorry about that!" Annie was panting a little too. As she treaded water, she continued to hold Esme up. "It's that darn steam engine! I knew it needed more wood because the lights began to dim. I hate it when it does that." A shadow of annoyance crossed her face. "Anyway, when I got outside, Henry was already adding wood. I hope you weren't scared in the dark."

"You know how to stoke a steam engine?" Tommy asked, mighty impressed. As they talked, they gradually drifted towards the edge of the tank.

Annie laughed. "I tapped you on your shoulders to let you know I was leaving the tank, but you two were too busy watching Madame Sage and Luis."

"Luis?" Esme asked. "Who's Luis?"

As they crawled out onto a small platform, Annie asked, "You haven't met Luis yet?"

"No," said Esme, trying to squirm out of her rubber fish tail. "Is he an old man?" She finally freed herself from her scales and stood on her own two legs again. "Because Madame Sage is really old. I'm kind of relieved because I had thought she was kissing Maxwell, and I couldn't imagine Maxwell and Madame Sage together as a couple." Esme paused. Then she added, "I don't even think Jane Austen could have imagined them as a couple."

Annie's gentle laugh made Tommy feel cheerful. For the first time, he noticed the dimple under her left eye. He thought, *Maybe Esme is right about her after all.*

"So who is this Luis?" Esme asked again.

"He's our very own Gentleman's Werewolf." Annie had said the word "werewolf" in a mighty spooky voice. "I'm surprised you haven't run into him yet."

"A werewolf?" Tommy stammered. "I thought there were no such thing as werewolves and vampires. I thought they were just a bunch of hogwash!"

"A real werewolf!" Esme murmured. Tommy could tell she was fascinated. With her love of danger, he reckoned she had a powerful hankering to leave right away to track the creature down.

So Tommy was amazed when Esme said, "I don't know about you two, but I want to go in the water again, without the tail this time. I think I might be able to swim underwater all by myself." She added hopefully, "Is that okay, Annie?"

"Sure!"

So Esme jumped into the water, taking off as smoothly as a little fish. They watched her go straight to an air tube at the bottom of the tank. She waved and gave them a "thumbs up" signal.

"I think she's got the hang of it," Tommy told Annie. "Or at least she's overcoming her fear of water."

"I'm glad she's having fun," Annie said, turning to look at him. Tommy thought, *How come I never noticed before that her eyes are a brilliant shade of blue?*

Annie added, "Let's join her!" and then she did a perfect dive into the tank.

Tommy paused, watching her swim to Esme. He'd had Annie all wrong. Well, maybe he'd been partly right. He did think she was dangerous. Not a "take-your-best-friend-away-from-you" sort of dangerous. Or an "unknown-sea-creature" type of dangerous. It was really even scarier.

Annie was dangerous because she could steal your heart.

ESME

Late that afternoon, it was so hot that Esme vowed never, ever to complain about winter again. Even if it was fifty degrees below zero. Even if she couldn't see over the snowdrifts. Even if she was shoeless and trudging in a blizzard! Right now she was sweating like a pitcher of Hatch's bitter tea. She sat back on her heels, and beads of perspiration trickled into her eyes, making them burn. She mopped her brow.

The afternoon had turned muggy. Esme and Grandma were in the shadows of the forest, yet it was still humid. They were digging up lady's slipper. It really was the sweetest little wildflower — white, with vivid splashes of pink. The delicate blossom would make a perfect cap for a fairy!

Kneeling by Esme's side, Grandma taught her that the flower's roots, which lay just below the surface of the ground, could be used to cure headaches, and ease pain, and help one sleep. Grandma talked as they worked, and Esme listened. Esme realized how much she loved these moments. She wished she could save them in her shiny locket, so she could take them out every so often and live them again.

She was only sorry that Tommy wasn't with them. Now that a thief was in their midst, Grandma thought they needed to keep a closer eye on their horses and gypsy wagon. So Tommy had volunteered to stay behind at the wagon that afternoon, which also gave him a chance to practice his knife throwing.

A shrill cry from an eagle overhead made Esme glance up. Sunlight dappled the leaves of the trees. *What a beautiful place!* They were very close to Lake Pepin, and mossy trees grew thick here, dense and deep. It was like an enchanted forest, or the greenwood from the Robin Hood tales. If Esme had been Maid Marian, she would have loved visiting Robin in a pretty forest like this. It would have been awfully romantic!

"I think this is enough," said Grandma. She stopped working and leaned back to rest against a lofty cottonwood. Searching her many, many pockets, she found her pipe and began to fill it. "Remember, we must always leave some roots in the ground for the next year."

She took a draw from her pipe and sighed. "I daresay we are in an interesting situation! The detective is contacting Arthur, and I'm heading back to the telegraph office soon to see if there's a message. I am amazingly excited! And you, my dear granddaughter, are wholeheartedly trying to solve the mystery facing the circus. Tell me, do you have any theories about who is behind the bedlam?"

Esme put down her jackknife and stretched out on the ground. With her hands behind her head, she stared up at the canopy of branches. "You know, Grandma," she began. "I'm really starting to suspect Madame Sage." Esme told her about seeing Madame Sage sprinting out of the tent while Esme had swung on the trapeze. "And then I saw her kissing a werewolf when we were swimming, and . . ."

"Excuse me, dear," Grandma interrupted her. "Did you just say a *werewolf?*"

"Yes, Grandma. I haven't met him yet, but Annie says he's a werewolf! Are werewolves real? Have you ever met one?"

"I've met a wolf in sheep's clothing," Grandma said, with a smile. "Yet I cannot say I've ever met a werewolf."

"Well, all of this makes me very suspicious of Madame Sage. But you know, Grandma, the circus is full of surprises." In her best Madame Sage voice, Esme intoned, "Things are not always what they seem."

Grandma chuckled. "That's very true, my dear. In a circus, people make their living doing magical acts, making us believe that what we see is real. I think that if we uncloak the illusion, we're disappointed, for we like to hope there's a little magic in the world."

Grandma stood and raised her arms to the sky for a good stretch. Using her top skirt as an apron, she filled it with their lady's slipper roots. "I'm longing to know if there's news from Arthur," she exclaimed as they started back to the gypsy wagon. "It's all so exciting! I wonder what he's been doing all these years, and if he's greatly changed."

"I'm excited too, Grandma. I keep trying to imagine what he'll look like. In my mind, I see him as a little, old man with white hair and a knobby cane."

Grandma laughed. "I picture him as I remember him, except that he's now grown larger. In my imagination, he still has red hair."

This made Esme smile, for she hadn't known that Grandma imagined things too. *I'm getting mighty curious about this long-lost, thought-to-be-dead relative of mine.*

Esme and Grandma stepped out of the forest and strolled to the gypsy wagon. There, Esme paused to pet Bess while Grandma stroked the muzzles of Joe and Zinjiber.

Suddenly Esme jumped because Mr. Wright streaked from the wagon. Tommy hurtled right behind him, screaming, "Snake! Snake!"

TOMMY

It was that lowdown snake, Creampuff! Tommy had been sitting in the gypsy wagon, trying his best to clean his glasses and not think of Annie, when — good gravy! — that snake came slithering right out of Papuza's bedchamber!

Well, Tommy lit out of there mighty quick. Even if Creampuff wasn't venomous, she still had that troublesome snakelike ability to scare him half to death. As he raced down the wagon's back steps, he spotted Esme and Papuza near the horses, so he made a beeline over to them. "Snake!" he hollered. "Snake!" He didn't stop running. He rushed right

by them, into the woods and behind an oak tree.

Leaning against the oak and panting, Tommy waited a minute before he peeked out to see what was happening. Papuza was heading towards the wagon, and Esme was ambling in his general direction, carrying Mr. Wright.

"Tommy!" Esme called. "Tommy! Where are you?"

He stepped out from behind the tree, and she hurried up to him with a happy grin. "Grandma's taking care of the snake. Are you all right?"

Still panting, he nodded. "That danged snake dropped down from Papuza's bedchamber. It must have been up there watching me the whole time. Just the thought of that critter lurking nearby gives me the shivers." He shuddered.

And then he shuddered again. Did the circus villain put that snake up there? *Am I the next target?*

Papuza called from the wagon, "Children, would you mind coming here, please?"

They headed to the wagon, where Papuza held the door open for them. Esme flew up the stairs, but Tommy dawdled behind. *After all,* he thought, *how can I be sure the wagon's free of vipers?*

"It's fine, Thomas," Papuza reassured him. "Our wagon is now officially snake-free!"

Slowly he entered the gypsy wagon. As Papuza ushered him in, she told them, "I was looking in all the nooks and crannies to see if we have other surprising visitors, when I came across something rather puzzling." She sat down on a bench and stirred uneasily. "Tommy, after we worked on Buttercup, did you bring back some bottles of mandragora potion? I feel ever so sure that she didn't drink all of them."

"Yep, I brought back four bottles and put them where I'd found them. Why?"

"They're gone," said Papuza.

Esme stammered, "What?"

Anxiously Papuza rubbed her forehead. "In the hands of the wrong person, they could be very dangerous. Very dangerous indeed."

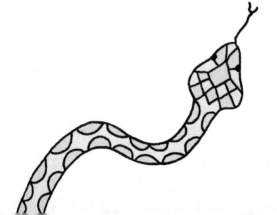

ESME

Orange and yellow flames licked the night sky, while sparks flew into its black abyss. The heat from the glowing bonfire pushed people back, as the blaze consumed the storm's debris. The crowd was lively, and the chatter was loud. Esme watched quietly.

The firelight cast ominous shadows on the people of the circus. The naturally handsome face of Maxwell the Magnificent looked threatening, and even Henry the Eighth's face took on an almost sinister leer, reminding Esme of the evil giant in *Jack and the Beanstalk*.

She stepped a little closer to Tommy, who held Mr. Wright. Her cousin was in a keen conversation with Bernardo, discussing the knife-throwing lesson they'd had after supper. This time Esme hadn't gone to watch. Instead she had spent an hour with Buttercup. They'd had wonderful fun playing the dousing trick on a pair of unsuspecting clowns.

As Esme gazed into the bright fire, she thought of the elephant. She swore she had never been so taken with an animal. She felt such a powerful bond with Buttercup that it almost seemed as if Esme could read her mind. Esme wondered if she could possibly sneak Buttercup home with her when they went back to Zumbro Falls. How did somebody kidnap an elephant? *Probably very, very carefully.* She imagined covering Buttercup with a pitch-black blanket and smuggling her away in the middle of the night. But she couldn't do that to Maria and Katrina because it would break their hearts. And besides, Esme knew that kidnapping was wrong.

As she dwelt on her predicament, she also thought about the joyful news that Grandma had shared after her latest trip to the telegraph office. My stars, she'd heard from Arthur! His telegram said he would meet them in Wabasha in two days. Grandma practically bubbled with delight, and she hummed and sang and even whistled for the rest of the afternoon.

However Grandma had also told them about a worrisome telegram she'd received from Tommy's pa. Hatch and Groggs were missing, so they all needed to be extra watchful. *Crumbs. Crumbs. Crumbs.* Oh, why couldn't Hatch just go off and get shipwrecked for sixty-six years? That would solve everything!

Esme was so deep in thought, imagining Hatch and Groggs shipwrecked and bickering on a desert isle, that she jumped when a hand touched her shoulder.

Jessamina, the Bearded Lady smiled down at her. At least Esme thought it was a smile. It was hard to tell with that flowing beard of hers. Jessamina wore a shawl trimmed with shiny threads that picked up sparkles from the firelight. "Katrina said I have you to thank for zee return of my jewels," she spoke gently. "Your honesty, it means more to me than I can possibly say."

"You're welcome," Esme said with a smile. "I'm just happy they were found. And I'm really glad no one thought we stole them!"

"Quite zee contrary," said Jessamina. She leaned close to Esme and confided, "I suspect Luis the Werewolf is behind zee thefts. He is terribly jealous of me! My beard is much longer than his, and I draw zee biggest crowds."

With a silvery laugh, she added, "I have come up with zee perfect plan for stopping zee villain." She glanced around to make sure no one was watching. Then she lifted her beard. Oh, good gravy! Beneath her beard, she wore at least a dozen necklaces. Looped through the chains were rings, bracelets, and earrings. Gemstones glittered. Esme gasped at the dazzling display and hoped the plan wouldn't put Jessamina herself in danger. Perhaps someone should warn her against strolling down dark alleys.

A breeze lifted embers from the fire and spun them into the crowd. A few embers landed on Jessamina's beard, which she began to pat wildly. "Oh, no!" she cried hysterically. Esme wondered, *Will her beard go up in flames?*

In a flash, Maxwell the Magnificent was at their side. He threw the contents of his punch cup at Jessamina's face and beard, successfully extinguishing the embers.

Jessamina looked stunned. Finally she stammered, "Th-Thank you, Maxwell. Merci." Wiping her face and wringing out her beard, she bade them good night and faded away from the bonfire.

"Jeepers! It's lucky you turned up!" Esme told Maxwell.

"No, it's lucky that Bernardo had just filled my punch cup. I didn't need to rely on my magic to come up with anything liquid!" He laughed his marvelous laugh. Then he knelt down to Esme's height and pulled an egg from behind her ear. He cracked the egg on top of her head, and confetti rained down all over her! "That was supposed to be a yoke," he chuckled, which made her giggle.

Just like that, he was off again, looking for another innocent bystander who might enjoy his pranks.

Esme began to search for Annie, keeping an eye out for Tommy too. She heard a voice in the crowd say, "He's still out completely. It's amazing that branch didn't kill him." *Oh, they must be talking about Angus.* She'd have to ask Grandma tonight how he was doing.

As Esme scanned the gathering, she realized how many people she didn't know. She hated to admit it, but this mystery was turning out to be more challenging than she'd expected. How many people worked for Katrina's circus? By jingo, a lot!

She continued searching, trying very hard to keep her imagination from getting the best of her. Distorted shadows lent the gathering an eerie feel that gave her goose bumps. As she glanced around, her eyes came to a jarring stop, and she almost jumped right out of her bloomers!

A werewolf slouched six feet away from her.

At least, he sure looked like a werewolf. Hair covered every inch of his face, except his glowing eyes. Esme looked at his hands to see if he had claws, but his fingers were surprisingly normal. She felt a crazy mixture of fascination and terror. She promised herself she would visit the sideshow attractions tomorrow, so she could study the werewolf in full, safe, secure daylight. *Are Jessamina's suspicions correct?*

Then Esme noticed Madame Sage standing far back from the bonfire, close to the woods. Mordecai the Raven perched on her shoulder. In the smoke and shadows, the fortune-teller seemed grimly mysterious. She nodded very slightly before she crept into the forest.

A second later, the blonde and elegant Emmeline followed.

They left the gathering so sneakily that Esme was instantly wary. *Why would they go into the woods at night? What are they up to?*

Quickly she looked around for Tommy. *Where did he go?* He suspected both Emmeline and Madame Sage, so Esme was sure he'd love to know about this secret meeting. But she couldn't see him.

She didn't really relish the idea of plodding into the woods all by herself, but what else could she do? This could be the very clue they needed, and if she didn't hurry, she would lose their trail. So she slipped out of the gathering as casually as she could, and she followed them into the silent, black forest.

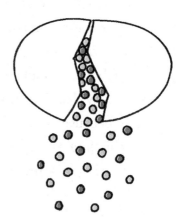

TOMMY

It was quite a bonfire, and people seemed to be in good spirits. Tommy learned that Henry the Eighth really loved baseball, and he'd even seen Cy Young pitch in the World Series last summer. Holy smoke! They chattered for ten minutes before Tommy realized he'd forgotten all about Esme. She had been at his side earlier, but now she was gone. *Where is she?*

Tommy looked all around the bonfire, but he didn't see her. And then, because she was so little and easy to miss, he searched all over again. Shucks, there was no doubt about it. *She ain't here.*

Where the heck had she gone? You really couldn't leave her alone for a minute because off she'd go and do something dangerous. That was Esme, all right.

Maybe she was just singing to Buttercup again. So sighing, Tommy started down the trail to the riverbank, where the elephant was tethered. His little cousin had sure taken to that big critter. Tommy thought this was a mistake because what would happen when Esme got back to Zumbro Falls? There was no way she'd be able to get an elephant for a pet.

Tommy reached the spot where Buttercup was tethered, but there was no sign of Esme. He scratched his head. Maybe she was off with Annie. Thinking of Annie made him sigh.

Maybe Esme had gone back to the gypsy wagon, and she was already sleeping. Tommy reckoned he'd head back to the wagon because at least he knew where *that* was.

Whistling as he moseyed along, he began to daydream about being a knife thrower. Bernardo said he had real potential. Yep, he was a natural, that's what Bernardo had said. Maybe if Tommy practiced every day, he'd get to join a show in a couple of years. Maybe he could talk Esme into being his target. He could just imagine her spinning around and around on a bull's eye and having a grand old time. *The way she loves danger, you'd think it would be right up her alley.*

He reached the gypsy wagon, and as he climbed the back steps, he pulled Mr. Wright out of his bib pocket. Papuza was inside the wagon, tidying up. "Where's Esme, dear?" she asked.

Now Tommy was getting worried. "She ain't here?"

"No, Thomas. I haven't seen her all evening."

Suddenly he felt mighty uneasy. "Shucks, where can she be?"

ESME

In the night woods, Esme tried to be quiet, but creeping around in a forest is a lot noisier than one might think. Sticks and twigs snapped beneath her tiptoes — and she had really *tiny* tiptoes.

As she crept along, she grew more and more anxious. Sounds of the night made the forest forbidding and eerie. It was the same place where she'd rooted with Grandma that afternoon, and back then, Esme had thought it was enchanting. But now, in the dark, the forest felt haunted.

When she saw lantern-light ahead, she paused. Hiding behind a tree, she waited for her heart to stop pounding loudly, so she could eavesdrop. She knew that eavesdropping was not a very nice thing to do. Even so, she considered herself to be somewhat of an expert at it.

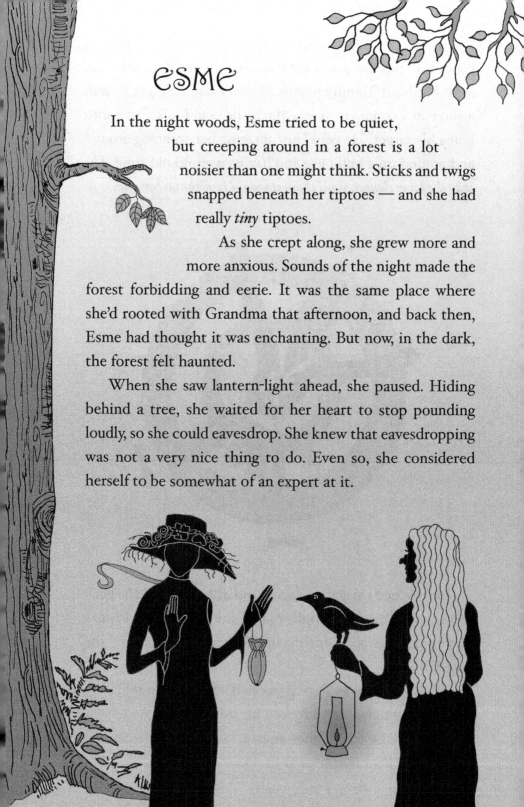

She had come to the spot where Madame Sage and Emmeline were holding a secret meeting. Madame Sage clutched a lantern, which cast dismal shadows on her face. With Mordecai the Raven perched on her hand, she looked, for all the world, like one of the witches in *Macbeth*. Or maybe like the witch in *Hansel and Gretel*. Or maybe like the wicked queen in *Snow White*. Or maybe . . . Stop it, Esme told herself. *She looks wicked, and that's that.*

"Will it work?" Emmeline moaned. The magician's assistant looked miserable, with tears trembling on her beautiful face. Sobbing, she pleaded, "I'm desperate. If I don't do something fast, it will be too late. I'm losing him to Maria."

"Then be quick, dear. Take this potion, put it in one of his drinks, and recite this spell I've written down for you." Madame Sage offered Emmeline a slip of paper and a pouch that dangled from a golden cord. Emmeline took them in her gloved hands and brushed away her tears to read the spell. Then she slid it into her pocket.

Ah, it must be a love potion, thought Esme. *But for whom?* Her guess was that it was probably meant for Bernardo because he seemed quite taken with Maria.

Awkwardly, Emmeline seized the fortune-teller's hand. "I'm most thankful to you."

Madame Sage patted Emmeline's arm. "No one should suffer."

Pressing her handkerchief to her mouth, Emmeline sobbed, "I've suffered more than I'd ever thought possible. When Bernardo turned his affections to Maria, I thought I would die."

So it is Bernardo, thought Esme. Maybe Tommy had been right about Emmeline all along. And wasn't it interesting that just that afternoon, Emmeline had told Esme that her troubles with Maria were over? *Why did she lie to me?*

Madame Sage studied the distressed young woman. "Remember, you can't hurry love along. It tends to take its own course."

"But I *have* to rush it along," Emmeline groaned in frustration. "He's falling more and more in love with Maria every day. Ever since she had that accident, he hasn't even looked at me." She buried her face in her hands and started crying again.

"There, there," Madame Sage soothed. "But since you mentioned it, I've been hearing rumors about the accident. You wouldn't have any idea who would do such a thing, would you?"

Why would she ask that? Extremely curious, Esme waited for Emmeline's response.

Emmeline gasped. "Surely you don't think I had anything to do with it?"

"No, no, dear," Madame Sage hurried to say. "I was just wondering if you saw or heard anything."

Laughing through her tears, Emmeline said, "I only know that people have suspicions about our new fortune-teller."

Madame Sage cackled. "You mean me? Well, isn't that a surprise." She and Emmeline laughed as they slowly began to stride away from their meeting spot.

Esme held her breath and remained very still, as Madame Sage and Emmeline walked by, a few feet from where she was hiding. Esme waited until they had passed, and their lantern-light had faded. Then she stole after them.

Slinking along, she stepped on a twig. It cracked loudly! Oh, mercy!

"Caww!" Mordecai the Raven responded.

Esme froze.

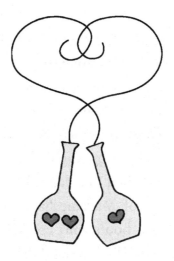

TOMMY

Papuza had sent Tommy back to the bonfire to search for Esme, but shucks, it looked like he was too late. Everyone was gone, and the fire had burned low. He had hoped the party would still be going, and he'd find Esme.

But she wasn't here.

Where can she be?

Loud cawing came from the forest, sounding like Mordecai the Raven. Why did that bird like to peck at him so much? What had he ever done to it?

"Good evening," rasped Madame Sage.

Tommy jumped sky high. *Where did **she** come from?* He stammered, "I-I-It ain't nice to creep up on people." Alarmed, he edged away from the fortune-teller.

She cackled, and then her danged bird cackled too. A dead flower fell out of Madame Sage's white hair as she muttered, "The devil's boots don't creak."

Tommy mumbled, "Well, yours didn't creak either." Was this her way of saying she was like the devil? *By gum, she won't get no argument from me about that.*

Madame Sage cackled again. "You'll never know when I'm nearby."

Tommy thought, *Your pesky bird **never** lets me forget when you're nearby.* But he didn't say that out loud. He was nervous, which was actually better than he usually felt in Madame Sage's company. At least he wasn't choking and gasping for air this time. Thankfully, he watched her limp away and fade into the starry evening.

Someone tugged on Tommy's overalls, making him jump. He glanced down, and relief flooded him. "It's just me," Esme whispered.

"Where the heck have you been?" he whispered back.

"Let's get back to the wagon, and I'll tell you all about it." So they skedaddled to their abode, where Papuza and Mr. Wright were very happy to see them. They settled in for the night, discussing what Esme had overheard in the forest.

Some parts of the puzzle seemed to fit perfectly, but to Tommy's mind, others didn't fit at all. Papuza brought up the points of the planted jewelry and the missing sleeping potion. She couldn't see why Emmeline would be mixed up in those shenanigans if she were only interested in Bernardo.

Tommy cleared his throat. A little embarrassed, he asked, "Do those love potions work?"

"Well, my Gran sold more love potions than anything else," said Papuza. "I certainly made plenty of them for her when I was a girl. Yet I can't say I hold much faith in them. Love isn't that simple. It can't be bought or created by magic."

Tommy wondered if Maxwell had ever created love accidentally while he was trying to do a completely different magic trick.

"If Emmeline's not the one who's been doing all these bad things, then I really feel sorry for her," Esme said compassionately. "You should have seen her. She was miserable!"

"Maybe we'd better save Bernardo from that love potion," said Tommy. "Just in case it truly works." *We men have a hard enough time, without getting tricked into love!*

243

He couldn't help but think of Annie.

After a moment, Esme asked, "Oh, Tommy, did you see Maxwell tonight? He wore his magician's cape, and in the firelight, he looked just like Dracula!"

"He's about the only person I *don't* suspect," he told her. "He's just too happy to be doing all this no-good business."

"Well, children, shall we see what tomorrow brings? I think we'd better get some sleep now." Papuza blew out the kerosene lantern, and darkness descended on the wagon. "Good nights" were said all around.

Tommy rolled over and immediately rolled back. He tried to think of something happy to help him sleep, and his mind went to knife throwing. Then his thoughts shifted to Annie, although that just made him toss and turn all the more.

Finally he drifted off. In his dreams, he was throwing knives at a target. It wasn't easy work, and pretty soon he was mighty thirsty. Esme strolled by, holding a tray, and on that tray, there was a glass of water. Tommy reached for it and gulped it down in front of a cheering crowd. It sure tasted funny! It wasn't like any water he'd ever drunk before. Suddenly he left his act and started wandering around the circus grounds.

Before long, he ended up at Madame Sage's wagon. Very cautiously, he opened her door. She was waiting for him with open arms!

Jeepers, he had to get out of there. And fast! But then Esme appeared and told him it was too late. His helpful little cousin said she'd accidentally dropped a potion in that water he'd drunk, and now he was going to fall in love with Madame Sage!

Oh, Tarnation! Botheration! Thunderation! That cackling, old biddy wanted Tommy to kiss her!

She puckered up her lips, and they were a sickly color. Her breath smelled like the fires of Hades.

His dream was so horrible that it woke him, and he jolted upright. His whole body was sweating, and he realized he needed to warn Bernardo. *It's my duty as a fellow male.* No one should have to go through what Tommy had just dreamed. Yep, tomorrow he'd find Bernardo right away and tell him not to drink anything!

VILLAIN

Planting Jessamina's jewels in their wagon turned out to be a colossal flop. I thought they'd be led away in handcuffs, but instead I saw Jessamina smiling and laughing with them. I need those kids and their grandmother gone.

I watched her on the trapeze this afternoon. Her joy was quite annoying.

The sleeping potion I stole from their wagon should work nicely tomorrow. With any luck, those meddlers will even be blamed for the "accident."

ESME

The following afternoon, Esme observed the werewolf closely. He sat at a roll-top desk, reading a book, while dressed in a tuxedo. The painted backdrop for his stage was covered with fascinating portraits of "Luis: The Gentleman's Werewolf." One of the lifelike pictures showed him standing by Queen Victoria while another portrayed him playing a violin to a fashionable audience.

Esme studied the paintings and then looked back at Luis. He seemed engrossed in his book. She found herself thinking, *What do werewolves like to read?*

The heat in the small tent was almost unbearable for her. *It must be even worse for Luis,* she thought. He was dressed in a suit and tie and fur. She wondered if he ever felt like shaving.

Earlier that morning, she had glimpsed Luis in a peculiar situation. Esme was dragging a reluctant Mr. Wright away from the breakfast tent, and in the distance, she could see the back stoop of the fortune-teller's wagon. The werewolf was handing Madame Sage a bouquet of flowers! Gee whillikers! Esme thought they were an unlikely couple, but maybe a witchy woman and a werewolfy man made a perfect pair. Luis tried to kiss the fortune-teller's hand, but she pulled it away. Hmm, very curious. *Are Luis and Madame Sage somehow involved in the wicked deeds against the circus? What would they have to gain?*

Then Esme's mind flew to some of the people she had met that morning. The Fat Lady was very funny, and Esme really enjoyed talking with her, although it bothered her a little that the Lady wore baby doll clothes. Maybe she wanted to look younger? Tommy said it could be a new fashion that hadn't yet reached Zumbro Falls.

They continued to explore the circus, and they actually met a grown-up who was smaller than Esme! Only by an inch, but even so, the posters said she was the smallest human being in the world. The cousins tried to talk with her, but she ignored them, which hurt Esme's feelings. Tommy said it was because she viewed Esme as competition, which only made Esme punch him.

Now Esme was in the Gentleman Werewolf's tent, sitting on the ground, near the back canvas. The touch of the grass felt cool on her hands. A few other people were viewing his exhibit, and Esme tried to hide behind them while still getting a good look. As she studied the werewolf, her mind kept returning to that morning.

At daybreak, Tommy had insisted that they *had* to find Bernardo. Tommy had had a powerful dream about a love potion and said he needed to warn Bernardo. Immediately! Yet when they did find Bernardo, he merely shook his head and claimed he didn't believe in such things. "Besides," he added with a dazzling smile, "in love I am already with Maria."

Later, Esme ran into Annie. Esme helped her drag hay to the circus horses, and afterwards, they shared a strawberry soda. Gosh-almighty! It was the first soda Esme had ever tasted, and it was delicious! She wished she could take oodles of bottles home to all her friends.

After that, she spent a few quiet minutes with Buttercup. She didn't think it was her imagination that the elephant was beginning to love her too. Just thinking about Buttercup made her smile.

Esme also stopped by Angus' wagon to see how he was doing. She was sad to hear there had been no improvement, even though Grandma had been doing everything she could to help him. Grandma said his recovery would take some time.

Then Esme visited Maxwell the Magnificent, who was in his sideshow tent, practicing a new trick. He was trying to turn a scarf into a dove, but the scarf wasn't obeying because it kept turning into a fan. When Maxwell saw Esme, he fluttered the fan and cried cheerfully, "Hello, my dear! It's so nice of you to drop by."

He took a break from practicing, and they sat on the edge of the stage, dangling their feet and chatting. Esme asked him who *he* thought had put the box of doves ringside.

"Whoever it was, they must have some knowledge of handling birds. I have a heck of a time getting those doves to cooperate. In fact, I've been thinking of cutting the act completely. I told myself a dove act is strictly for the birds!"

Esme laughed at his joke, although she found herself thinking that Emmeline had some bird-handling knowledge. It seemed like the blonde magician's assistant was inching ever closer to Esme's "Yes" column of suspects.

All in all, it had been a very busy morning. Esme was determined to meet everyone in the circus, to help her solve the mystery. Yet jiminy, after hours of walking, and talking, and questioning, and contemplating, she still didn't have an answer. She wondered if Sherlock Holmes had ever been frustrated in the middle of an investigation.

Suddenly Esme realized that the other spectators in the werewolf exhibit had shuffled out and left her alone in the tent with Luis. Oh, no!

Esme rose silently, hoping to sneak away quietly because, honestly, he scared her.

The werewolf startled her by asking, "Are you done studying me?"

His voice was melodious, heavily accented. He slunk down from the stage and approached her, and her misgivings increased by the second. Even in the dimly lit tent, his dark eyes glistened like black cherries. Stepping back, Esme was now pressed into the canvas. As she stared up at him, icy fear twisted around her heart.

"I'm very hungry," he whispered, "and you are just the right size for a meal."

Opening his mouth, he displayed long, pointy teeth.

KATRINA

Katrina was in her wagon, an hour before showtime, when a soft knock on the back door interrupted her thoughts. "Missus, if you please . . ." When she opened the door, a clown dashed in, saying, "This gentleman says he has a very important message." The clown pointed to a stranger in a bowler hat, who waited on the back stoop.

The stranger stepped forward. "I have strict orders to hand-deliver this message to the owner of the circus." He presented a telegram to Katrina, which read:

To: The owner of the Kirkkomaki Circus

Dear Sir, A tiger has appeared in our fair town. By any chance, are you missing one? Please respond. —R. J. Brusse, Mayor of Zumbro Falls

It had to be Tasha! Thank goodness she was all right. Katrina told the stranger, "I will handle this right away." He nodded and departed.

Immediately Katrina left the circus grounds to go to the telegraph office. There, she responded to the mayor:

Dear Mayor Brusse, I am the owner of the Kirkkomaki Circus. Yes, I am missing a tiger. Please do not hurt her. She has no teeth. I will offer a handsome reward if Tasha is returned safely. Please respond. —Katrina Kirkkomaki

Within minutes, she received a reply from the mayor of Zumbro Falls.

Dear Mrs. Kirkkomaki, Thank you for responding. Your tiger is fine. She is currently holding two citizens hostage in a tree at a local farmer's residence. Any advice on how to contain her? —R. J. Brusse

A few minutes later, Katrina sent off another message:

Dear Mayor Brusse, Please tell the people who are trapped in the tree that I send my heartfelt regrets, and I've paid for two train tickets for them to attend the circus in Wabasha for free. I will put them up, in hopes of helping them forget the troubles that my tiger has caused. As for securing Tasha, try tuna fish. It's her favorite. Put the tuna in a portable cage or crate, and she should venture right into it. Please let me know if that works. —Katrina Kirkkomaki

Promptly she received a short response from the mayor:

Dear Mrs. Kirkkomaki, We will do our best to secure the tiger. I will tell our two citizens in the tree about your offer, and I will let you know when the situation is resolved. —R. J. Brusse

Katrina sighed with relief. She would see her Tasha again!

Surely Papuza and the children were acquainted with the two people from Zumbro Falls. What a nice surprise this would be for all of them!

HATCH

"Go find a ladder!" Hatch growled at her brother. They were stuck in a maple tree, held hostage by a tiger.

"And how am I supposed to do that?" he asked scornfully.

"Just climb down and find one, you lazy good-for-nothing."

She was mortified to be caught in this humiliating situation. But then again, she should have expected trouble from the way things had started out. Hatch had ordered Groggs to steal eggs from Farmer Schmidt's henhouse, but her dolt of a brother had said he'd just gotten out of jail, and he had some "catching up" to do on his moonshining. *Lazy maggot.* He refused to steal eggs all alone, so Hatch had to haul him to the henhouse. There, they got the shock of their lives, when this vile tiger showed up!

They were lucky they had made it up the tree. Even so, they'd been here all night, and nobody — absolutely nobody — had been any help. Hatch sneered at her brother on the other branch. "Climb down, I tell you!"

"*You* climb down," he drawled, chewing on a toothpick.

Hatch scanned the people below them, on Farmer Schmidt's porch. She knew the sheriff had been looking for her, but there was no sign of him in the crowd, which suited her just fine. She glared at the group because no one was eager to come too close to that tiger. Instead they were waiting for something interesting to happen, while they stayed within arm's reach of the screen door of the farmhouse.

Groggs peeked down at the tiger and blathered, "You know, she really looks kinda pretty. She don't look mean. A feller can always tell if a critter has a sweet nature. And that there tiger has a mighty sweet nature. Yes, siree . . ."

Hatch snapped, "Would you shut up, you worthless piece of scum! I'm trying to think of a way to get out of this!"

"I reckon I've heard about enough of your griping!"

"Keep your voice down!" Hatch yelled. "We're enough of a spectacle already. I'm warning you . . ."

"Or what? Whatcha gonna do if I keep on talking?" Defiantly, Groggs crossed his arms. Sometimes Hatch thought he might be smarter than he looked, which wouldn't be very hard. To her surprise, he reached over to her branch and began to shake it. He shook it for all it was worth!

Furious, Hatch swung her fist in his direction and punched him in the nose. The crowd gasped as he toppled over backwards. Now he hung upside-down from the branch by his knees.

"Get up, you milksop!" she snarled. "Or better yet, fall off and let that beast eat you, so I can run away."

Righting himself on the branch, Billy Groggs waved to his admirers on the porch. In return, the crowd gave him a smattering of applause.

"Stop that right now," Hatch ordered. "You're making an even bigger fool of us, and . . ."

"Say," Billy interrupted, "someone's coming!"

Hatch swung her head in the direction of the farmhouse. She hated to say he was right, but he was right. Someone was actually stepping out from the crowd. It looked like that young Schmidt girl — the one who was followed by a slew of animals wherever she went. She walked straight towards the tiger, carrying a bushel basket. Hatch realized, *It's filled with cans.*

Immediately the tiger raised its ferocious head and smelled the air. It began to lick its lips.

Then Hatch noticed that a few men had dropped a sizable crate behind the girl. The girl approached the tiger and calmly set down an open can of tuna fish. Slowly she stepped backwards and placed another can on the ground. And then another. She created a trail of tuna cans, leaving the final can inside the crate.

It was a tiger trap, and it worked like a charm. As soon as the tiger was shut inside the crate, the crowd cheered.

"She doesn't have any teeth, and she's supposed to be the gentlest of tigers," a man in overalls called up to Hatch. He leaned a ladder against her tree branch and helped her down.

When she reached the ground, she shoved him away rudely. *Someone is going to pay for making me a laughingstock.*

And very soon, it dawned on her who would be doing the paying. The mayor told them the owner of the carnival had offered them a free day at the circus. Of course Hatch would take her up on that offer. She'd accept the train ticket to Wabasha, and when she reached that woman, she'd sue her and make her pay! A tight smile crossed Hatch's face.

PAPUZA

That will do, Papuza told herself, pulling the last of the white, cotton wrappings from their makeshift clothesline. The wrappings were clean and ready for the next time they would be needed. Papuza hoped that wouldn't be for a good, long while.

As she worked, she thought about Esme and Tommy. *Such good children. Such good friends.* She was so very proud of both of them.

Her mind turned to her own cousin, Arthur. Their communication yesterday had been by telegram instead of telephone, so she still hadn't heard his voice. She had so many questions! She wondered if his father had survived the shipwreck also. Or had Arthur been all alone on that island? The thought of it made her shake her head sadly. *What a lonely life he must have led.*

Then Papuza's thoughts switched to another survivor — Buttercup. If the branch had pierced the elephant more deeply, things would have gone poorly. Papuza was very glad the elephant had pulled through the ordeal.

And Papuza felt ever so thankful that Maria's arm was also on the mend. *I daresay,* thought Papuza, *things are looking up for the circus.*

Except for those missing bottles of sleeping potion.

The sound of cawing made her peer up at the ragged clouds. A murderous-looking raven flapped towards her, landing on her hand. This was probably Mordecai, whom the children had mentioned. Papuza glanced around for his owner, but there was no sign of an approaching Madame Sage. *How curious.*

The raven tilted his head to one side, watching Papuza. Then it flew a short distance and stopped.

He gazed back at her, waiting.

He wants me to follow him, she thought. Although she was reluctant to leave their wagon alone, she could tell that the bird was trying to communicate with her.

Fortunately she saw Maria striding towards their wagon. Full of high spirits and her natural good will, Maria thanked Papuza again for setting her arm and helping Buttercup.

"Would you have the great goodness to do me a favor?" Papuza asked, keeping an eye on the restless raven. "I would be very much obliged to you, Maria, if you could watch my wagon. I should be back shortly."

Maria said she would be happy to help, so Papuza left, following Mordecai. When the dismal bird reached Madame

Sage's wagon, he flew to the roof and cawed loudly. The door was slightly ajar, so Papuza knocked.

There was no answer.

Cautiously she opened the door the rest of the way.

The body of a woman, who she assumed was Madame Sage, splayed across the table, lying very still.

Very still indeed.

ESME

As Esme peered up at the looming figure, a grisly fear swept through her. *I am going to be eaten by a werewolf.* Of all the ways to die, she'd never, ever imagined this. She clutched her lucky locket as her mind darted to the gruesome story of Dr. Jekyll and Mr. Hyde. This must be like the suffering of Mr. Hyde's victims, and Esme realized she should have felt more sorry for them. Her heart beat so hard her whole body shook. *What does Madame Sage see in him? He's horrifying!*

Luis opened his mouth further and pulled out his fake fangs. He threw back his head, and instead of howling like a werewolf, he roared with laughter. In fact, he laughed so hard he had to wipe his eyes. "I'm sorry," he apologized, trying to be serious.

As Esme realized it had all been a joke, she let out her breath, which she hadn't even known she'd been holding. Luis assured her, "I didn't mean to give you such a fright! Your eyes were as big as pie tins! Forgive me."

Ducking his head, Henry the Eighth entered the tent. He boomed, "What's going on in here?"

"I'm afraid I gave this little one quite a scare." Luis bent down on one knee and extended his hand to Esme. Gallantly he declared, "I'm at your service."

Tentatively, she stretched out her hand. She still felt a little afraid of him. But then he smiled at her, and she found herself smiling back. Yes, he'd scared her terribly, but then she remembered all the times she'd scared Tommy. She made a solemn vow to never scare her cousin again — or at least not within the next few hours.

Taking a deep breath, she began to relax. She tried to sound grown-up as she told them, "No harm done."

"Thatta girl," Henry smiled down at her. "There's no room for fear at the circus. Everyone should be having fun!" Awkwardly, he knelt down. "Put her on my shoulder, Luis."

Without further warning, Luis scooped her up and set her on Henry's shoulder. As Henry began to stand, Esme quickly wrapped her arm around his neck. He ducked out of the tent and then rose to his full height outside. "How's the weather up there?" he teased her.

"It's grand," she cried.

And it was.

She felt taller than the man on stilts. It wasn't often that she could see the tops of things. *This is how Henry sees the world,* she thought. *My goodness, it's so different from what I see!*

"We're missing the show," Henry thundered. "Let's go."

As he carried Esme to the big top, Luis accompanied them. Esme spotted Tommy standing by the entrance, holding Mr. Wright and waiting for her. She waved furiously, hoping to catch his attention.

When he finally saw her, he gave her a happy grin. "Hey, I've been searching all over for you," he called up to her. She admitted she rather enjoyed her new position in life, where she was taller than Tommy.

"I was busy. I was almost eaten by a werewolf." From her lofty height, she introduced Tommy to Luis.

"May I stay on your shoulder for a while?" she asked Henry.

"For the whole show, if you'd like. You're as light as a feather."

They entered the tent and paused by the end of the bleachers. The circus was in full swing. From Esme's vantage point, it looked different from last time. For one thing, the clowns seemed shorter than before. They were in the middle of an act where a pig was shoving around huge, bouncy balls with its snout, and the balls were knocking over clowns. Esme giggled so hard that she almost fell off Henry's shoulder.

Katrina was busy with her big cats, coaxing them to jump through flaming hoops. Meanwhile, acrobats warmed up overhead, and Esme noticed Bernardo, who was climbing the ladder to the platform. Vividly she remembered yesterday and how wonderful it had felt to fly through the air.

When Bernardo reached the platform, he swayed a little uncertainly, which made Esme nervous. *My gosh, that's not at all like the Bernardo of yesterday.* She wondered if Emmeline *had* given Bernardo the love potion.

Quickly she scanned the tent, looking for Emmeline. Esme spotted her with Annie in the bleachers, where they were staring up at Bernardo as they ate popcorn and drank sodas. Esme wished she could read Emmeline's face.

An uneasy feeling grew inside her as the trapeze bar swung back to Bernardo. He stood on one end of the platform, waiting for the bar to arrive. When it reached him, he grabbed hold, which reassured Esme.

But seconds later, as he was flying, his grasp broke.

Oh, mercy! He fell!

A gasp went up from the crowd as they watched in horror. Bernardo fell head over heels, his body limp. He landed on the edge of the net and bounced up again, this time being thrown out of the net's reach.

The clowns were performing directly below him, and looks of terror crossed their faces when they realized what was about to happen. Esme thought, *I can't bear to watch!*

As luck would have it, instead of smashing into the ground, Bernardo hit one of the colored balls that were part of the clowns' act. His body bounced up in the air like a rag doll before it dropped in the sawdust with a thud.

"Oh, no!" cried Esme. Pandemonium broke out. Screams and cries filled the tent as people dashed towards the fallen acrobat. Reaching up to steady her on his shoulder, Henry started to run.

PAPUZA

Papuza hurried to Madame Sage and placed her fingers on the fortune-teller's neck. Thank goodness, there was a pulse! The soothsayer was alive, but what in the name of wonder had happened? Had she had a heart attack? Or a seizure?

As Papuza leaned Madame Sage's body back into her chair, she noticed something surprising. The woman's long, white hair was actually a wig! It was pushed back from the fortune-teller's forehead, and the hair underneath was blonde. Upon closer inspection, Papuza also realized that a rubber nose was covering the woman's own. Papuza thought, *What can be the meaning of this?*

Madame Sage's eyes were closed. When Papuza pried open an eyelid to look at the fortune-teller's pupil, the woman mumbled something incoherent. Papuza found the pulse in the woman's wrist and silently counted for a few seconds. Madame Sage's heartbeat was normal, which was a good sign, and Papuza saw no suggestion of injury on her body. So what had happened?

Papuza glanced around the wagon for clues. An empty bottle sat on the table with a sherry glass by its side. The glass held a few drops of a red liquid. Was Madame Sage a drinker? Had she drunk herself into a stupor?

Papuza picked up the crystal glass and sniffed it. This was definitely not sherry. Tasting a drop, Papuza nodded. Without a doubt, it was the sleeping potion that had been stolen from her yesterday.

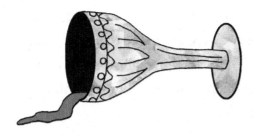

TOMMY

Tommy thought, *He's breathing! Thank goodness he's alive!* But would Bernardo survive? Or walk? Or ever perform again?

Henry lifted Bernardo's unconscious body and carried it out of the ring. The band struck up a sunny tune, making Mr. Wright stir from his nap in the bib of Tommy's overalls. Samuel, the ringmaster, tried to put a brave face on things by announcing that everything was fine — even though Bernardo sure didn't look fine to Tommy!

Esme and Tommy had to run to keep up with Henry's gigantic strides. He was carrying Bernardo to their gypsy wagon to get Papuza's help. Some of the clowns trailed behind them.

When they reached the wagon, and Maria saw Bernardo, she looked so stricken that Tommy worried she might faint. And then Emmeline charged up too, followed by Annie. But Papuza wasn't there!

Maria said Papuza had asked her to watch the wagon. One of the clowns volunteered to find Papuza, and he took off running.

Tommy seriously doubted that they could all fit into the gypsy wagon. After all, it had been mighty cramped in there when they'd helped Maria, and Bernardo was bigger than Maria, and there were even more people today. So Tommy blurted out, "There ain't enough room in there!" He rushed inside the wagon and brought out a comforter, which they spread on the ground.

As Henry laid Bernardo gently on the comforter, Esme murmured, "Good thinking, Tommy." He felt himself blushing.

Bernardo lay lifeless. Well, pretty much lifeless, for Tommy could see his chest just barely rising and falling. The group gathered around the stricken trapeze artist, waiting for Papuza, and unsure of what to do. Maria was on her knees, holding Bernardo's right hand and crying. Emmeline was on her knees too, holding Bernardo's left hand and crying. *Shucks,* thought Tommy, *maybe it's a good thing he's asleep.* Which one would he pick, if he were awake?

Bernardo's leg was so crooked it was obvious that something was wrong. "It looks like his leg is broken," Esme muttered to Tommy. "If Grandma were here, she'd cut off his tights."

Esme gave Bernardo a thoughtful squint, and then she raced into the wagon and brought back a tiny pair of scissors. By gosh, Tommy really hoped she knew what she was doing. He also hoped she wouldn't get any ideas about giving Bernardo a haircut.

Carefully, Esme cut Bernardo's tights away from his right thigh, exposing his leg. His injury looked even worse without his leotard. The hand-holding females let out a collective gasp and started to cry even louder. Tommy swore they made matters worse. If Bernardo could hear them, he'd be convinced that he was dying and heading to the Great Beyond. *Maybe,* thought Tommy, *he already is.*

Then, for gosh sakes, Bernardo's two admirers started bickering with each other. "This never would have happened, if he hadn't been distracted," Emmeline said snidely.

"I can't take it," Maria moaned. "How can you be nasty at a time like this?"

"Well, obviously, he wasn't focused." Emmeline glared at Maria with eyes like that venomous, green sky that tells you a tornado is coming.

"Stop it," Maria cried.

I reckon we've got us a real squabble, thought Tommy. He rubbed his forehead. He and his brothers fought — but not like this!

"Ladies," Henry boomed. His voice was firm.

"Maybe he wasn't feeling well," Esme said shyly. "Maybe he ate or *drank* something that didn't agree with him."

By jingo! Tommy had forgotten all about that love potion! He guessed Bernardo hadn't listened to his warning that morning. Tommy peeked at Emmeline to see if she looked guilty. Her face crumpled, and she began to sob.

Poor Bernardo. How could a fellow put up with this? When Tommy glanced at him, his heart jumped. He didn't see Bernardo's chest moving anymore. Holey buckets! *I think he's dead!*

ESME

Where in the world is Grandma? Things looked dire, and if Grandma didn't show up soon, Esme didn't know what would happen to Bernardo. Scooting close to Maria, Esme put her ear on Bernardo's chest. She could hear a heartbeat, yet it seemed like he was barely breathing.

Then, thank goodness, Grandma appeared. "What happened?" she asked. Quickly they told her about his horrible fall.

Grandma asked Maria and Emmeline to move back, so she could assess the situation. She produced smelling salts from her pocket and placed them under Bernardo's nose. Esme scolded herself, *Now, why didn't I think of that?*

But Bernardo didn't respond to the smelling salts. Nor did he respond when Mr. Wright stole up and began to nibble on Bernardo's mustache. Grandma pried open one of the patient's eyelids and confirmed that his pupil looked normal. "Hmm." She pondered the situation, as Tommy pulled Mr. Wright away.

Bernardo's two admirers were still crying. They reminded Esme of two comely maidens weeping over a slain knight. But oh, my stars, they sure did carry on! Their sobbing and blubbering reached such a pitch that finally Grandma told them they had to leave, so she could concentrate on Bernardo. She nodded at Henry, who led the women and Annie away.

"Whew," Tommy muttered. "At the rate they were going, they might have caused a flood."

Studying their patient, Grandma asked, "Now, who cut his clothing?"

"I did," Esme said, worrying a little that she might have done something wrong.

Instead, Grandma said, "Good work, my dear," which made Esme beam.

Grandma finished examining Bernardo for noticeable injuries. "Quickly now, let's try to set his leg while he's still unconscious. Esme, kindly fetch the clean wrappings from our table in the wagon. And Tommy, please search the woods for some straight and sturdy branches. I need a few that are roughly three feet long."

Esme and Tommy hurried to help, and as soon as they had the wrappings and the branches, they all went to work. *It's like setting Maria's arm,* thought Esme, *only a lot bigger.*

First Grandma pulled Bernardo's leg to straighten it. Then Tommy held the splints in place while Grandma and Esme wrapped white, cotton strips around the splints and Bernardo's leg. Esme really loved this doctoring business, and she especially liked doing these wrappings. She felt sure she had a special knack for them (or at least that's what she imagined until she tied Tommy's finger in one of the knots).

As Esme finished a knot, Bernardo blinked slowly. Drifting in and out of consciousness, he was having trouble waking up. Grandma studied him. Then on a hunch, she leaned over his mouth and sniffed.

Sitting back, she rubbed her chin thoughtfully. "I rather expected him to stir as we set his leg. I do suspect he unwittingly consumed a sleeping potion. His breath has a particular aroma."

Clearly Esme would need to wait to ask Bernardo her burning questions, such as, "Did you drink anything before you started your act? And if you did drink something, did it come from Emmeline?" It was so very hard to wait for answers. It made her wonder if Sherlock Holmes ever wished that unconscious victims were more considerate.

"By the way, where did you go, Grandma?" Esme asked her. "I was worried when we got here, and you were gone."

Grandma laid her hand on Esme's shoulder. Then she told the cousins how Mordecai the Raven had led her to unexpected discoveries in the fortune-teller's wagon. Madame Sage was wearing a wig *and* a false nose!

"Would you two be darlings yet again?" asked Grandma. "Tommy, could you find Katrina and bring her here? And Esme, would you kindly run to Madame Sage's to check if she's awake? I'm very curious to hear how she came by that sleeping potion. If we learn who gave it to her, we just might discover the villain."

So Esme dashed to Madame Sage's wagon and knocked on the door. A groggy "Enter" reached her ears, filling her with excitement. Jim-dandy! Here was a place where she should be able to ask some questions!

Esme opened the door.

If possible, the dimly lit wagon held even more mysteries than before. Madame Sage sat slumped at the table, looking as if she'd been run over by Hatch's horse and buggy. Even though Grandma had warned Esme about what she would find, she was still shocked to see blonde hair slipping out from beneath the fortune-teller's white wig. The woman's nose was lopsided too! Mordecai the Raven was perched on her shoulder. He tilted his head and waited.

Esme cleared her throat. "How are you, Madame Sage?"

"Tired," she groaned. Her usually brilliant eyes seemed weary. "Had a powerful nap. So strange in the middle of the day."

Esme sat down on a chair, thinking about what to say, and where to start. Meanwhile she noticed an empty soda bottle resting on the table, and she remembered the strawberry soda she'd shared with Annie earlier that day. *Could Annie be the villain? That's impossible.* Puzzled, she stared at the bottle.

Madame Sage mumbled, "You look as if a ghost just passed through you."

Esme's mind spun in confusion, and she struggled to form the right question. Slowly she asked, "Did you have a busy day?"

The old (or was she young?) woman snorted. As she yawned, she rubbed her neck. "Not at all. Nobody crossed my threshold except Annie. We shared a birthday toast." To Esme's dismay, Madame Sage nodded at the soda bottle on the table.

"Today is your birthday?"

"No, it's Annie's birthday. She turned sixteen today."

"She can't be! She doesn't look sixteen!"

Madame Sage cackled. "Things are not always what they seem."

ESME

As the evening came on, Esme wrote rapidly in her journal. She sat in the gypsy wagon, which was riding on the circus train. She and Tommy had helped Henry load the gypsy wagon onto the train while Grandma was away, tending to Angus and Bernardo. The cousins hadn't seen Grandma since Esme's return from Madame Sage.

As Esme wrote, her thoughts swirled. She had so many emotions to express. She described the bonfire, and her eavesdropping, and the news of Arthur, and how they'd be meeting him soon. And then Esme wrote about Bernardo's fall from the trapeze, and his two admirers, and how she and Tommy and Grandma had doctored his leg. The more Esme wrote, the more she yearned to write. But her writing hand was starting to hurt because it couldn't keep up with her thoughts.

She began to write down her worries about Annie. She felt very torn up about her friend. Esme had told Tommy everything she'd seen and heard, and he thought she was plumb crazy.

"You have to be wrong, Esme," he said convincingly. "I mean, yesterday she practically saved your life in the fish tank. It can't be Annie."

Well, this certainly surprised Esme. His views on Annie had definitely changed.

He interrupted her thoughts by saying, "You need to tell your grandma how you feel. I bet she'd stick up for Annie too."

Esme put down her pencil and rubbed her hand. "I'm going to. But first I want to talk with Annie. I don't want to falsely accuse her." She remembered the story of *The Count of Monte Cristo,* who was falsely accused and suffered miserably.

That afternoon had been pure chaos. After Esme had left Madame Sage's, she *did* search for Annie but couldn't find her anywhere. Then the circus had packed up and loaded onto the train, and everything had been in an uproar.

Tommy added, "Maybe Annie has a logical explanation for everything."

And Esme really hoped that Annie *did* have an explanation for everything. Because Esme considered her to be a friend and maybe a future sister. It gave her a sick feeling to think that Annie might be deceiving her and everybody else.

Esme sat silently while Tommy fiddled with his jackknife. The train rumbled down the tracks, rocking back and forth, speeding from Lake City to Wabasha.

Esme closed her journal. For some reason, she didn't want to wear her hair like Annie's anymore, so she braided it in her old style. She felt terribly unsettled. She asked herself, *Is Annie the guilty party?* And then she thought, *She can't be.* Yet Esme had nagging suspicions that wouldn't go away.

I can't wait a minute longer to know the truth.

Jumping up from the table, she said, "I'm going to find Annie. If we hurry, we can clear this up before this train even gets to Wabasha."

"I'm going with you." Tommy put his knife away, slipping it into his pocket. "We'd better leave a note for Papuza. If we ain't here when she gets back, she'll be worried."

"Good idea." Esme looked around for some paper. She didn't want to rip a page out of her journal, but she needed to write on *something.* So Tommy fished around in his pockets and pulled out a crumpled candy wrapper. He smoothed it out, grabbed a pencil, and wrote:

Papuza — We went to talk with Annie. Esme has a crazy idea that she might be the villain.

He left the scrap of paper on the table.

Esme patted Mr. Wright's head and told him, "Take good care of the wagon while we're gone!"

ESME

Esme and Tommy hurried out of the gypsy wagon and headed to the door at the end of their boxcar. There was a sign (with pointing hands) that said, "Danger! Do not open this door. This one here. This very door."

So, of course, they tried to open the door immediately.

Esme and Tommy tugged and pulled, and eventually the door opened. The evening wind rushed in, feeling brisk against Esme's face. After a few seconds, her eyes adjusted to the darkness. She could see the tracks moving beneath the edge of the platform, and a mishmash of fear and excitement swept through her.

She stared down at the connector that joined the boxcars. If she slipped, the train would crush her. It felt like she and Tommy were on a hair-raising adventure straight out of *The*

Three Musketeers, one of Esme's favorite novels. But since there were only two of them, it would have to be called *The Two Musketeers.*

"Say, Esme." Tommy sounded worried. "This could be quite a leap for you. Are you sure you can you make it?"

Although Esme knew he was being nice, she couldn't stand it when he thought she was too little to do things. So fearlessly, she leaped to the platform of the next boxcar.

Tommy grinned and jumped across too. As they stood on the new platform, the wind whipped their hair. Sunset was almost over, leaving just the slightest touch of orange against a night blue sky.

Esme said, "I think I saw Buttercup being loaded into this boxcar before we left Lake City."

Tommy struggled with the new door. "I wonder how many cars we'll have to pass through before we find Annie."

When they entered the new boxcar, Esme noticed it was loud inside — as loud as it had been outside. Yet it wasn't as dark as she'd thought it would be. Light was coming from somewhere.

"Hopefully, we'll find her sooner rather than later," Tommy mumbled.

And they did.

Annie was in that very car. She was sweeping up animal dung and sawdust with a broom and shoving it out the boxcar's open side door. A lone kerosene lantern swung from above. Its beam of light swayed back and forth, in rhythm with the train.

Esme held her finger to her lips, sending Tommy a signal to be quiet. They sneaked behind a wagon and watched

Annie as she swept. Could she really be the villain? Why would she do it? *And how in the world,* thought Esme, *am I going to ask her?*

Gathering her courage, Esme stepped out from behind the wagon. Annie jumped, startled. At first she gave Esme a friendly smile, but she must have sensed Esme's worries because right away, her warm expression vanished.

Wind rushed in from the side door, blowing across Esme's bangs. She felt a sudden chill. Goose bumps rose on the back of her neck, but they were not from the evening air.

Esme swallowed. "Happy Birthday," she said kindly.

"You must have been talking to Madame Sage," said Annie. Esme didn't care for the look in Annie's eyes. Maybe it was just the shadowy lighting, but suddenly, she remembered the first time she'd seen Annie — when she was a spooky-looking mermaid.

Softly Esme added, "I didn't know you were sixteen."

"What else did that old hag tell you?"

Esme was surprised by the hostility of her reply. This was not the girl she had thought was her friend. Her heart beat faster as she tried to decide what to say. "Madame Sage was sleeping," she began, wondering if this was a good way to start the accusation. "Someone gave her my grandmother's sleeping potion."

Annie stepped towards her. Then she saw Tommy by the wagon and stopped. He came further into the light, to stand by Esme's side.

Esme added, "I bet you anything that same someone gave Bernardo the sleeping potion."

She could see the wheels in Annie's mind spinning. *She's trying to figure out what to say.* And then, with a great certainty, it hit Esme that she was looking at the guilty party. Her stomach knotted.

It *was* Annie.

ESME

"Why?" Esme asked. "Why would you hurt all those people?"

Annie didn't even try to deny it. Her shoulders slumped. All the fight had gone out of her, and she stared at them with the saddest face.

"I don't know if you can understand." She spoke so softly that Esme and Tommy stepped closer. Esme saw the glint of tears in Annie's eyes, so she reached out and placed her hand on Annie's arm.

It seemed as if that simple act of kindness did Annie in, for she crumpled to the floor of the boxcar. Esme and Tommy plopped down beside her, and she started to share her story.

Annie had had a magical childhood, growing up in the circus. Her father, mother, and uncle came from a long line

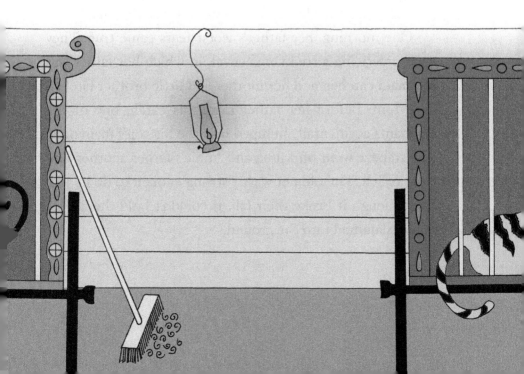

of trapeze artists who had performed for generations. Annie and her brother were raised as aerialists, taught by the very best. Her earliest memories were of flights on the trapeze, being caught by her father's strong arms.

Day after day, her family did what they loved, and Annie was happy. "So very happy!" she said. Sniffling, she wiped her nose on her sleeve.

However five years ago, when the circus stopped in Wabasha, her life came crashing down. Her family needed a new net, for they had mended and mended the one they were using. Her father went to Samuel, the ringmaster, who controlled the circus' finances. Samuel was grieving over his wife's death. "But even so," said Annie, "he still should have paid attention to the circus."

There was a bitter squabble, for Samuel wanted everyone to make do until the end of the season. But Annie's father wore him down, and reluctantly, Samuel ordered a new net.

Day after day, they waited for the new net, and in the meantime, Annie's family had to use the risky, old net.

One morning, her father's worst fears came true. They were practicing a tricky maneuver, in which her father was the main catcher, and her mother and little brother latched onto him. Before her father made his catch, one of the elephants accidentally bumped into the big top's main pole. The trapeze went off-kilter, and Annie's father, mother, and brother fell. The old net wasn't strong enough to do its job. Even though it broke their fall, it couldn't hold them. Her family slammed into the ground.

Annie and her uncle had been standing below, and they watched the fall with horror. Barely eleven years old, Annie felt a helplessness that she would never forget.

Her family survived, but their injuries were severe. Both her parents had broken arms, legs, ribs, and more. Her little brother had suffered the worst, with a broken back. Annie blamed Samuel for not buying a new net earlier, and the accident planted a seed of revenge in her mind.

More tragedy struck soon. The doctor who treated Annie's family had a drinking problem. The day after the accident, he gave Annie's family some medicine, so they would sleep. As he sat in their wagon to oversee them, he drank. Clumsily, he knocked over a kerosene lantern, and the wagon went up in flames.

Annie was in the food tent when she heard people shouting, "Fire!" She ran to help, not realizing it was her own wagon that was burning. When she reached the flames, she was horrified.

The drunken doctor managed to stumble out of the wagon, but nobody else escaped.

The other circus performers tried to hold Annie back from the flames, but she charged towards the wagon, doing her best to save her family. The heat was so intense that she couldn't make it past the door. Henry the Eighth pulled her back and held her, as her family burned to death.

Her little brother must have woken up, for she could hear him screaming. With his broken back, he couldn't move. "His screams still haunt me," she told Esme and Tommy. She feared she would hear them for the rest of her life.

The doctor blamed himself, yet all his apologies couldn't bring Annie's family back. He disappeared from the circus the very next day.

Out of guilt, Samuel bought the aquarium, so Annie and her uncle could have a new act. As she swam around in her fish tank, one year after another passed, and her resentment grew.

Annie stopped talking. Tears glistened on her pale cheeks, and she smothered a sob. Gazing at Esme and Tommy, she asked, "Now do you understand?"

TOMMY

Tommy couldn't help but feel sorry for her. Jeepers, who wouldn't? Her story made his heart hurt. He reckoned they needed to get some answers, so he asked, "Did you put Jessamina's jewelry in our wagon?"

"Yes." Annie sighed. "I hoped the police would find them, and you'd have to leave the show."

"But why did you want us to leave so bad?" asked Esme. Tommy could tell that she was mighty hurt.

"Your grandmother helped Maria through her accident. I'd been hoping Samuel would have to watch his daughter die." Annie paused. "I suppose you've told your grandmother all about me."

"I haven't told her anything," said Esme. "I didn't want to falsely accuse you. I still can't believe you wanted to get rid of us."

"You got too curious. I didn't want you to stop my plans."

She was making Tommy feel mighty uneasy. "And what are your plans, exactly?"

"It's been five years since my family died. And now we're heading back to Wabasha. I think there's a kind of justice in wrecking the circus in the very place where my own life was destroyed."

Esme drew an anxious breath. "What do you mean? What are you going to do?"

"I've been planning to set the big top on fire during the first show. But I wanted Samuel to suffer for more than just a day, so I started scaring him early, a few weeks ago."

"So you want to burn down the circus?" Tommy asked. "The only home you've ever had? And *then* what would you do?"

"I'll meet up with a boy named Eddie, who used to work for the circus," said Annie. "We've been writing to each other secretly, ever since Maria forced him out unfairly. He helped me plan some of this."

"How could you hurt so many people?" asked Esme. "Does your uncle know about this? Is he in on your plans?"

Annie scoffed. "He doesn't have a clue. When my family died, he seemed to have died too. He plays poker every night and is oblivious."

Tommy thought of his pa, who had hurt so much when Ma had died. Somehow Pa had kept going — maybe because his thirteen sons still needed him.

Esme and Tommy were quiet, mulling things over. Suddenly Tommy asked Annie, "Why did you give Madame

Sage that sleeping potion?" He thought, *Not that I'm complaining about that.*

"I saw you use it on Buttercup when she had her accident. But I didn't know how long it would take to work on humans, so I tested it on Madame Sage. I didn't want Bernardo to take the potion too soon and fall asleep before he climbed to the trapeze."

Esme cried, "But how could you do that to poor Bernardo, after what your own family went through?"

"By hurting Bernardo, I hurt Maria. And by hurting Maria, I hurt Samuel." She sniffed haughtily. "Besides, Bernardo isn't the greatest trapeze artist. They never should have hired him to replace my parents."

Tommy didn't like hearing such talk, for Bernardo would always be one of his particular heroes. He studied Annie's face and her beautiful blue eyes. *How could someone with such a sweet face be so evil?* Curious, he asked, "Are you really sixteen?"

"Yes. I don't look my age. My mother was very tiny, and my father wasn't large either. It runs in my family. I'm the perfect size for an acrobat."

Then Tommy remembered another question that had nagged him earlier. "Did you know that Buttercup was going to throw us in the river?"

Annie actually laughed. "That dumb, old elephant! I didn't know for sure that she'd do it, but I hoped she would."

"She's not dumb!" Esme looked across the boxcar to where Buttercup was resting. The elephant gave Esme a loving gaze. "And what do you mean you hoped? You'd just met us."

"Before I even walked up to you on the fairway, I knew you would be traveling with the circus. I eavesdropped on Mama Kat and your grandmother in the big top."

"So you didn't like us from the very start?" Esme asked in astonishment. "Before you even knew us? All this time you were just *pretending* to be our friend?"

Annie's expression softened. Bowing her head sadly, she rose and picked up her broom. She leaned on the handle as if she needed it for support.

Tommy thought, *She looks plumb exhausted.*

Miserably, Annie shuffled over to the boxcar's open side door.

Then she inched even closer.

Shucks, Tommy didn't like where this was heading. He started to feel anxious about how close she was standing to the edge.

He moved to her side, ready to grab her in case she was thinking about jumping. "What are you going to do?" he asked uneasily. Esme had followed him, and now they both stood by Annie.

Annie mumbled, "I guess I'll have to turn myself in. I'll tell Samuel and Mama Kat the truth. I've told you everything, so there's no hiding now." She stared straight ahead into the black night. Shadowy landscape rushed by below.

She shrugged her shoulders. "Or I could just jump and end it all."

Tense, Tommy stood ready. He couldn't let her do it. *I have to save her.*

She turned and faced them. "Or I could tell you that things are not always what they seem." Suddenly she looked like the wicked mermaid they had seen on the first day they'd met her.

In a flash, she stepped back and used her broom to shove Esme and Tommy off the moving train!

They screamed, as they flew into nighttime.

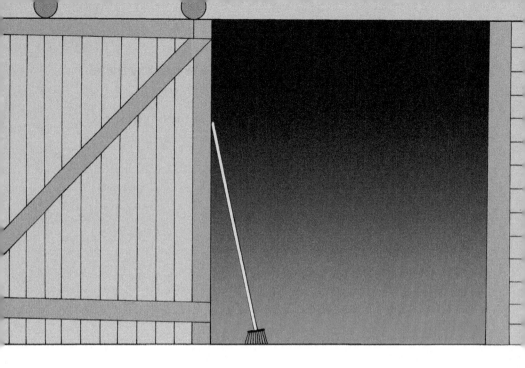

ANNIE

Annie thought the look on their faces had been wonderful. Especially the one on Esme's. It wasn't fear. It was surprise. Esme had been dumbfounded that Annie had deceived them yet again. *Well, what did she expect? That I would get this far and give up on my plans?*

Annie only wished that she could have seen their landing. She was sure they'd splattered nicely. At the speed the train was going, there was no way they could have survived the fall. Even though Annie had stuck her head out of the side door, the train had been moving too fast in the dark for her to see anything.

But she'd heard their screams.

For a second anyhow.

Of course there would be questions about their whereabouts. The grandmother would be nosing around, so it was good they hadn't told her anything. All in all, Annie wasn't too worried. She'd fooled everyone so far. Everyone in the circus just saw her as a sweet, little orphan.

By tomorrow night, it would all be over. She would finally, *finally* have her revenge.

MR. WRIGHT

They were gone again, off to who knows where. They disappeared at the strangest times, and when they returned, they were usually so excited they jabbered away quickly. Their rapid speech was hard for him to decipher — except for his own name, of course, which he could always pick out. They had named him "Mr. Right," which fit him perfectly!

If he were a worrying sort of raccoon, he would be wondering about the company they'd been keeping. The other morning at breakfast, an alarming woman sat down next to Tommy. Mr. Wright didn't think her hair had ever experienced a comb. She surprised Tommy so much that he spat out what he'd been chewing. When Mr. Wright rushed to claim it, he was absolutely thrilled to learn it was a chunk of sausage, but just as he was about to sink his teeth into it, it was stolen! Yes, he was robbed by a nasty raven named Mordecai, who told him that things were not always what they seemed. Mr. Wright told the boorish bird that it and its manners were *exactly* what they seemed.

Thinking about that lost morsel of sausage made Mr. Wright hungry, so he was happy to see that Esme and Tommy had left him a treat! It was a small offering — just an appetizer, but it did smell delicious. He would eat this candy wrapper, on which they had scribbled something, and he hoped Esme and Tommy would bring him the main course when they returned.

PAPUZA

Papuza could see that Bernardo was in good spirits, despite his injury. His happy mood might have been due to the fact that Maria was feeding him grapes while he lounged on plump pillows. The two lovebirds whispered endearments to each other, in English and Italian, as the train rocked them back and forth.

Good for them, thought Papuza. They'd both taken nasty falls, and they deserved some enjoyment. Not for the first time, Papuza told herself that tenderness could be the best medicine in the world. Her herbs, potions, and remedies contained nothing as powerful as love. She left the sweethearts in peace, closing the door to their wagon.

Papuza made her way through several boxcars until she reached the car that held her gypsy wagon. Once she was inside, she was surprised to see that the far door, with the "Danger" sign, was wide open! Something was amiss. She hurried up the steps of the gypsy wagon and discovered that the children were gone!

Only Mr. Wright remained, sitting on the table. He peered at Papuza expectantly. She scanned the wagon for a message, and she even shifted Mr. Wright a few inches aside, in case he happened to be resting on a note.

But there was nothing.

She tried to calm herself. Logically, she knew there were many safe places where the children could be. Yet her mind was struggling with her heart. *Why is that boxcar door open?*

"Where are they?" she asked Mr. Wright as she stroked his soft head.

The baby raccoon merely raised his eyebrows.

Maybe the children would return any minute. Nevertheless, a keen sense of foreboding flooded Papuza. *Something is very, very wrong.*

Esme

Esme gasped when she opened her eyes. *Where am I?* It was so dark. She felt totally disoriented, and she had no clue as to where she could be. *Am I dreaming?* She wondered if this was how Alice had felt when she'd tumbled down the rabbit hole.

Unable to sit up, Esme groaned. She was soaking wet, weighed down with a heaviness that made it difficult to even breathe. *What on earth happened?* And then it all rushed back to her.

Annie.

She'd pushed them from the train.

It had happened so quickly that they hadn't been able to catch themselves. And really, there hadn't even been time to get frightened. All Esme remembered was feeling shocked. The venomous look in her so-called friend's eyes was the most startling thing of all. *I can't believe I wanted her for my sister.* The betrayal made Esme sick to her stomach.

She grabbed for her locket. Oh, thank goodness! She still had it! The protecting presence of her talisman gave her hope.

"Tommy?" she sputtered, struggling unsuccessfully to sit up. She couldn't see anything — not even her hand, as she waved it in front of her face. Maybe she'd died during the fall, and that's why everything was so dark. Well, jiminy, if she were dead, one would think the Great Beyond would have some lanterns, so people could see where the heck they were.

The sound of crickets made her realize she was probably

still alive, and she sighed with relief. *But what happened to Tommy?* Her eyes were slowly becoming used to the darkness. She could see her hands now, but nothing beyond them. Such a primeval blackness enveloped her that she feared she'd never find her cousin.

An unbearable thought popped into her mind. *What if he didn't survive the fall?* "Tommy!" she cried into the emptiness.

Only the chirp of night insects came back.

Esme tried again to sit up, but she couldn't. She was tangled in . . . what? What had captured her? It felt like thick grass or weeds, and something covered with ooze. "Oh, Tommy, please answer!"

In response, she received a brutal silence.

Frantically, she tore at her restraints. As she battled, something soft whapped her cheek. She froze, listening.

She only heard the sound of her racing heart.

Wondering what had just touched her face, she stretched her arms up and cautiously moved them around. As she felt the plants above her, it dawned on her that she had landed in a bog of cattails!

Undoubtedly, the bog had given her a soft landing, which had probably saved her life, yet getting free from the mud seemed nearly impossible. Esme wrestled and fought, and after a great effort, she was finally able to stand.

An instant later, her feet sank into the muck.

"TOMMY!" she shouted as loudly as she could. How could she find him if she couldn't walk? What if he'd landed face first in this mud and was suffocating this very minute? Or just as awful, what if he hadn't been thrown into the mudflat, and he'd landed on solid ground?

Desolation swept over her.

She took a deep breath. *Don't panic,* she told herself. *Calm down. Think logically.* How would she get unstuck?

The plants were taller than she was, and in desperation, she seized some cattails above her and tried to pull her feet free.

She tugged hard on the cattails, and jeepers, her right foot started to loosen! Hope began to grow inside of her.

She pulled again.

And again.

With a sucking sound and the near-loss of her boot, her right foot finally jerked free of its muddy prison!

"Tommy?" she called, checking for him again.

Oh, my goodness, she heard a groan nearby. *It's Tommy! It has to be!*

"Tommy, are you okay? Where are you?" Esme remained quiet for a moment, hoping to hear another groan.

And then she did.

It sounded like it had come from over on her right. "Tommy, help me find you. Could you groan again?"

"Esme?"

It was a feeble reply, yet nothing had ever sounded sweeter to her ears. *He's not dead!!!*

A surge of willpower helped her free her left foot. *We'll get out of here. Some way. Somehow.*

Tommy groaned again. "Esme, I reckon I'm hurt. Where are we?"

"We landed in a bog of cattails. It's almost impossible to get out of this mud, but gosh sakes, you're alive! Can you move?"

"Something is mighty wrong, Esme." She heard him gasp. "I think my leg is b-b-broken." *Oh, poor Tommy!*

He sounded like he was close by. If only they had some light. Moonlight would be a miracle, and she'd even settle for some starlight. In truth, the light of one lone star that had died a billion years ago would be better than what they had now.

As if it could hear her thoughts, a firefly landed nearby. It barely illuminated the cattail where it was perching, yet it gave Esme hope. Maybe she could gather oodles of fireflies, and they'd create enough light for her and Tommy to see.

She tried to catch the firefly, but it flitted away. Crumbs!

"Tommy, keep talking, so I can find you." Fearing she'd sink into the mud again, she tried to walk as lightly as she could.

She heard breathing. He couldn't be far away. Quietly she asked, "Tommy?" She took a cautious step.

"AAAHHHHHHHHHH!" Tommy's scream pierced the night, making Esme almost jump out of her skin. "GET OFF!" he cried.

Unknowingly, she had stepped upon his broken leg.

TOMMY

Bright colors flashed behind Tommy's eyelids. Aaargh! *It's the worst pain I've ever felt.* And he'd suffered through some mighty awful pains.

"I'm sorry, I'm so sorry!" Esme scrambled to get off his leg.

He'd never known the human body could hurt like this. The pain was so sharp he could barely breathe.

"Thank goodness I found you!" Esme cried. "Thank goodness you're all right!"

Believe me, thought Tommy, *I'm the furthest thing from all right.* He was lying on his back, in the mud, in the dark, and he'd be amazed if he'd ever walk again. Yet maybe he could live with that, if only the pain would go away.

"I need to get you out of here," said Esme. "Can you move your arms?"

He could lift one arm out of the mud, but it wasn't easy. Any motion caused him pain. He could feel Esme's hand on his arm, but where was she? It was pitch-black. He couldn't see her at all.

Oh! There she was. Now he could detect a faint outline of her head. She was only inches away. "I'll help you sit up," she warned, tugging on his arm.

"NO!" he cried. "Please stop," he panted. "It hurts too much."

"I know it will probably hurt, but bear with me." She tugged again.

He snatched his arm away from her. "Nope. You're gonna have to leave me and get help. Or just leave me here to rot."

Esme grew quiet, and he could tell she was thinking. Yep, he could almost imagine the cogs in her brain spinning around, and he dreaded her upcoming words. After a full minute of waiting, he finally said, "Well?"

"We have to get you out of here. I can't do it alone. You're going to have to use your strength too."

Tommy groaned because right about then, he didn't *have* a lot of strength.

Suddenly her hand seemed close to his face. "Hey, you still have your glasses. That's lucky! Now, don't get mad at me."

Before he could wonder what she was going to do that would make him mad at her, she went ahead and did it. She grabbed his nose and gave it a vicious twist.

"OHH!" he roared, bolting straight up from the mud. "What in the world . . ."

"You did it!" she sang gleefully. "I wasn't sure it would work. At least you're sitting up now."

Talk about kicking a feller when he's down! As his rage started to

subside, he realized she'd been right. But he wasn't about to tell her that.

She came around to his back and slipped her arms beneath his armpits. "I'll try to pull you out, but you've got to help too."

She tugged at him while he tried to wriggle his body out of the muck. After a valiant struggle, they made it to firmer ground. Tommy's leg throbbed something awful, but at least he was free from his prison of mud.

"How's your leg?" asked Esme.

"I ain't never had anything hurt this bad."

"I'm so sorry . . ." She froze because a far-off train rumbled in the distance.

"Tommy, do you hear that?"

PAPUZA

They were gone. No one had seen them, and Papuza had asked everywhere.

When they'd arrived in Wabasha that night, Katrina had called a meeting of all the circus performers, asking for their help in locating the missing children. Papuza had held out hope that maybe Annie would know of their whereabouts, but the girl seemed just as surprised and worried as the rest of them. Papuza thought, *It's as if they vanished into thin air.*

To say she was worried was an understatement. Something must have happened to them on the train. Like all children, they were naturally curious. Papuza could picture Esme and Tommy wanting to jump from boxcar to boxcar — and then slipping. The thought of it shattered her.

She was packing up to ride back in the dark to search for them. Even though she dreaded what she might find on the tracks, she had to go. Her thoughts flew to William. *How can I possibly tell him that Tommy is gone?*

She closed the door to the gypsy wagon, which she had parked near the performers' wagons. As she saddled Zinjiber, her hands shook. *Be strong,* she scolded herself. Desperately, she needed to choke back her forebodings. Taking a deep breath, she glanced up at the shrouded night sky. It was grim, without a spark of light or hope.

She rechecked her supplies. Her saddlebags brimmed with things she might need, and her rope and lanterns were secure. She tightened the cinch beneath Zinjiber's belly. Papuza was ready.

"I can go with you. You might need someone along." From his booming voice, she knew it was Henry before she even spun around.

Papuza turned to thank him. "No, it would be better if you stayed here with my wagon, Henry, as we discussed. I do, indeed, appreciate your help." Reaching up, she placed her hand gently on his arm. "Remember to feed our little raccoon, please."

"We'll keep the home lights burning," Maria said, joining them. "Things will be nice and cozy when they get back." Her good nature was trying to cheer Papuza's sore heart.

Katrina arrived and hugged her. "My thoughts will be with you," she whispered in Papuza's ear. Tears pricked Papuza's eyes.

Papuza mounted her horse but paused before she rode away. "If I'm still gone when Arthur arrives, tell him that only this dire situation could have kept me from meeting him. Please ask him to wait! I'll be back, for better or worse."

Katrina and Maria called up to her, "Good luck!" Remaining quiet, Henry raised his hand in farewell.

Nodding, Papuza turned Zinjiber around and headed north.

ESME

Esme heard the train growing louder, but she still couldn't see any light. All the same, it filled her with hope, for she imagined running towards the train and flagging it down. They'd be saved. And by gum, if they were saved, the circus would be saved too. She sighed with relief. *It will all work out.*

However, when she finally saw the train's lantern-light, it was above her! She tried to hurry towards it, but the mud made it impossible to move fast. "You ain't gonna make it," Tommy called.

Yet she kept trying.

As the train neared, its light revealed their situation, and Esme realized Tommy was right. Her hopes were completely crushed.

The gaslight from the locomotive shone down on them as it rattled by. Esme was quite a ways below the train tracks. Massive boulders supported the tracks through this infernally marshy area.

She felt so frustrated! After the train passed, they were in darkness again, with only the sound of the retreating locomotive.

Soon even that was gone.

The night insects resumed their chorus, and Esme slogged back to Tommy in defeat. He said, "You know, that looked like the Orphan Train we saw back in Zumbro Falls."

Dropping down by his side, Esme sighed. She never would have thought she'd want to change places with those poor orphans. Yet right about now, she'd rather be anywhere than here.

They sat quietly, thinking their separate thoughts. Fireflies flickered on and off, and their glowing orbs provided the only light. As Esme watched them, she thought, *I wish* **we** *had wings, so we could fly away too.*

She told Tommy, "When the sun comes up, I'll be able to see to set your leg — unless you want me to doctor you now, in the dark."

She heard him groan.

"I ain't gonna make it up those rocks," Tommy muttered. "I don't even think I'll make it out of this bog. You're gonna have to leave me here, Esme, and get help."

"I won't leave you, Tommy," she said stubbornly.

The chirping of crickets filled the silence between them as Esme thought about what she'd just said. It reminded her of a day several years ago when Tommy hadn't left her alone in her time of need. Quietly she asked, "Do you remember the Bright Star award?"

He sighed. "How could I ever forget?"

Suddenly, Esme was reliving Tommy's attempt to win the Bright Star medal. He'd gone to school early every day to help the school marm, Miss Blomgren, by toting wood for the fire, and carrying out the ashes, and cleaning the chalkboards, and sweeping the floor. Another pupil, Andy Clauer, was also trying to win the award. Tommy and Andy showed up early each morning — rain or shine, blizzard or drought, in sickness or in health — hoping to win the coveted prize. Tommy had taken it very seriously because none of his brothers had ever won a medal, and he would have been the first Dooley boy to live up to his presidential name. But mostly, he just wanted to make his pa smile again. His pa had been so sad since Tommy's ma had died.

On the last day of the year, when Miss Blomgren would be announcing the winner, Esme woke up early to ride with Tommy to school. They were both on Bess, and Esme fell off, which made her nose bleed something awful. There was blood everywhere, but especially on her dress. Esme couldn't go to school that way, yet she couldn't go back home either because Hatch would be sure to punish her for ruining her clothes.

Esme begged Tommy to go on without her, but he wouldn't hear of it. He insisted they could still make it to school on time if they hurried.

Riding back to Esme's abode, they decided she would climb the trumpet vine to her bedroom window and change clothes while Tommy kept a lookout for Hatch. But just as Esme started her climb, Hatch appeared around the corner.

When Hatch saw how Esme had bloodied her dress, she

flew into a rage. She grabbed Esme by the arm and threw her into their old, abandoned well — the place that Esme feared most of all, because all kinds of scary and horrible things lived down there. Especially rats!

Tommy didn't leave her, even when Hatch yelled at him to skedaddle. He merely slipped into the woods and hid until Hatch left.

As time ticked by, he must have realized he was losing his award by helping Esme. And he *did* help her! Why, she'd probably still be in that well, and she might have even died down there, if he hadn't thrown her a rope to save her.

But it had all taken time. Tommy had to wait for Hatch to leave before he could help Esme out. And then Esme had to clean herself up. By the time they made it to school, Andy Clauer was wearing the Bright Star medal around his neck. Tommy was heartbroken.

"You didn't leave me, Tommy," Esme said quietly, remembering how horrible she had felt about his defeat. Just thinking about it made her eyes fill with tears. "You've always been my best friend, for as long as I can remember. Probably even longer than I can remember. So I'm *not* going to leave you in this bog."

Suddenly Tommy laid a grateful hand on her shoulder, and she realized he must have been afraid of staying here alone.

After a moment, he pulled his hand away. His voice wavered as he said, "You made me a medal out of cardboard."

"Tommy, are you crying?"

"No!" he answered, a bit too loudly. He always claimed that he never, ever cried.

Esme looked up to where the Big Dipper would have been, if the sky hadn't been pitch dark. She felt as lightless as the stars, but for Tommy's sake, she tried to sound cheerful. "At least it's a beautiful night."

As soon as she said it, they felt the first raindrops.

TOMMY

Tommy swore she brought on the rain.

And just when he thought things couldn't get more worrisome, he heard a sniff.

And then another one.

Oh, jeepers, she was crying.

He couldn't stand it when she cried. She hardly ever cried, so she must have been at the bottom of her barrel.

"Esme . . . ," he began. But he didn't have the words. He didn't know how to cheer her up. *She's always the one who does the cheering-up.*

Nevertheless he tried. "Come on, Esme," he mumbled.

"Oh, Tommy, I don't think I've ever been so low." She sobbed the saddest sob he'd ever heard. "Grandma, and the circus folks, and the spectators, and the animals will all die, if Annie burns down the big top." Her voice trembled. "How could she be so evil?" Esme paused to wipe her face on her sleeve. "I never told you this, but secretly, I was hoping we'd adopt her. I thought she'd be a wonderful sister."

Since they were telling the truth, Tommy offered up, "I think I was falling in love with her."

Esme gasped.

"And then she went and tried to kill me!" he exclaimed. "I've always heard that love is a dangerous thing!"

Half laughing and half crying, Esme murmured, "Oh, Tommy, I'm so sorry." She cleared her throat and sighed again. "This all feels like a nightmare. I keep replaying in my mind how she pushed us off the train."

"I thought she was gonna jump."

"So did I!"

"I've been thinking about her story," Tommy said. "She's had an awful time. But shucks, you can't go around killing people." He may not have always paid the closest attention in Sunday school, but he did know that murdering wasn't a neighborly thing to do.

Esme asked, "Do you think she tried to kill us in the fish tank too? When the air tubes stopped working?"

315

"'Afraid so, Esme. Maybe she ran into Henry outside and knew he'd suspect her if we drowned."

"I can't get over how I thought she was my friend," Esme mumbled. "I feel so betrayed. I've never had this feeling before, and it makes me sick to my stomach."

"Yep, she done us wrong," he agreed wholeheartedly.

"You know, we were always taught that when someone does you wrong, you turn the other cheek. But honestly, I don't know if I'll ever be able to forgive her."

A sad silence stretched between them. Eventually Tommy said, "She did all those bad things because she's never been able to forgive Samuel. She carried that anger around for years. I reckon it destroyed her."

Quietly, Esme thought about Annie, as well as another angry individual, who was all-too-familiar. Finally she said, "I wonder what happened to Hatch to make her such a miserable person."

"Her father used to beat her," said Tommy. "With a hickory stick."

Shocked, Esme asked, "What? Who told you that? When did you hear this?"

"It was during our Great Silence," Tommy joked.

"Well, I'm glad you can josh about that now. But where did you hear this?"

"My brothers were talking about it. They heard gossip in town about Hatch and her jail sentence. People were saying, 'What else can you expect from the likes of her? After all, she had a mighty bad childhood.'"

Esme asked softly, "Was it really bad?"

"Well, they say her mother died when she was eight, and she was the oldest of six children. Hatch had to be the mother for her brothers and sisters, and her father beat all of them. One time, their neighbors caught him whipping Hatch because he didn't like her beef stew."

"Oh, Tommy," Esme cried. "For the first time in my life, I feel sorry for her. I mean, I know what it feels like to disappoint people with my cooking. At least I didn't get whipped for it. I really feel like I have something in common with her. Poor Aunt Hatch!"

Startled by the idea that Esme might have something in common with that old battle-axe, Tommy gasped. The movement jarred his leg, which made him groan.

Esme said, "I bet I could wrap your leg with cattail leaves. They'd be strong enough. Remember when Mrs. Mehrkens came to Sunday school and showed us how to make baskets out of them?"

"I remember her banana bread."

"Yes," Esme agreed, "she does make the best banana bread I've ever tasted."

"And carrot cake."

"And chocolate chip cookies." Esme added longingly.

"And cherry pie." Tommy's stomach began to grumble.

"And apple pie. Oh, jeepers, we have to stop this. We're making ourselves even more hungry!"

"Yep." Tommy sighed.

"But I brought up Mrs. Mehrkens because of her basketmaking. Maybe I could take these cattail leaves and weave you a wrapping for a splint!"

Tommy could tell she was starting to perk up, so he wasn't going to say he had serious doubts about the usefulness of cattails.

"Do you still have your jackknife?" she asked. "Or did you lose it when we fell off the train?"

He felt in the bib of his overalls, and he still had his knife! It seemed like a tiny miracle, after everything they'd gone through, and it boosted his spirits. *We ain't without resources in this dark, wet, lonely wilderness.* "Yep, I've got it."

"Oh, good!" She sounded as relieved as he felt. "When it gets light enough, I'll start cutting." The rain pelted down harder, and Esme scooted closer to Tommy for warmth.

The pain in his leg had become a dull ache. Not a throbbing, stabbing, out-of-your mind kind of pain, but it still hurt mighty bad. He didn't know if he'd be able to sleep, given that he was so wet and hurt.

But exhaustion took over, and sometime before dawn, he and Esme nodded off. It was a hard sleep — the sleep of the dead, which was a flock he thought he might be joining in the very near future.

Then he felt a nudge.

And another one.

"Wake up!" Esme chirped.

Unwillingly, he cracked open an eyelid.

She gave him an optimistic smile. "I've been cutting cattail stalks and gathering branches to set your leg."

Tommy moaned. He knew her, and he might as well accept that there was no way to talk her out of this. So he scowled at her and grumbled, "Okay."

He glanced around. Now that it was dawn, everything looked different. They were mighty close to the Mississippi River. In fact, it sparkled just a few yards away. The train tracks ran above them on a trestle bridge. Climbing the rocks up to the tracks would be impossible with his broken leg. *How am I gonna make it out of here?* He told Esme his worries.

"I've been thinking about that too." Raising her chin proudly, she declared, "And I just might have an answer!" She pointed to a log in the water, at the edge of the bog. "We can float downriver on that log. We're bound to find *somebody* who can help us — and if not, at least we'll be heading towards Wabasha."

He realized she had a point there. It wasn't a bad idea. Before he could comment, she started cutting the bottom of his pants with his knife, so she could set his leg. *Gosh-almighty,* he thought, *I ain't looking forward to this.*

When she opened his pants leg, they could see that his leg was broken below his knee. She told Tommy to lie back and close his eyes, and on the count of three, she'd set it.

"One . . . ," she began, and then he saw stars explode behind his eyes. He let out a ferocious scream.

PAPUZA

Papuza heard a scream, and she could have sworn it was Tommy. Yet she only heard it for the briefest second. Immediately it was masked by the cawing and shrieking of birds — hundreds of birds, from the sound of it. *Was the scream just a figment of my imagination?* She wanted so desperately to find the children that maybe her mind was playing tricks on her.

A storm had blown in last night, and she and Zinjiber had to halt until it was over. The hours she'd spent by the side of the tracks, wrapped in her rain poncho, were miserable. She had tried to focus on Arthur, but even her anticipation of their cherished reunion could not curb the sickening worries she carried. Her thoughts were bleak, and her chest felt as if it would burst from heartache.

After the rain had passed, Papuza had struck out again, dreading what she might find. She steeled herself for tragedy.

However the farther she went down the tracks, the more puzzled she became. There was nary a sign of them, nor evidence of an accident. *Could they possibly be alive? How could two children disappear into thin air?*

She still had much ground to cover along the tracks. If her mind hadn't been in such a wretched state, she would have loved a leisurely ride through this stunning landscape. Without a doubt, Lake Pepin was magnificent.

Yet there was no way she could appreciate the vista. With every mile she traveled, she feared she was closer to finding what she didn't want to find.

This is no task a grandmother should ever have to do.

ESME

Esme knew it must have hurt something awful. *Poor Tommy!* She pulled his leg down, and it looked a lot straighter. She thought that was a good sign.

Then she tried to use the cattail leaves, but they didn't work very well. They came undone as soon as she tried to tie them. So she cut his pants leg into strips and added cattail stalks and branches to keep his leg straight while she bandaged him up.

What if she messed this up? What if Tommy would need crutches for the rest of his life? What if he could never play baseball again? She couldn't live with that. She had to try her very best to do right by her cousin.

She worked as quickly as she could, hoping to keep his suffering to a minimum.

When she finished setting his leg, she helped him wriggle over to the log, and he stretched out on top of it while Esme pushed him away from shore. Getting out of the shallow, muddy water was a fierce battle for her, and Tommy couldn't help much, with his broken leg.

As they made their way into the river's current, Esme began to feel exhilarated. By Jove, they could do this. She knew it! And she refused to worry about the fact that they'd never done this before. And they didn't know where they were going. And she was just learning how to swim.

Within minutes, restless clouds covered the sun, like an ominous warning. The water was fearfully cold, and it dragged at her sailor dress while she tried to kick. Sometimes she felt things brushing against her stockings. The thought of a sea monster lurking just below the surface made her kick all the harder.

They hugged the shoreline. In places, the banks were shallow, and they had to use all their might to shove away from them. Esme soon learned to avoid low-lying tree branches that reached out to snare them. The best route seemed to be a little ways from shore, yet she constantly worried about veering into the middle of the river. She thought, *We don't want to get run over by a paddle wheel boat.*

Esme kept glancing at Tommy. At least once a minute she asked him how he felt, and she could tell it was starting to irritate him. "Wabasha can't be that far," she chirped, trying to sound cheerful.

She could see he was pretty gloomy. The weather seemed to match his mood, with the sky getting darker by the second. *Please don't let it rain,* she silently prayed.

Esme thought about what she'd do when they got to Wabasha. First, she'd find Grandma. Esme went back and forth between fearing that Annie would kill Grandma and assuring herself that Grandma would outsmart Annie.

Grandma can take care of herself, thought Esme. *I hope so, anyway.* Believing anything else was just too awful.

Second, Esme would find Katrina and tell her everything. Katrina would call the sheriff, who would haul Annie away. *That's what will happen,* Esme tried to tell herself. *If only we can get there in time.*

She thought she felt a splash from the river, but then she realized it was raindrops. Tommy muttered, "Esme, I think a storm is coming."

Oh, good gravy, it hit them like a monsoon! Rain came pouring down, as if someone were emptying the sky with buckets. Esme yelled to Tommy, "Let's head to shore. Maybe we can wait it out under a tree."

They tried to veer the log to the right. A strong wind swept down from the bluffs, pushing them in the opposite direction, making all their efforts useless.

As they drifted farther into the channel, Esme cried, "What's happening?"

"It's the wind. We can't fight it!"

Kicking furiously now, Esme still made no headway, and the wind forced them even farther from shore. Stinging rain pelted them angrily. She heard a rumbling noise and wondered if it was thunder, but it didn't go away. Instead it only grew louder.

The river rounded another bend, and the noise became deafening. She glanced ahead and stared in horror.

"Tommy! It's a logjam! We're heading straight for it!"

TOMMY

Holy Toledo, it was a logjam! Gigantic logs filled the entire river, from bank to bank. Tommy thought, *We're in a heap of trouble.*

He knew about the dangers of logjams, and not just from Papuza's stories. Why, every kid in Zumbro Falls had heard about Clarence Taylor's older brother, who had died in a logjam. He'd tumbled into the water, between the logs, and the rushing logs had covered him and blocked him in. He'd never made it back up to the surface.

Across the way, Tommy saw a narrow boat that held loggers with long poles. If he and Esme could somehow get their attention, maybe they would help. The cousins screamed and yelled, but given the sounds of the falling rain, and the roaring river, and the logs crashing into each other,

none of the loggers heard them. None of them turned their way.

The closer Esme and Tommy grew to the snarled mess of logs, the more Tommy's hopes sank.

"What can we do?" Esme shouted.

"Hang on!" he yelled back. But they already were. Both of them were gripping their log with all their strength. They were going to crash into the logjam, and there was nothing they could do about it. Tommy thought, *We're goners!*

Esme couldn't swim. Not really, anyhow. She looked terrified, and Tommy could only imagine how scared she must be. At least he could swim, but his leg was in a splint. *I reckon I'll sink like a stone.*

He called to her, "Whatever you do, don't let go of the log." He aimed to sound strong, yet that was about the last thing he felt. Fear twisted his stomach into a cold knot. He closed his eyes and thought of home.

ESME

Esme's mind raced with hundreds of scenarios of how this could turn out. She couldn't pretend to herself that any of them were promising.

Over and over, the river slapped her face as they jolted through choppy water. Esme had to wipe her eyes to see what was happening. Ahead of them, a man balanced on top of a log and held a long pole. He had his back to them, and Esme tried to get his attention. "Help!" she screamed.

But the noise of the wind, and the rain, and the river, and the logjam were deafening. "Help!" she cried again.

Several yards from the massive logs, she darted a desperate look at Tommy. His face was so pale it made his freckles stand out. Esme wondered if this would be the last time she'd look upon the face of her best friend.

KRAK!! Their log smashed violently into another log, throwing Esme and Tommy in the river.

Within seconds, she was deep underwater.

It was cold and dark and terrifying, and nowhere could she see Tommy. She kicked and struggled to rise to the surface. This was nothing like Annie's fish tank. Nothing at all!

Reaching the surface, she gasped for air. Immediately she began to sink again. She had no time to scream for help, no time to grab onto anything. Even though she thrashed her arms and legs, she couldn't stay above water.

Just as she sank again, a pole with a hook was thrust down beside her. The hook caught her locket! Instantly, the

pole was jerked up, breaking her chain! Esme grabbed for her locket, just missing it.

It was swept away.

Oh, no! She felt like her luck had run out, and now she would surely drown.

She tried to claw her way upwards, yet the more she struggled, the deeper she sank into her grim and watery grave.

Esme couldn't hold her breath any longer. Her lungs burned, needing oxygen. She thought of the wonderful air tubes in Annie's tank, and she felt wretched in so many ways.

She wondered if Tommy was drowning too.

And she thought of Grandma, picturing her loving face. Esme's heart hurt, tortured by a haunting image

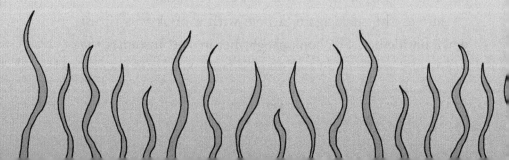

of Grandma in flames. *I'm failing everyone. Not just myself, but everyone.*

Suddenly Esme felt a pole by her side again, and she clasped onto it. Oh, my stars! It was pulling her upwards.

Astonished, she broke through the surface, gasping for air. A man stood in a boat, holding the other end of the pole. Quickly he grabbed her, pulling her safely into his vessel.

Panting hard, she looked around but didn't see Tommy. She shouted to the man, "There's a boy with me. Red hair. Do you see him?"

Esme rose in the boat, scanning the massive logjam. Rain played tricks with her vision, so she kept rubbing her face to see better. *What happened to him?*

Not seeing him anywhere, she grew despondent. Hysterical.

"Tommy!" she screamed.

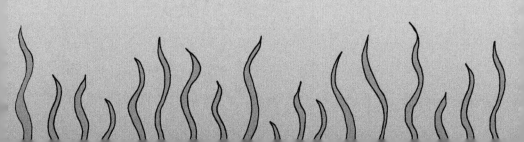

GROGGS

Hot diggity dog! Groggs had always wanted to go to the circus. Heck, he'd always wanted to be *in* the circus. He felt pretty sure he would have made a mighty fine acrobat. He had the physique and the natural grace for it — unlike his sister. Why, if she were up on that flying trapeze, she'd

probably pull the whole tent down on top of herself. The thought of her buried and thrashing in canvas made him laugh out loud.

His harpy of a sister hauled off and whapped him on the back of his head.

"Hey," he grumbled. "Why'd you up and do that?" He gave her a shove and then leaped across the train aisle before she could shove him back.

Sitting by himself next to the window, he admired his reflection and tried to forget that his ornery sister existed. She sure knew how to ruin a feller's good time.

If you asked Groggs, *he* deserved to go to the circus a whole lot more than she did. *He* was the one who'd taken on that ferocious tiger all by his lonesome. Hatch had just sat on a branch and hollered at him. And bellowed at him. And generally cussed at him without mercy.

Yet there wasn't any way on this green earth that he could have talked her out of coming along on this trip. She'd been avoiding the law, keeping out of sight, so she jumped at the offer of a free ticket out of town. And then there was also the matter of compensation. She figured the circus owed her considerably for putting her through vexations and humiliations.

Groggs wondered if that nice lady who'd sent them the telegram had any idea of the storm that was heading her way. Yes, siree, she was in a mighty heap of trouble.

Maybe when she had to deal with Hatch, he could lend her a hand. And maybe she'd be so grateful she'd offer him a job in her circus.

As Groggs imagined helping that sweet damsel in distress, he puffed out his scrawny chest with pride.

Well, heck, he thought, with an optimistic grin, *if I just use my manly magnetism, I'll probably own the whole shindig by the end of the week.*

ESME

Esme scanned the logjam with the loggers, looking for Tommy. Rain limited their visibility. Moisture covered her face, and she repeatedly wiped her eyes, hoping to see better.

And then she saw him! Tommy was floating facedown by a log, his body lifeless. Esme pointed to him and shouted, and the loggers steered the boat over to him. *He has to be okay,* she kept thinking. *He just **has** to be.*

Using their hooked poles, the loggers snagged Tommy's limp body and rushed to pull him into the boat. They laid him on his back and felt for his pulse. Panic welled within Esme, and she held Tommy's hand, willing him to open his eyes.

A logger began pumping on Tommy's stomach.

Nothing happened.

Rain continued to pummel them, and Esme watched in horror as the determined logger tried again and again. *Oh, please, Tommy, wake up,* she kept begging.

And finally, he did!

His eyes flew open, and he sputtered and coughed up massive amounts of river water. Still in shock, Esme began shaking with relief.

One of the men told Tommy, "You were *very* lucky."

"Oh, Tommy, I don't think I've ever been so scared." Esme was still holding his hand, kneeling by his side. His glasses were crooked, and he looked dazed, which she thought was a pretty normal reaction for someone who'd just come back from the dead.

"Thank you, sirs." She looked up to the rugged loggers standing above her. Her voice broke as she said, "Thank you for saving our lives." The whole experience had been so horrible that she didn't think she'd ever go near water again. *Ever!*

Esme felt their boat lurch to a stop. Glancing up, she was surprised to see they'd reached a dock, and a village loomed before them. A sign on the dock said, *"Reads Landing."*

"Here you go, then," a logger told them kindly.

Esme asked him, "Are you stopping here?"

"No, we're heading downriver. This run has been nothing but headaches. We'll be happy when it's done."

"Oh, but please, sir," she pleaded. "Could we go as far as Wabasha with you? It's very important."

"Sorry, miss. It's against company policy to transport people. I could lose my job, and I have mouths to feed at home. Besides, you're lucky you survived the river. I wouldn't tempt fate, if I were you."

Esme thought about what he'd said, and it made a lot of sense. They'd have to find another way to get to Wabasha — a less dangerous way. She wondered how far Wabasha was from Reads Landing. *Will we make it in time?*

In the wind and rain, the cousins thanked the loggers. Tommy shook their hands, and Esme hugged them and said she'd never forget them.

On the shore, Tommy couldn't put any pressure on his leg, so he used Esme as a crutch. As he leaned on her and hobbled along, the loggers shoved away from the dock. Rain made them look blurry, and they grew smaller and smaller. Soon, they slipped through a curtain of rain and disappeared.

ESME

Esme helped Tommy through the rain towards the closest building. It seemed to be a tavern. She sighed. "Oh, Tommy, that was so scary."

He remained silent, stoically limping along.

The rain was unrelenting. Esme had been in wet clothes since the previous night. Her stockings and boots rubbed on her heels, and blisters were starting. She felt like a drowned river rat, and she longed to be warm and dry.

Yet she couldn't complain — not after what Tommy had been through. He wasn't saying anything, but Esme was pretty sure she knew what he was thinking. It wasn't at all positive.

She told him, "We're going to have to find a ride to Wabasha. We won't be able to walk. Not with your leg."

"Just leave me here. I ain't feeling right."

"Once you get out of this rain, you'll feel better," she said hopefully.

They reached the door to the tavern. With Tommy's help, Esme finally swung open the creaky door.

Inside, the atmosphere was loud and lively. The tavern was crowded, considering it was still morning. Clouds of cigar smoke made Esme cough, and her spirits sagged when she looked around. *Who will help us?* Not one person in this gathering seemed like a knight in shining armor.

They plodded to the nearest booth, where Tommy fell into the seat. Esme wiped back her wet bangs and straightened her drenched dress, as best she could. Glancing around the tavern, she tried to find a kindly face. "Now, stay here," she told Tommy.

But she hadn't needed to say that because from the looks of him, he wouldn't be moving. He slumped down in the booth with his eyes closed.

Worried, Esme felt his sweaty forehead. And then she felt her own. Tommy's forehead wasn't cold and clammy like hers. Instead his brow was burning up. He had a raging fever. *Is it from his broken leg? Did I set it wrong?*

Esme wished Grandma were here. She would know exactly what to do. Esme realized that the best thing she could do for Tommy was to find him a doctor. She should leave him in a doctor's care while she went on to Wabasha alone.

Through the rowdy men, she caught glimpses of the barkeeper. *He would know where to find a doctor.* So even though Esme wasn't sure if Tommy could hear her, she told him she'd be right back. She started weaving her way between the legs in the crowd.

Once she reached the bar, she climbed on top of an empty stool and stood there, waving to catch the barkeeper's attention. He was too busy to notice her, but she kept waving. In fact, she waved and waved and waved until she thought her arms might fall off. She even put her fingers in her mouth and let out a shrill whistle. But it was all for nothing.

Esme noticed that a white-haired man sitting next to her was eating. Instantly she was ravenous. *When did we last eat?* She didn't think she'd ever been so hungry. Her knees began to buckle, and she had to sit down.

The old man shoved his plate of pickled pig's feet her way. Oh, jeepers! Esme knew he was trying to be generous, but as hungry as she was, she couldn't bring herself to eat them. In fact, she worried that she might be sick.

The stately regulator clock on the wall said it was eleven o'clock. Its pendulum swung back and forth, and every second counted. The circus show would start at two o'clock, so Esme had only three hours left. *We're running out of time.*

She thought of Tommy and everything that had happened since last night. It made her cover her face with her hands. She fought back tears of frustration.

"Say," said the codger who was eating pig's feet, "you look like you've been pulled through a knothole backwards."

Surprised that someone had noticed her, Esme turned to look at him. He seemed like a nice man. Even though he was filthy, and he was missing some teeth, and he smelled bad, and his clothes were rags, if there was one thing she'd

learned on this journey, it was that things were not always what they seemed. For all she knew, she could be talking with the king of England.

"I need help," she said urgently. "I really need help." Anxiously she bit her lip.

"Well, then. Maybe I can help you work it out. What seems to be the problem?" He started to pack his pipe, and that quiet gesture reminded Esme of Grandma.

Maybe he really *would* be able to help. Esme decided to tell him her story. She took a deep breath before she began, "We were . . ."

Gunshots rang out in the tavern.

At first Esme didn't understand the loud, shocking noises. There was shouting and shoving, and then there were more shots. She couldn't tell where they came from, and her heart pounded wildly! The codger lifted her from her stool and set her down behind it, on the tavern floor. He warned her to duck down.

Kneeling beside her, he casually smoked his pipe during the bedlam. At one point, he shouted to her over the confusion, "It wouldn't be Reads Landing, if there wasn't a shootout every day." He paused to take a puff. "There used to be five murders here a week. It's slowed down some, now that they don't bring as many logs down the old Chippewa."

Esme couldn't believe he wasn't more worried. Why, he was giving her a history lesson in the middle of a gunfight! Suddenly a man collapsed close to her hiding-place, and blood flowed from his shoulder. Esme screamed!

Will I be shot to death? Out of habit, she reached for her lucky locket, but of course it was gone. And what about

Tommy? Was he all right? She needed to get back to him, so she started to rise from her crouched position.

The old man grabbed her hand. "Wait 'til this blows over," he advised. "If you thought you had troubles before, just try standing up."

TOMMY

Gunshots woke Tommy from a feverish dream. *Where am I?* It took him a moment to recognize the booth where he was lying. Then it all came flooding back to him.

As he struggled to sit up, he saw a regular gunfight all around him. *Shucks, I must still be dreaming.* Or maybe he was delirious from the fever. *Because this ain't real,* he thought. *It can't be.*

Something hit his leg! The force made him cry out in pain. By gum, maybe this gunfight truly *was* real. *Was I struck by a bullet?* As Tommy tried to check it out, a stray bullet — he was sure of it, this time — whizzed past his head. Dangerously close!

Immediately he slouched back down in the booth, with a powerful hankering to hide even lower. He decided to slide down and take cover beneath the booth's table.

It wasn't easy.

His splint made it hard to move, and as he squirmed and twisted, his heart thumped because he felt sure a bullet would hit him any second. After what seemed like an eternity, he successfully made it under the table.

Tommy sat on the floor, with his legs stretched out in front of him. He reckoned he'd be bleeding if he'd been shot, but he didn't see blood anywhere. All the same, he felt so delirious that he might have been shot and hadn't even realized it. So he patted his chest and arms and legs, checking for blood. By gosh, he felt flabbergasted to find a bullet in his splint bindings!

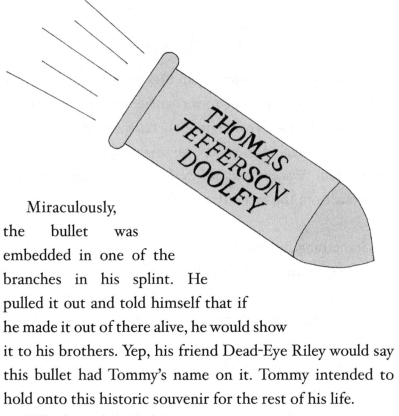

Miraculously,
the bullet was
embedded in one of the
branches in his splint. He
pulled it out and told himself that if
he made it out of there alive, he would show
it to his brothers. Yep, his friend Dead-Eye Riley would say
this bullet had Tommy's name on it. Tommy intended to
hold onto this historic souvenir for the rest of his life.

Which might only be a minute more.

Wondering if anybody had died yet, he peeked through
the table legs, searching for Esme. The tavern was in an
uproar, and Tommy couldn't see her anywhere. *Is she okay?*

Maybe she made it behind the bar and was hiding there,
out of harm's way. But what if there was a bullet with her
name on it too? Anxiously he kept watching for her through
the smoke and the hullaballoo. Was that her on the ground?
Was she shot?

ANNIE

It was so very easy to get money from her uncle. Annie reminded him that he'd forgotten her birthday, and she needed some new clothes. He must have felt guilty because he handed over ten dollars. That was more than he'd ever given her, and definitely more than she'd expected.

In the hardware store in Wabasha, she was probably the best customer of the day. They were only too happy to sell her a lot of cans of kerosene.

Annie believed in justice. An eye for an eye. And she could tell that justice was on her side, for the rain was starting to let up. She foresaw a beautifully sunny afternoon, where her inferno of revenge could be seen for miles.

ESME

An extremely loud BOOM sounded, and the chaos in the tavern came to an abrupt halt. Esme still didn't dare lift her head, but the old man next to her gave her a nudge.

"It's over," he said. "When Marty gets out his rifle, he's had enough."

Rising cautiously, she looked around at the carnage. Four men were wounded (or worse) on the floor. Esme turned and saw the weathered barkeeper standing behind the counter, with a scowl on his face and a rifle in his hands. "Get out of here now, all of you! Out!" He shouted so ferociously that she ducked in fear.

Crouching low, she scrambled over to Tommy, who was hiding beneath the booth table. "Oh, my gosh, Tommy. Can you believe it? Are you all right?"

He showed her the hole that the bullet had made in his splint, and Esme knew he would make the most of this story. Just thinking about him telling his brothers made the corners of her mouth turn up.

"Call for Doc Charlie," the barkeeper yelled at the departing patrons.

Marvelous relief filled Esme. There was hope, and it was coming in the form of a doctor! Maybe everything could still work out. *If I only had my lucky locket, I'd be **sure** that things are going to work out.*

She and Tommy kept hiding under the table as the riffraff left the bar. Esme worried that the barkeeper would find them and make them leave too. But they hadn't caused any problems. They'd probably been the best-behaved customers in the tavern (although that really wasn't saying much).

The old man who had helped her was sitting at the bar again, smoking his pipe and opening his morning paper. Esme studied the bodies on the floor and felt relieved to see that all of them were moving. Granted, some of them were just barely twitching, but others were trying to stand.

"How are you?" Esme put her hand on Tommy's brow. It was just as hot — if not hotter — than before.

"About as well as a feller can expect," he mumbled. "Coming back from the dead." He lapsed into a weary silence.

Just then, Esme noticed the legs of a well-dressed man coming through the door. She peeked out from the end of the table and saw a tall man, with black hair and a dashing mustache. He wore a bow tie and carried a doctor's bag. *It has to be the doctor!*

Esme crawled out from beneath the table, and then she helped Tommy up too. As soon she got him standing, he collapsed back down in the booth.

Doc Charlie examined a man on the floor — the one with the shoulder injury — who'd fallen by Esme earlier. The wounded man was now sitting up, which was a considerable improvement.

Tentatively, Esme approached the doctor, wishing she didn't need to trouble him, yet agonizing over every second that slipped by. As he rummaged around in his doctor's bag, she clasped her hands and stepped forward. She spoke as politely as she could. "Please, sir, I wouldn't interrupt you if

I didn't have an emergency, but my cousin and I need your help."

Doc Charlie gave her a quick once over, probably noticing her wet and bedraggled appearance. Then he saw Tommy sprawled in the booth behind her. Raising his dark eyebrows, the doctor asked, "Did he get shot?"

"No, he's not hurt. I mean, he's not hurt from the gunfight. But he has a real high fever, and I'd appreciate it ever so much if you could look at him."

"Hang on just a second," Doc Charlie said distractedly. He returned to the man's wound.

Esme glanced at the regulator clock and felt sick to see it was almost noon. If everything went smoothly, maybe she could still make it to the circus in time. *Yet nothing at all has gone smoothly this morning.*

She noticed the old pipe-smoker again, and she got an idea, so she dashed across the room and hauled herself up on the stool next to him. "Excuse me, sir."

He set down his newspaper and turned his kindly face to her.

"Is there a sheriff in town?" she asked, hoping for help with her dire situation.

"Yep, but he's up north right now. Fishing." He puffed on his pipe.

Drats! That was no help. Esme's mind searched for other solutions, and she realized that maybe she could send Katrina a telegram, to warn her. Esme asked the man hopefully, "Do you have a telegraph office?"

"We do." Casually, he picked at his plate of pickled pig's feet. "But the storm a few days ago knocked down the lines. I don't know when they'll be up and going again."

Double drats! Now Esme really racked her brain. *How can I get to Wabasha?* She brimmed with frustration, and anxious words burst out of her. "What does a girl have to do around here to get any help?!"

"Well, maybe I can be of some help," the codger said kindly.

For the second time that morning, Esme stared at him. Eagerly, she asked, "Do you have a horse?"

He shook his head no.

She groaned in disappointment. "I have a monumental emergency, and I *have* to get to Wabasha. In less than two hours!"

"Well, then, why don't you walk?" He gave her a smile, showing off his few, discolored teeth.

"Walk?" she asked, puzzled.

"Why yep, it's only a couple of miles from here. You could make it in plenty of time!"

Jumping Jehoshaphat! She was so happy she could have kissed him, except he was eating those pickled pigs' feet, and he didn't smell too kissable. So instead, she extended her hand.

They shook hands, and Esme thanked him and told him she'd never forget him, and actually, she didn't know what all she said because she was so relieved that she blabbered on and on.

"Miss," Doc Charlie interrupted her. "I can see to your cousin now." So Esme jumped down from the stool and hurried over to Tommy, with Doc Charlie close behind her.

With his eyes closed, Tommy stretched out in the booth. The doctor started looking him over and soon asked, "Did you break your leg?"

Tommy took an agonizingly long time to nod his head. In the few minutes Esme had been away, he had slipped deeper into delirium.

"How did you break it?" Doc asked.

Esme's infinite patience died. She couldn't wait for her feverishly slow cousin to talk, so she answered for Tommy. "We were pushed off a moving train."

The doctor's eyebrows shot upwards. "Well, who in the world put this splint on him?"

"I did," said Esme.

Doc Charlie's eyebrows crept even higher. "Were you caught in the storm? How did he get so wet?"

"He drowned about an hour ago. Some really nice loggers brought him back to life."

The doctor's eyebrows shot so high upon his forehead that Esme wondered if they'd ever come down again.

"I'm worried about his fever," she explained. "Just feel him. He's burning up!"

Doc Charlie put his hand on Tommy's forehead. "Hmm, he is rather warm. It'd be best if he'd come back to my office, so I could give him a good looking over. I have some new medicine that might help."

"Oh, that would be wonderful!" Esme gushed appreciatively. "I was hoping I could count on you. And now I have to get going because there's an honest-to-goodness emergency in Wabasha. It's a matter of life and death. Trust me when I say that people's lives are in danger!"

As Doc Charlie stared at her, she realized she'd forgotten her manners. After all, if he were taking care of Tommy, it might be nice if he knew her cousin's name. From the looks of it, Tommy wouldn't be able to remember it himself.

"I'm sorry. My name is Esme Dooley. And this is my cousin, Tommy Dooley. I promise I'll come back for him. Hopefully, I'll have some money to pay you for your services."

Clasping Tommy's hand, she told him, "I'll be thinking of you the whole time. I know the doctor will help you. It's the best place for you right now." Esme gave his hand a tight squeeze.

Quickly she thanked the doctor, and before he could make any objections, she raced out of the tavern.

A moment later, she dashed back in, crying, "Which way is Wabasha?"

ESME

It had stopped raining! The sun was shining, and the sky was so blue it was as if Mother Nature was trying to make up for her previous bad behavior. *This is a good sign.* Esme took off running as fast as she could. Soon she left Reads Landing and was heading to Wabasha.

The ground was still wet from the rain, and at one point she slipped and fell. She leaped up quickly, telling herself to go more slowly.

But she couldn't.

As Esme rushed along, she waited to hear the sound of a horse and buggy. Surely, *someone* must be going to Wabasha. Especially now that it had stopped raining. One would have thought the road would be *loaded* with buggies.

But it wasn't.

Esme's side began to ache as she hurried along. The danger of the gunfight had made her completely forget her hunger,

yet now it was returning, and she felt faint. Moreover, her clothes were so wet they rubbed uncomfortably against her skin. The painful blisters on her heels were getting worse.

She thought about the task that lay ahead of her, and she recalled the last time she'd been in Wabasha, when she'd attended the wedding of Lavinia Hobbs. It had been so good to see Lavinia's parents again, Mr. and Mrs. Hobbs. Esme couldn't help but smile at the lasting memories.

Since she knew the layout of Wabasha — at least somewhat — she tried to imagine where the circus would have set up. She predicted she'd find it down by the river. She remembered a spacious park there, which would be the perfect spot. *Wherever it is, I'll find it!*

Esme was growing tired, yet she pushed on. She charged up a small hill, which became bigger, and bigger, and even bigger still. Jeepers! Her mind went to Sisyphus, in Greek mythology, who'd been condemned to an eternity of rolling a boulder uphill. Just the thought of him made her side ache even more.

As she neared the top of the knoll, she was panting so hard she couldn't hear anything except her jagged breathing and pounding heart. At the top, she jumped. Oh, good gravy! A motorcar was heading straight at her!

HATCH

It hadn't been easy to drag her mindless brother away from the sideshows, especially the Bearded Lady's tent. He claimed he'd been struck by Cupid's arrow. Hatch longed for a bow, so she could shoot at him too.

He kept calling that whiskered Frenchie his "honeybunch," and then he started singing to her, crooning off-key about love at first sight. *Ridiculous Romeo.* Who knew how long he would have stood there mooning over her, if Hatch hadn't yanked him away?

And how was she to know he would reach out and grab that woman's beard, just as Hatch was pulling him aside? The hussy's bloodcurdling scream still rang in Hatch's ears.

She didn't have time for her lovesick brother's nonsense. She had to track down that circus owner and see how much she'd pay for all the pain and suffering her tiger had caused. Maybe Hatch could corner her before the two o'clock show.

As Hatch and her gangly brother stalked through the maze of wagons, looking for the circus owner, Hatch spotted something else altogether! It was that gypsy wagon that belonged to Esme's abominable grandmother. *What are they doing here?* Quickly, Hatch pulled her derelict brother behind a tent, so they could spy on Papuza's wagon. "Do you see that?" she hissed.

"Say, that's their wagon. We should go over and say howdy," he said in his moronic way.

Hatch slugged him. "Go over and say howdy, my foot." She seethed. "Here's our chance to get back at them. Go see if they're in that wagon."

"*You* go see," he said belligerently. "I'm going to light out and apologize to Jessamina."

Hatch roared, "Who?"

"The Bearded Lady. She . . . OUCH!" He yelped, as Hatch hauled off and slapped him. Gloomily, he asked, "Why'd you up and do that?"

"Just peek in their window, you ignorant clown!" She lunged towards him.

He sprang back. "Well, *you* could get off your lard-butt and look. But alrighty!" Casually, he moseyed towards the gypsy wagon. As he neared his destination, he plunged his hands in his pockets and started whistling. Hatch didn't think he could look any more suspicious.

Reaching a window, he peeked in. "Aargh!" he howled, falling backwards. A raccoon had leaped up to the window and scared the bejesus out of him.

The smallest of smiles formed upon Hatch's lips.

Recovering from his eye-opener, Groggs slouched to another window and peered in. After a moment, he waved to his sister and shouted, "They're gone! Coast is clear!"

She groaned. Didn't he understand that they needed to be quiet? He was yelling loud enough for the whole big top to hear. Hatch hurried to the gypsy wagon to shut him up. "Keep your voice down, you idiot!" She glanced around in all directions, and when she was sure no one was watching them, she made a beeline for the wagon door. Groggs followed.

Once they were inside the wagon, Hatch slammed the door. *Hmm,* she thought sarcastically, *doesn't this look cozy? And because of **them**, I'm homeless.* It sent her pulse racing, and her temple started to throb. It made her want to tear up the wagon — and maybe she would — after she'd stolen as much as she wanted.

A firm knock on the door made her jump. A man's voice rang out, "Papuza? Are you back yet?"

Neither Hatch nor her greasy brother moved an eyelash until they finally heard footsteps walking away.

Then that slippery raccoon launched from the bedchamber and landed on her brother's head, setting him hopping helter-skelter, as he tried to shake off that rascally creature.

"Stop it!" Hatch snarled. The last thing they needed was to create a ruckus and attract attention.

Then another knock came at the back door. Hatch laid an iron fist on her brother's arm to keep him from squirming, which was hard for him, since that raccoon was digging into his filthy hair.

They waited in silence for this second interloper to leave. When the stranger finally did, Hatch grabbed that varmint from her brother's head and flung it as hard as she could onto the bench. The animal lay deathly still.

Good, she thought. *One varmint down. Three to go.*

PAPUZA

On reaching Reads Landing, Papuza tethered Zinjiber to the hitching post outside a tavern. Her search had been fruitless, and she felt a mixture of emotions. Obviously she was relieved she hadn't found their dead bodies, yet the mystery of what had happened to them was bewildering.

The dark night of searching had fatigued Papuza, and she needed a hot cup of coffee before she faced the staggering task of notifying Tommy's father. Wearily, she trudged into the tavern. She thought it was rather quiet for this time of day. There were only three customers and a scowling barkeeper. Papuza sat down at the counter and ordered coffee.

Her mind was so full of worries that she paid no attention to a conversation that was taking place next to her. She sipped the steaming coffee thankfully. After a bit, she felt its effects.

"She was no taller than a grasshopper's knee," the man beside her told the barkeeper.

Instantly, Papuza was wide-awake.

"For a young'un that small, she sure had some big worries. 'A monumental emergency,' she said. But I'll be danged if she ever told me what that emergency was!" The gentleman chuckled and took a bite of his pickled pig's feet.

Papuza's pulse pounded. Trying not to get her hopes up, she turned to the man and did her best to speak calmly. "Forgive me, sir, I couldn't help overhearing. Were you referring to a small girl, about this high?" From the top of the counter, she raised her hand not quite four feet. "With long, brown hair?"

The man nodded.

"And by any chance, was she traveling with a redheaded boy?" Papuza's voice broke slightly.

"Yep, that's her all right. She was a feisty little thing."

"When did you see them?" Papuza could no longer control her emotions, and tears sprang to her eyes.

"Less than an hour ago, I reckon."

Oh, thank goodness! Thank goodness! Papuza's relief was so enormous she began to tremble. She fished her drawstring coin purse from her pocket and pulled out a silver dollar, which she set by the man's plate to pay for his meal. "Thank you, sir. What wonderful news! Have you any idea where the children might be now?"

"Well, the girl took off on foot, but the boy is with Doc Charlie."

"Doc Charlie?" she asked.

"Yep, Doc Charlie. His office is just down the street. You can't miss it."

Papuza rushed outdoors and dashed in the direction he'd pointed. Soon she found the doctor's office. Hurrying through the door, she received an impression of a sunny room with engraved prints on the walls, but most importantly, she saw Tommy lying on a table. Feeling overwhelmingly thankful, she tiptoed towards him. He was fast asleep.

"Do you know this lad?" a tall man asked, rising from his desk. Papuza assumed he was the doctor.

"Yes, he's my granddaughter's first cousin. By any chance, have you seen her too?" Quickly, she added, "Oh, dear, my name is Papuza Dobbs, and this is Tommy Dooley." She extended her hand.

"Doc Charlie," he said, shaking her hand. He gave her a thoughtful smile.

"The girl I spoke of, my granddaughter Esme. Do you, by any chance, know where she is?"

"She said she was heading to Wabasha, but she would be back."

Then Papuza realized that Tommy's leg had a splint. In her relief to find him, she hadn't noticed it before. Anxiously, she asked, "What happened to his leg? Is it broken?"

"I was just about to take off the splint and examine him. I gave him some aspirin twenty minutes ago." He paused and felt Tommy's forehead. "It seems to be working. He's much cooler. Now he'll feel more comfortable when I remove his splint."

"But what happened to his leg?"

He studied her, as if he were weighing how much to tell her. "Your granddaughter said they were pushed from a moving train."

She shuddered. *Who in the circus could be capable of such evil?* How in the world had the children survived?

She stood beside Tommy, who slept so soundly she didn't have the heart to wake him. What a joy to see his sweet face again! Protectively she placed her hand on his arm.

"When did Esme say she'd be back?"

"She didn't say," said the doctor. "She just said there was an emergency in Wabasha."

Papuza clasped her hands uneasily. "Did she tell you the nature of the emergency?"

"Papuza," Tommy mumbled, opening his eyes slowly. "Am I dreaming, or are you really here?"

"It's me, child. What a relief to have found you!" She brushed back his bangs and kissed his forehead.

"Papuza," he said worriedly, "Esme went to Wabasha to stop Annie. Annie is the one who's been doing all the bad things at the circus. She's the one who pushed us from the train . . ."

Papuza interrupted, astonished. "But she's just a child!"

"She's sixteen. And evil." Tommy struggled to sit up. "What time is it? Esme's trying to stop Annie from burning down the circus!"

"Good gracious!" cried Papuza. *What alarming news!*

"If we hurry," Tommy pleaded, "maybe we can help Esme. A lot of people's lives are depending on it!"

ESME

Esme sat up in the ditch. To her astonishment, the energetic gentleman with the driving goggles was none other than Mr. Hobbs of Wabasha — the same Mr. Hobbs who had invited them to his daughter's wedding, and who had crashed a few motorcars into altars and porch posts. *That* wonderful Mr. Hobbs! Esme looked heavenward, thanking her stars and garters. Ignoring the bruises from her tumble, she rushed to his automobile.

"Oh, Mr. Hobbs!" she panted. "I don't think I've ever been so happy to almost get run over! I desperately need a ride to Wabasha. Can you help me?" She had spoken so fast and breathlessly that she wasn't sure if he'd understood.

"Esme! What a surprise! Didn't know you were in my neck of the woods. Of course."

Mr. Hobbs bounded out of his vehicle to open the door to the back seat. He bowed and waited for Esme to enter.

"Mr. Hobbs, you have a new horseless carriage! It's beautiful!" Esme scrambled into the upholstered seat, taking in the smell of new leather. *Oh, jiminy,* she thought, *it's like climbing into a jewel box.* Unconsciously she tried to brush the mud off her dress.

"Just came in today. Mum's the word to Mrs. Hobbs. Put her foot down about me ever buying another vehicle. Quite contrary."

The horseless carriage twitched and throbbed and thrummed, shaking and rattling Esme. This was the first time she'd ever been in a motorcar, and she tingled with excitement! *Now I'll **surely** make it to the circus in time!*

Mr. Hobbs shut her door and strode back around to the driver's side. Swiftly he slid into his seat and strapped on his goggles. "Hang on!" he laughed, as he shifted gears.

And they were off!

Esme didn't want to miss a thing, so she stood on her seat, clutching the seat in front of her. The wind licked her face as they gained momentum. *Oh, this is lovely,* she thought. *Like flying, only closer to the ground.*

They zoomed by green pastures, where cows forgot to graze, as they gazed upon the strange and noisy carriage. Rushing past rolling fields, Esme breathed the sweet smells of corn and cut hay. Farmers paused in their work to watch the motorcar shoot by.

Over the rumbling of the engine, Mr. Hobbs called, "So what's the rush? Where are you going?"

Esme was about to answer, but they spotted a delivery cart coming towards them, tugged by a pair of horses. Immediately the deliveryman pulled over to the side of the road, barely avoiding a head-on collision. His horses whinnied and reared up in a frenzy, as the automobile swept by. Esme waved to the startled man.

As they neared the outskirts of Wabasha, Esme felt absolutely certain that she'd make it to the circus on time. But then suddenly, they came upon a sharp turn in the road. Mr. Hobbs was approaching the corner at an alarming speed!

Oh, mercy, she should have thought twice (or at least once) before she hopped into his horseless carriage. Now she recalled that he'd wrecked a fair number of vehicles, and that's why Mrs. Hobbs had put her foot down. "AIEEE!"

Esme screamed, as the motorcar tipped on its side and balanced precariously on two wheels.

Esme gripped the seat in front of her again, trying to stay upright. Shouting to be heard above the engine, she cried, "Mr. Hobbs, please slow down!"

He just chuckled. The automobile settled on the road again, with all four wheels touching the earth.

With the wind swirling past Esme's ears, they roared into Wabasha. She had such forebodings of doom that she wanted to be out of that motorcar more than anything in the world.

And then it happened.

As they bolted down Main Street, a black dog darted out, right in front of them.

To avoid hitting it, Mr. Hobbs turned the wheel violently, making Esme shriek.

He swerved into the boardwalk, splintering a ladder that held up a sign painter. As the poor painter toppled to the ground, Mr. Hobbs was already veering in the opposite direction. Esme was shocked to see that they were on a collision course with a flour wagon!

Zigzagging to miss the wagon, Mr. Hobbs crashed straight into a porch post. Esme was thrown from the vehicle, hurling through the air like a circus performer who'd been shot from a cannon. Tumbling head over heels, she closed her eyes tightly, afraid to see where she would land.

PAPUZA

Away rode Papuza, holding Tommy in front of her. Zinjiber's galloping strides shook and jarred the poor boy and his broken leg. The short trip to Wabasha was agonizing for him. At times, Papuza caught glimpses of his face, and he was gritting his teeth against the pain.

As they rode, Tommy managed to tell her why Annie had committed her crimes against the circus. Truly it was a tragic tale that would sadden any heart.

Papuza and Tommy watched for Esme along the twisty road, but to their dismay, they never saw her. They earnestly hoped she had found a shortcut.

As they trotted into Wabasha, they passed an angry crowd gathered around a wrecked motorcar. Dear me! *Could that be Mr. Hobbs?* Papuza vowed to come back later to see if her assistance was needed, but right now she needed to hurry to the circus.

Before long, they reached the circus grounds, where they were very relieved to find nothing burning. Papuza wanted to warn Katrina about Annie, and she thought, *I have to find Esme!*

But first she'd take Tommy to their gypsy wagon, to ease his suffering. There he could rest. She would also be able to search for Esme more quickly, if she were alone.

They reached their beloved wagon, which was always a reassuring sight. Papuza dismounted, lifting Tommy off Zinjiber. As she carried him indoors, WHAP! Something struck her on the head.

Her world turned black.

TOMMY

It was Hatch! She'd been hiding behind the door with a frying pan, and when Tommy and Papuza had entered the wagon, WHAP! She smacked poor Papuza so hard that Tommy feared Hatch might have killed her.

Papuza fell to the floor, dropping Tommy as she keeled over. Tommy landed on the floor too, banging his broken leg. A sickening agony slammed through him. "Papuza?" he gasped. He dragged himself closer to her to try to check on her.

Hatch stopped him. She grabbed the straps of his overalls and hoisted him from the floor. She yelled over her shoulder, "Get down here, you lazy sack of bones!"

The curtains of the bedchamber swished, and Groggs slid down drowsily, walking along the tabletop before he hopped to the floor. Hatch snapped at him, "Hold this ugly hoodlum while I look for a rope." Dangling Tommy by his overalls straps, she handed him to her brother.

"Wait!" Tommy cried. "Y-Y-You're making a big mistake. Papuza needs to warn . . ." He was cut off in mid-sentence because Hatch stuffed a dishtowel in his mouth.

"That should keep you quiet," she sneered. She stomped outdoors.

Groggs pinned Tommy's arms behind him, holding him tightly, so he couldn't run away — as if Tommy could have run anywhere, anytime soon with his bad leg. Mournfully, Tommy stared down at Papuza on the floor. He thought she was breathing, yet it was hard to be sure. *Will she be okay?*

Then he noticed Mr. Wright crumpled on the bench. *Tarnation, what happened to him?* He looked even more lifeless than Papuza. Tommy longed to check on both of them, so he wriggled to break free, but that only made Groggs grip him tighter.

Just when Tommy thought things couldn't get much worse, he saw Annie outside the window, carrying a metal can. Jumping Jupiter! *No one has stopped her yet!* Esme must not have made it here. So now it was up to Papuza and himself. *But how can **we** stop her?*

Tommy watched in horror, as Annie started to douse the back of the big top with liquid from her can. *Oh, what did I ever see in her?* Somebody had to do something! And fast!

Hatch returned with horse reins and tied up Papuza and Tommy. She didn't just bind their hands. She tied their feet too, which almost made Tommy pass out because she jostled and squeezed his broken leg. By the time she was done, Tommy and Papuza were probably tied up tighter than Hatch's whalebone corset. She left them on the bench where Mr. Wright lay. Tommy nudged the poor raccoon, hoping he'd respond.

But he didn't.

Hatch told her brother, "Keep an eye on them while I find my sniveling niece. If these two are at the circus, that little upstart is bound to be here too."

Groggs grumbled, "But I wanted to see the show . . ."

Hatch smacked him. "You can see the show tonight, you whining fool. Right now, we need to take care of business." She spun on her heel and stormed out of the wagon.

Watching through the window, Tommy saw her stride towards a cluster of circus wagons. And then he saw Annie again! She was sneaking towards their gypsy wagon with her deadly metal can.

Tommy had been squirming so hard to free his hands that he was sure he'd rubbed all the skin off his wrists. He heard a moan, and when he looked over at Papuza, she was moving slightly. Oh, thank goodness, she's alive! *Please wake up,* he begged silently. They hadn't gagged her, so if she could only wake up and see what was happening, maybe they could stop Annie. At least Papuza could scream, which was a lot more than he could do.

He saw the evil-yet-still-pretty Annie creeping outside their wagon, pouring kerosene, or gasoline, or something even worse, all around them. Surely Groggs must be seeing this too. But no. When Tommy glanced over, he saw Groggs snooping through the many, many drawers where Papuza kept her herbs, and her recipes, and her feathers, and —

well, you name it, it was in those drawers.

"Looky here." Groggs beamed, as he uncorked a bottle. "Hair tonic." He took a sniff and made a face. Peering at the label, he read aloud, "Apply generously for vigorous and abundant hair growth." He didn't hesitate at all before he slathered the tonic all over his chin. With admiration, he gazed in the mirror and waited.

What in tarnation?! They were about to go up in flames, and Groggs was worried about whiskers? How could Tommy get his attention? Tommy screamed, but since he was gagged, it came out weaker than a pathetic whimper. Desperate, he banged his head on the table, but Groggs ignored him. He just kept smiling in the mirror and rubbing hair tonic on his chin. "Can't let that sweetheart outdo me," he mumbled. "In a romance, the feller's gotta have the bigger beard."

Tommy rolled his eyes and groaned, in a muffled sort of way.

Groggs sang to himself, "Oh, my darling, oh, my darling, oh, my darling Clementine — I mean Jessamina." He preened in the mirror.

Peering out the window again, Tommy saw Annie pouring a trail of liquid away from their wagon. *Of course,* he thought. *When she sets us on fire, she'll want to be a ways away.* The realization that they could be burning in a few minutes made his heart do flip-flops in his chest.

Tommy thought of home and his pa and brothers. He was sure they'd miss him. Well, at least he hoped they would. He remembered how much his twin brothers had wanted his pocketknife, and he really wished he could hand it to them now, before it burned up.

Then he thought of Esme. *Where is she? Why didn't she make it here? Is she in trouble?* A wave of protectiveness washed over him, as he realized Esme might be in danger. She had done her very best that morning when she'd set his leg, and put him on that log, and helped the loggers save him. She was the best friend he'd ever had, and if they both happened to live, he was going to tell her that.

ESME

From the horseless carriage, Esme hurled head over heels through the air. With no idea where she'd end up, she squeezed her eyes shut and hoped for the best.

PLOOSH!! She landed on something soft. *Thank goodness it wasn't a pointed weather vane.* Sitting up, Esme was bewildered to find herself in a thick fog. Swatting the air, trying to clear away white dust, she wondered if she was in a cloud. But what was that odor? It seemed very, very familiar.

Then she recognized it. Why, it was the smell of flour.

As she struggled to stand, her foot sank into a soft surface. Voices reached her through the haze. "Sakes alive," someone cried. "Not again!"

Esme tried to call out for help, but she couldn't because she needed to cough. Flour dust caught in her throat. She squinted through the white dust to see where she'd landed. Jeepers! She was on top of the wagon that Mr. Hobbs had swerved to avoid — the wagon filled with flour sacks!

She crawled over to the edge of the wagon to look down, and there was nothing but chaos below. A crowd had gathered around the crashed motorcar, where a dazed Mr. Hobbs sat slumped behind the wheel.

A ladder was attached to the side of the flour wagon, and Esme used it to climb down. She bumped into a long-nosed woman in a wide-brimmed hat, who said in a withering voice, "That's the fifth devil-wagon he's wrecked this year. The fifth one!" Feathers quivered on the woman's hat, as she shook her head reproachfully.

Women with pastel parasols and men in summer suits

crowded the street. Esme edged through the swarm of buzzing onlookers until she finally reached the horseless carriage. For a man of constant motion, Mr. Hobbs sat fairly still, just rocking back and forth slightly, holding his head. "Oh, Mr. Hobbs," cried Esme. "Are you all right?"

He looked at her with surprise — maybe because she was completely covered with flour. His voice shook as he asked, "Are *you* all right?"

"I'm fine."

"My secret's out," he groaned miserably. "Mrs. Hobbs will banish me to the henhouse."

In the distance, Esme heard a faint melody from a calliope. "I have to leave now, Mr. Hobbs, but I'll come back later to see how you're doing." She reached up and squeezed his hand in farewell.

Sprinting in the direction of the calliope music, she spotted the peak of the big top and was overjoyed to see no smoke! Maybe Grandma had solved the mystery of the misdeeds, and a sheriff had already taken Annie away. Esme fervently hoped that was the case, but she couldn't be sure, so she had to keep running.

As she sped past the main entrance, the ticket seller's mouth dropped open in surprise. That could have been due to the fact that she hadn't paid him, or maybe it was because she was still dusty with flour. Either way, she headed straight for the big top.

Once she got there, she heard laughter and applause coming from inside the tent. She decided to dash around the outside of the big top, to see if she could find any trace of her so-called-friend, her once-hoped-for sister. For at that very minute, Annie might be poised to strike the fateful match.

Esme made it halfway around the tent without spotting any sign of Annie. She started to feel confident that Annie truly *had* been caught and sent to jail.

Unfortunately, when Esme reached the very back of the tent, she saw Annie.

Annie's back was turned to Esme, and she was splashing the big top with kerosene. It was so utterly evil that Esme had to gasp.

Silently, Esme sneaked up behind her, so she'd have the advantage of surprise. When she was a just a few feet away, she charged into Annie's back and knocked her to the ground.

As Annie fell, she dropped her metal can, and kerosene splashed on both their dresses. Its smell lay heavy in the air. When Annie saw who had tripped her up, she froze in shock.

"It can't be," she muttered. The surprise of seeing Esme had totally undone her. Making the most of this opportunity, Esme picked up the kerosene can and flung it as far away from the big top as she possibly could.

Annie scrambled to her feet. Drawing herself to her tallest height, she towered over Esme, and her face was a savage mask of rage. "You are *not* going to stop me!"

Thinking fast, Esme said, "I already have. I've told Henry, and he's coming with the others." *If only that were true,* thought Esme.

Disbelief flashed in Annie's eyes. "Even if they came running around that corner right now — and I doubt that they will — it's too late. I've already drenched the big top and all around your grandmother's precious wagon." She nodded to the right.

Esme glanced over and noticed their gypsy wagon for the first time. It was parked by the river's edge, and Buttercup and their horses were tethered to the trees next to it. *If the wagon burns, will they burn too?*

Then she saw Tommy! He was in their gypsy wagon, shaking his head, and it looked as if something was stuffed in his mouth. *But that's impossible,* thought Esme. *I left him in Reads Landing.* What in the world was going on?

Annie stepped closer to Esme, pulling a box of matches from her pocket. "What should I burn first? The big top or your wagon?"

Annie took a match from the box and struck it.

Oh, jiminy! This was a hanging-by-a-thread sort of moment. Esme didn't know which way Annie would fling the match. Would she throw it towards the big top, where hundreds of innocent people were watching the show? Or would she toss it towards the gypsy wagon, where Tommy sat with his broken leg?

All Esme knew was that she had to stop Annie! Without knowing how things would end, Esme jumped at Annie to knock the lighted match from her hand.

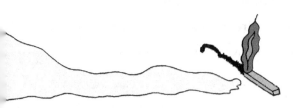

TOMMY

From the gypsy wagon, Tommy had watched in horror as Annie had struck the match. Then out of the blue, Esme had leaped at her!

Now they were probably wrestling on the ground. Tommy couldn't see them anymore because they were below his range of view. Esme was so much smaller than Annie. How could Esme possibly win? *What's happening?*

"Oh, my darling, oh, my darling, oh, my darling Jessamina." Groggs continued to sing to himself, as he gazed in the mirror and rubbed hair tonic on his chin.

And then Tommy saw it.

The trail of fluid that Annie had poured to their wagon was on fire. Flames were heading right at them!

ESME

Esme was able to knock Annie away from the tent, but they landed in kerosene that had spilled on the ground, and when Annie's lit match hit that patch of grass, a crackling fire flared up and engulfed both of them!

Panic welled in Esme's throat, and Annie must have been terrified too because she jumped to her feet, shrieking. The color drained from her face as she tried to pat out the flames on her arms. Esme wasn't sure why, but she *wasn't* on fire. *Maybe I'm fireproof?* But then Esme realized she didn't possess any supernatural powers. Instead she was simply wearing soggy clothes, covered with flour!

Flames spread rapidly over Annie. Pictures flashed through Esme's mind of all the pain that Annie had caused. On account of her, Esme had needed to face down that tiger. And it was Annie who'd spooked Maria's horse. And it was Annie who'd planted Jessamina's jewels in their wagon. And it was Annie who'd given Bernardo the sleeping potion. And it was Annie who'd pushed Tommy off the train, which had broken his leg.

All of Annie's dark deeds were villainous, yet Esme knew in her heart that she couldn't let Annie burn.

So Esme leaped into the flames to save her enemy. She jumped at Annie again, knocking her onto safer ground, trying to smother the flames, and hoping to get her to roll. "Roll, Annie!" screamed Esme.

Annie's hair caught on fire! Esme tried to pat it out, but her hands were definitely not fireproof. They recoiled from the heat. Esme watched in horror as Annie's yellow hair

378

burned like straw, vanishing before her very eyes. The smell was sickening.

"Roll!" Esme kept screaming, and finally Annie listened. Within seconds, Annie smothered the flames by rolling on the ground. Esme hurried to her side to see if there was anything she could do to help.

Annie was burned something terrible, and her golden hair was all gone. Her face twisted in agony. Her eyes were closed, yet she was moaning, so Esme knew she was still alive.

Sadness squeezed Esme's heart.

There was a place on Annie's arm where she wasn't burned, and Esme laid her hand there. Annie opened her eyes and looked up at her. "I'm sorry," Annie whispered.

Esme didn't even get a chance to take this in because she suddenly realized their gypsy wagon was burning! Holy smoke! She jumped up, telling Annie she'd be right back, and then she raced as fast as she could to the wagon. *What if Tommy is still inside? And where are Grandma and Mr. Wright?*

As Esme rushed to the wagon, she didn't see Tommy in the window, but she did see Bess and Joe and Zinjiber going crazy with fear. Over and over, they reared up on the riverbank, where they were tethered. Next to them, Buttercup looked on nervously.

And that's when it hit Esme.

"Thirsty, Buttercup!" she yelled, pointing to the wagon. "Thirsty!"

It was clear that Buttercup understood her because right away, she filled her trunk with water from the river. As Esme ran towards their wagon, Buttercup sprayed it with water. Esme shouted, "Thirsty" to Buttercup again and again, and Buttercup kept spraying.

When Esme reached the back door, it was wide open. Through the smoke, she could see that the wagon was empty. Thank goodness for that! *But where is Tommy?*

Esme darted outdoors to keep encouraging Buttercup. The elephant was making great progress, and the fire was nearly out, when someone grabbed Esme by her collar and hoisted her off the ground.

It was Hatch!

She gripped Esme's collar so tightly that she was choking her. "Going somewhere?" Hatch cackled sinisterly.

ESME

The next afternoon, Esme was on the circus train, dressed in a red sequined leotard and a fluffy feather headdress. She was scrawling rapidly in her journal because so much had happened since her last entry!

As she tried to come up with the perfect word for a sentence, she scrunched her eyebrows together in concentration. Her headdress slipped down her forehead, so she pushed it back up and continued to write:

I was stunned. Completely, absolutely, utterly stunned. Hatch was the last person I'd ever, ever expected to see. She held me close to her face, sneering. The look in her eyes was pure evil. I saw that her mole hair on her jowl had grown back, and it was twitching like an angry snake.

My horror and shock must have been plain to see because Hatch crowed, "You weren't expecting me, were you?"

"Put her down!" Tommy yelled, to my surprise. I whipped my head around and saw him leaning against a tree, about thirty feet away from me. Near him, I spotted poor Grandma tied up like a trussed turkey and lying on the ground. Mr. Wright was licking her face.

Hatch sneered at Tommy, "Make me."

And then, holey moley, Tommy did something that I'll never forget until the day I die. Balancing on his good leg, he aimed his pocketknife at us and threw it!

Time stood still, as I watched the knife flip end over end, coming closer to us. I sincerely hoped Bernardo's lessons would pay off.

And they did!

The knife stabbed Hatch in her upper arm, making her throw back her head and howl like a raging hippopotamus! Not that I really know what that sounds like, but I imagine it would sound just like Hatch did. Immediately she dropped me, which knocked the wind right out of me.

I couldn't breathe — literally — as I waited to see what Hatch would do. Tommy was watching her and waiting too.

Hatch continued to scream bloody murder as she tried to pull out the knife. When it finally came out, a blossom of blood spread over her sleeve like a blooming rose. I thought she'd throw the knife at me, but instead she turned towards Tommy and was aiming at him when a shadow fell over us.

It was Henry! He grabbed Hatch's hand and forced her to drop the knife.

Furious, Hatch yelled, "Let go of me this instant!"

Henry boomed, "Not until I know why you were holding Esme by her collar and aiming this knife at Tommy."

By now I could breathe again, and I jumped up from the ground. I rushed to Henry and hugged his shin, thanking him and thanking him, and I think I even kissed his knee before I took off running to Tommy and Grandma.

When I reached them, Tommy had just finished untying Grandma's hands. I fell to my knees at her side. Tommy said that Hatch had hit Grandma over the head with a frying pan and tied both of them up. Christopher Columbus!

I asked Grandma if she was okay. She patted my cheek. "It is I who have worried about you, child. During these last twenty-four hours, I've feared the worst." She hugged me lovingly.

Henry had followed behind me with Hatch in his inescapable grip. He shook Hatch and asked if she was responsible for striking my good, innocent grandma and tying her up. This made Hatch squirm, and cuss, and carry on like there was no tomorrow. Or any days after that!

Tommy told Henry that his pa and brothers back home were searching for Hatch because just last week, she'd shot at their window, and that he'd purt near lost an ear from that shooting. "A feller just doesn't know how fond he is of his ears until he's in danger of losing one," Tommy finished very seriously.

After hearing that, Henry decided to detain Hatch while the authorities were contacted.

Gee Christmas! Hatch hissed at Tommy, looking for all the world like one of Angus' snakes. And then she tried to lunge at me, but Henry held her back. She gave me such an evil look that I thought I might disintegrate into a little pile of ash and smoke right then and there.

That's when Henry marched her away, although Hatch put on such a show of kicking and spitting that I felt downright sorry for *him. Henry called over his shoulder that he'd lock Hatch up in an empty lion cage until he found the town's sheriff. Tommy mumbled that the cage didn't have to be empty.*

Grandma chuckled, and then she sighed. She became quite serious. "That poor woman," she said softly. "Her anger has ruined her life."

*I watched Henry haul Hatch away. Henry's size made her look like a small girl, and that made me remember what I'd heard about her childhood. I couldn't help but feel sorry for her. And Grandma was right. Hatch's anger **had** ruined her.*

After they were out of sight, I turned to Tommy and gave him a big hug, thanking him for saving me from Hatch. I wanted to know how they'd made it out of the burning wagon when they were all tied up.

Well, it turned out it was Groggs who had saved them! Tommy said that when Groggs finally realized that the wagon was on fire, he carried them all outside to safety. Jeepers! Well, what do you know? I guess Groggs isn't such a bad guy after all.

As soon as he got them outside, he moseyed off towards the fairway because he said he had "important bizness with a bearded woman."

Then Tommy wanted to know how I'd saved the circus from burning down. And he wondered what had happened to Annie.

Annie! Good golly, I'd forgotten all about her, what with the wagon burning, and Hatch, and everything else. I told Tommy and Grandma that she'd been burned something awful, and we had to go help her right away. So with Tommy leaning on Grandma as a crutch, I led us back to where I'd left Annie.

But she was gone!

I couldn't see her anywhere. I showed Grandma and Tommy the charred grass and described how Annie had burned. She'd been in such pain that I couldn't imagine how she could have moved.

We searched and searched around the tents and wagons, but we couldn't find her anywhere. She was simply gone.

We finally returned to our wagon, where Grandma studied the damage from the fire. She said the wagon might need new wheels but everything else was in pretty good shape. "You and Buttercup saved the day, my dear." She hugged me, and her words made me feel about ten feet tall!!

Then she checked Tommy's splint, taking it apart and looking at how I'd set his leg. "I couldn't have done it better myself!" she confessed, which made my heart soar.

I helped her put dry bindings on Tommy's leg, and that's when he said, "Yep, good job, Esme. I never would have made it out of that bog without you. You're the best friend and traveling partner a feller could ever have." His voice got a little choked up. I couldn't answer because it's really, really hard to talk when you have a lump the size of a rutabaga in your throat!

We told Grandma everything that had happened since we were pushed off the train. At the end, I described my glorious-yet-terrifying car ride with Mr. Hobbs.

"Good gracious!" Grandma cried. "It's a miracle you two survived!" She decided to send a note to the Hobbs' residence right away to ask how Mr. Hobbs was faring.

We kept talking about our adventures, and I said that of all the things that had happened, the one that hurt the most was Annie's betrayal. I had really believed she was my friend, and I had wanted her to be my sister.

Tommy mumbled that he felt betrayed too.

Grandma hugged us close and said that for our own sakes, we needed to be able to forgive Annie. And that through forgiveness, we'd also be helping ourselves because we'd be able to heal. I've been thinking about Grandma's words ever since.

Later, when Tommy was resting, and Grandma had gone to Katrina to tell her everything, I went to check on Buttercup. As I walked, I thought of my mother's locket, which I'd lost in the river. I realized it hadn't been protecting me. I had chased down Annie and stopped the fire without any help from my lucky talisman. So maybe I hadn't needed it after all. Maybe all I'd needed was to believe in myself.

The afternoon circus show ended, and word of what had happened spread like — well, I hate to say it — wildfire. We had everyone stopping by, thanking me. I told them all that Tommy had helped too, which made him blush.

Yet our news wasn't the only shocking thing that had happened that afternoon. Madame Sage was gone! She had eloped with Luis, the Gentleman's Werewolf!

And Madame Sage wasn't really Madame Sage. She was really Miss Peggy Gresham! A female detective! Samuel had hired her secretly to discover who was behind all the mishaps at the circus. Once the mystery was solved, Samuel no longer needed the services of the honorable Detective Gresham, who was really only twenty-five years old and said to be quite attractive when she wasn't wearing any disguises.

When Tommy heard this, he exclaimed, "Shucks, the whole time she was saying, 'Things are not always what they seem,' she was really talking about herself! I hope she took that brain-pecking raven with her."

We hadn't even finished laughing at that when Maria and Bernardo stopped by to thank us. Maria still wore my red ribbon around her splint. Bernardo hobbled on crutches, but he was full of smiles. He'd heard about Tommy's heroic knife throwing, and he slapped my tongue-tied cousin on the back and heartily shook his hand.

Suddenly Jessamina rushed up to thank us. She kissed my cheek, tickling me something terrible. She whispered that she had to hurry because a strange admirer named Groggs was in "zee hot pursuit," and she needed to stay ahead of him. Far, far ahead of him. As she sprinted away, Tommy called after her, "Does he have a beard yet?"

"No," she called back, "but his ears, they are sprouting hairs."

Then Maxwell appeared and told us that Emmeline had left his act. She found snakes—possibly Angus' snakes—in the reappearing box during the middle of a performance, and that was the last straw!

Still laughing, Maxwell bowed to us. "Thank you for saving our charming circus! Let me offer you a small token of my gratitude." He pulled from his cape an umbrella, and then he laughed at himself because it was supposed to be a bouquet of flowers. Tommy and I laughed too and gratefully accepted his gift.

Before he took his leave, Maxwell also told us that Angus was now sitting up and eating haggis and cullen skink, so he was on the road to recovery. As soon as I heard that, I just had to go see him. Tommy needed to rest his leg, and he still was a little leery of Creampuff, so I ran to Angus' wagon all by my lonesome.

Angus' door was wide open, and he called, "Come in, Miss Esme! Come in and have a proper sit-down!" So I did.

It was so good to see him back to his normal self. Well, pretty normal, that is, except for the big bandage around his head. He told me that he didn't know if someone had struck him with that branch,

387

or if it had fallen from a tree naturally, and he'd just had very ill luck!

I told him all about Annie, and he shook his head in disbelief. "Such a wee lass to be causing such big trouble," he muttered.

Then I asked him if he knew where all his snakes were, and he admitted that he had no idea, but he'd been contemplating a new act with a completely different species.

So of course I made the little suggestion of working with an elephant, and Angus warmed to that idea right away. By the time I left him, we'd come up with an act of Buttercup dancing while Angus played his bagpipes! I thought Buttercup would look lovely in a tutu. Angus said he'd try to think of a way to work me into his act! By jingo, I just might have my day on stage yet!

When I got back to our wagon, Henry had returned. He told us that the sheriff was dealing with Hatch. He also told us that a search party had looked for Annie. They'd found no sign of her, but they'd learned that Annie's uncle and his circus wagon were missing too.

People were speculating that Annie and her uncle fled the circus, so she could escape the charge of arson, which is a serious crime. When I think of Annie's burnt body, I can't help but feel that she's already been punished enough. And the way she apologized to me makes me think she truly was sorry.

My thoughts were interrupted by a knock on the wagon's door. It was a small man with a top hat and an endearing smile. At first, Grandma looked puzzled, and then her face lit up with joy.

It was Arthur!

Grandma and Uncle Arthur hugged and hugged. Tears sprang to her eyes as she murmured, "Oh, Arthur," in such a happy way that we were all wiping our eyes, even Tommy, who claims he never cries.

Uncle Arthur wasn't anything like I'd imagined him to be. For one thing, he didn't have white hair because he was completely bald, and covering his bald head were colorful tattoos of flowers and birds and even a panther! And he wasn't the lonely Robinson Crusoe figure I had imagined either. Far from it! He and his father were shipwrecked off the coast of South America on an uncharted isle, a tropical paradise of friendly people. Uncle Arthur said it reminded him of that island in "Moby-Dick" that wasn't on a map because true places never are.

Uncle Arthur married the island king's daughter, and eventually he became the king himself! A while ago, he turned over his duties to his only daughter. Since then, he's been very much enjoying his lack of responsibilities.

Recently however, a storm blew a British naval ship off course, and it landed upon their island. This gave Uncle Arthur a chance to address his only regret in life, which was that he'd never been able to tell his Cornish family that he was still alive. He only hoped it wasn't too late, and they hadn't all passed away. So here he was!

He said he has one child and thirteen grandchildren. At that point, I just had to interrupt and ask if any of his grandchildren were girls. Proudly he answered, "All thirteen of them are girls."

Oh, by jingo! I told Uncle Arthur that I'd love to meet them. Are they my third or fourth cousins? Or my second cousins once removed? I've never been very sure about how that all works.

"Well, you're in luck, Esme," he said, "because I brought them along." This made me clap my hands and cheer! Uncle Arthur explained that his daughter, the current queen, believed that some of her older girls are the right age for matchmaking.

Instantly my matchmaking hat came out! Of course I thought of Tommy and his brothers. Thirteen girls for thirteen boys! Gee whillikers! It couldn't simply be a coincidence. "Where are they?" I cried.

Uncle Arthur said they had wanted to clean up and look presentable after their train ride. He glanced out our wagon window and nodded. "Here they are now."

We all crowded around the window and stared. A line of females, clad in white dresses, walked in a slow procession to our wagon. Each one carried a white lace parasol.

They were led by a stately woman with a regal bearing. It was obvious that she was the queen. Her striking eyes shone in her delicate face, and her long, dark hair flowed free. It wasn't like the fashion in Zumbro Falls, where women pin up their hair. The queen had a deep red flower tucked behind her ear, and I thought she looked absolutely exotic.

Following the queen came her daughters, with the tallest girl in front, and the shortest girl at the end. The tiniest girl was just about my height! They were all so beautiful that I felt a little shy. I wondered what language they spoke, and I worried that I might not be able to understand them. Yet when I went outside and said hello and curtsied, they murmured hello right back, in the exact same British accent as Uncle Arthur's!

Tommy was carrying Mr. Wright, and all the girls just adored our shaggy pet. They'd never seen a raccoon before, and they all tried to hold him. I'm guessing it was too much for Mr. Wright because he jumped on top of one of their parasols, and then he continued to leap from one parasol to the next until he landed on top of the queen's, which made everyone laugh.

Later, Katrina and Samuel stopped by with huge smiles on their faces. They announced that the circus would be taking a break for the next two weeks to search for replacements for some of their acts.

After all, they needed either temporary or permanent replacements for a trick rider, a trapeze artist, a fortune-teller, a werewolf, a magician's assistant, and a mermaid. When Katrina said the word "mermaid," I felt a sharp stab of sadness.

Katrina believes it will take some time to replace these acts, and she can't think of a better place to regroup than in Zumbro Falls. There she can spend some time with her childhood friend and reunite with her beloved tiger, Tasha. Katrina added that she also wants to "thank two young heroes who saved our circus from being burned to the ground," and she plans to give free shows in Zumbro Falls in our honor!

Jumping Jehoshaphat! Tommy and I are absolutely over the moon! His pa and brothers will get to see the circus and meet our new friends! I can't wait for Buttercup to douse all my presidentially-named cousins!

Then Grandma invited Uncle Arthur to come to Zumbro Falls too. And he agreed! Now Tommy's brothers will be able to go to the circus with their new sweethearts that they don't even know they have yet!

We stayed up late last night, chatting around the campfire, under silver stars that filled the whole sky. I snuggled close to Grandma and listened to her and Uncle Arthur's stories about when they were children. As I nestled close beside her, the flames of the fire warmed me, and I felt completely secure. And incredibly thankful.

My mind jumped to the Orphan Train and how fortunate I was, compared to those poor kids. I vowed to follow through with my wish of adopting an orphan. Hopefully we'll find one who is not a deranged murderess.

And of course that made me think of Annie. I wondered how she was doing. I realized that if I held onto the memory of the harm she caused us, then I'd be carrying around this big ball of hurt inside of me, and I didn't want to do that. I didn't want to turn out like Hatch, all full of anger. And because I didn't want to be like that, I understood that I really did need to forgive Aunt Hatch. Thinking of her as a little girl with a sad childhood helped me feel sorry for her. So maybe this was a start on my road to forgiveness.

When Grandma said it was way past our bedtime, I found it impossible to sleep, even though I was exhausted. Swirling through my mind were images of ships, and tropical islands, and the circus in Zumbro Falls.

*Yet I **must** have fallen asleep because I woke with a start this morning when I heard an engine zooming past our wagon. Lickety-split, I looked out the window, and there was Mr. Hobbs driving his repaired vehicle, speeding around the circus grounds with Uncle Arthur by his side! The two men laughed uproariously, and I found myself smiling too. I sincerely hoped they wouldn't end up in a motorcar crash — especially after Uncle Arthur had traveled so far to find Grandma. Then I realized they're bound to be fine because there aren't any porch posts around here for Mr. Hobbs to hit.*

The circus was chaotic this morning as everyone worked to pack up. Tommy and I scrambled around, trying to help wherever we could. Everyone was still talking about Annie, but there was no news of her.

Right before we left the circus grounds, I went back to the grassy spot where I last saw Annie — the spot where I saw her burn. I placed my hand on the scorched grass. I told her that I forgave her and wished her no ill will.

I will probably never know her fate, but I know I will never, ever forget my time with her.

392

Oh, but now I have to go! The train whistle just blew, so we'll be in Zumbro Falls in a few minutes. I'm bursting with excitement! I'll be riding Buttercup, leading the circus parade down the main street of Zumbro Falls! I've been dressed in my costume for at least two hours. But I'm having trouble keeping this feathered headdress on top of my head. I can see how this could be a problem when I'm riding Buttercup . . .

"Esme, what in the world?" The train whistle woke Tommy, and he looked bewildered, staring at Esme like she was from Jupiter.

"Ta da!" Dramatically she stretched out her arms. "What do you think? Katrina wants me to wear this while I ride Buttercup. Now, doesn't this make you want to change your mind? You could get all gussied up too, and ride with me!"

"I said no because of my leg," Tommy grumbled. "Besides, I couldn't wear something like that! My brothers would never let me hear the end of it!"

Esme laughed, making her headdress slide off again, which made Tommy chuckle.

The train slowed down, and Esme and Tommy left the gypsy wagon and hurried to the window of the boxcar. Perched on bales of hay, they watched as the train pulled into Zumbro Falls.

Slowly they passed Mackey's General Store, where they noticed a fair amount of gaiety and commotion beneath its awning. Esme caught a glimpse of a fierce arm wrestling match between Red Kautz and Charlie Cliff. As the train rolled by, Red won.

Esme put two fingers in her mouth and let out a shrill whistle. Hanging out the window, she waved to the crowd, and they all waved back.

"You know, a feller could travel the whole world over," Tommy said, "But there ain't nothing like coming home."

Esme stood by his side, loving the sights of Zumbro Falls. "This homecoming seems extra special," she said, "what with Uncle Arthur and my thirteen girl cousins, who will soon be meeting my thirteen boy cousins . . ."

"Esme?" Tommy sounded mighty suspicious. "Just what do you have in mind?"

She simply smiled.

THE END

ACKNOWLEDGEMENTS

After visiting the Circus World Museum in Baraboo, Wisconsin, we were inspired to create Esme and Tommy's adventures at the Kirkkomaki Circus.

For Papuza's youthful tales, we drew from logging books, including *The St. Croix : Midwest border river* by James Taylor Dunn; and *The Wisconsin logging book, 1839-1939* by Malcolm Leviatt Rosholt; and *Time and the river : a history of the Saint Croix : a historic resource study of the Saint Croix National Scenic Riverway* by Eileen M. McMahon and Theodore J. Karamanski.

The staff at the Minnesota State Fair Archives provided information about the 1904 fair, and we are grateful for their assistance.

We give sincere thanks to Maria Donovan, horsewoman extraordinaire, for her help with the horse and elephant illustrations.

We would also like to thank friends and family who read this book as it was being written and illustrated. All of them offered thoughtful suggestions, especially David Trechter, Peggy Hrynko, Kathy Hoff, Jon Thomason, Ken Thomason, and our mother, Alice Thomason (1932-2014). We wish Mom could have held the final version in her hands.

CPSIA information can be obtained
at www.ICGtesting.com
Printed in the USA
LVOW05s1712041217
558589LV00007B/80/P